PRAISE FO

"Bestseller Shalvis (*Love fo*   ...rise
Cove series with a charmir   g a
cast readers will quickly con.
—*Publishers Weekly* on *The Family You Make*

"*Love for Beginners* is quintessential Shalvis, with humor and heat (whew, Emma and Simon give us heat), and a cast of characters you'll hate to leave behind when you turn the last page. But even so, we promise you'll finish this book feeling warm from the inside—and maybe the outside too. This is the summer's perfect beach read."
—Christina Lauren, *New York Times* bestselling author

"Jill Shalvis has a unique talent for making you want to spend time with her characters right off the bat."
—Kristen Ashley, *New York Times* bestselling author

"Sisterhood takes center stage in this utterly absorbing novel. Jill Shalvis balances her trademark sunny optimism and humor with unforgettable real-life drama. A book to savor—and share."
—Susan Wiggs, *New York Times* bestselling author, on *The Lemon Sisters*

"Jill Shalvis's books are funny, warm, charming, and unforgettable."
—RaeAnne Thayne, *New York Times* bestselling author

Better Than Friends

ALSO BY JILL SHALVIS

SUNRISE COVE NOVELS
The Family You Make • *The Friendship Pact*
The Backup Plan • *The Sweetheart List*
The Bright Spot • *The Summer Escape*
Better Than Friends

WILDSTONE NOVELS
Love for Beginners • *Mistletoe in Paradise* (novella)
The Forever Girl • *The Summer Deal*
Almost Just Friends • *The Lemon Sisters*
Rainy Day Friends • *The Good Luck Sister* (novella)
Lost and Found Sisters

HEARTBREAKER BAY NOVELS
Wrapped Up in You • *Playing for Keeps*
Hot Winter Nights • *About That Kiss*
Chasing Christmas Eve • *Accidentally on Purpose*
The Trouble with Mistletoe • *Sweet Little Lies*

LUCKY HARBOR NOVELS
One in a Million • *He's So Fine*
It's in His Kiss • *Once in a Lifetime*
Always on My Mind • *It Had to Be You*
Forever and a Day • *At Last*
Lucky in Love • *Head Over Heels*
The Sweetest Thing • *Simply Irresistible*

ANIMAL MAGNETISM NOVELS
Still the One • *All I Want*
Then Came You • *Rumor Has It*
Rescue My Heart • *Animal Attraction*
Animal Magnetism

Better Than Friends

A Novel

JILL SHALVIS

AVON

An Imprint of HarperCollins*Publishers*

HarperCollins books may be purchased for educational, business, or sales promotional use. For information, please email the Special Markets Department at SPsales@harpercollins.com.

FIRST EDITION

Interior text design by Diahann Sturge-Campbell

Title and chapter opener art © Danussa / Shutterstock

Library of Congress Cataloging-in-Publication Data has been applied for.

ISBN 978-0-06-335338-1
ISBN 978-0-06-335343-5 (hardcover library edition)

24 25 26 27 28 LBC 5 4 3 2 1

Better Than Friends

CHAPTER 1

Olive had three pet peeves: loud chewers, the word "moist," and . . . in the number one spot . . . love. And yes, she'd given it a try, several times in fact, and still had the occasional eye twitch to prove it, as she'd come out a big loser.

"You're breathing funny," Katie said. "You ate something with nuts in it again, didn't you."

Another example of how love hadn't worked out for her. Olive *loved* peanuts, so of course she was allergic. "No, and I'm fine," she said into her Bluetooth. Look at her, the master of the little white lie. After years of honing the skill, she could fool just about anyone, even her lifelong BFF. "And actually, I'm great. Totally great. Like one hundred percent great."

"That's sarcasm, right?"

Katie Turner-Brooks had an eidetic memory, could solve complicated mathematical problems in her head and recite years-old conversations verbatim, but sarcasm eluded her.

"Excuse me, it's called manifesting," Olive said. "Because I really *want* to be great." And *not* halfway to a panic attack . . .

"Then you will be."

Katie had never understood it wasn't that easy for Olive. She'd been a seriously awkward kid who'd been desperate to belong, and not much had changed. She exhaled and took in her view as she drove along Lake Tahoe, toward the small mountain town of Sunrise Cove on the north shore, trying not to feel like that lost girl all over again. "At my last stop for gas, I bought salami, an energy drink, and a chocolate cream pie, if that helps explain my emotional state."

"What are you worrying about? Almost no one remembers that time you ran over the town hero."

At Olive's silence, Katie sighed. "Aaaand, I still can't tell a joke right. I read a book on it and everything."

"It was a little funny." Emphasis on *little*. "But we both know everyone remembers what I did." Noah Turner, aka the town hero, was a lot of things. Voted most likely to make something of himself. Beloved son. Katie's twin brother.

And let's not forget Olive's high school *pretend* boyfriend.

"Why do you care what anyone thinks?" Katie asked.

"I don't. I'm just tired of not having my shit together."

"Gotta fake it to make it, babe," Katie said. "You once told me that."

The memories evoked an emotion that clogged Olive's throat, so she distracted herself by taking in the view. The sky was so bright and clear, the water such a deep blue, the mountains blanketed by endless pines, topped with caps of snow, all of it so stunning that if all of it hadn't been humming and teeming with such vibrance, it could've been a painting.

Into her silence, Katie said, "You also told me that no matter how many times you break, you can still put yourself back together."

"Yeah, well, past me had more hope. And it'd be great if you could try and forget all the dumb stuff I've said."

"How do I differentiate?"

Olive laughed. "Look at that, a joke!"

"Who said I was joking?"

"Ha-ha."

"Whatever." Katie cleared her throat. "Thanks for coming to help me with little Joey. The library gave me leave for as long as I need, but it'll still be so helpful to have you so I can spend more time at the hospital with Joe. It means a lot."

"Of course." Katie rarely asked for help, even though she'd given Olive everything her own parents hadn't been able to: safety, security . . . acceptance . . . "I'm all yours, whatever you need."

Noah and Joe, Katie's husband, were work partners, both ISB special agents—Investigative Services Branch of the National Park Service under the Department of the Interior—working out of the Yosemite station, about three hours south. They'd been investigating a series of car burglaries and thefts that had culminated in an ugly, dangerous high-speed chase. One of the suspects in the car had opened fire on Noah and Joe, blowing out their windshield and then two of their tires, causing their vehicle to flip.

Joe had been transported by helo to a Tahoe hospital, where a week later he still remained in the ICU. Noah had been released, though he was not cleared for duty, still healing from various injuries including his right leg. Actually, that was a re-injury, from when Olive had accidentally run him over all those years ago. Things she'd put away in the Don't Think About It Right Now file. "How's Joe?"

"Still in a coma," Katie said. "Which is the short story. The long story is that he's in a state of unarousable unconsciousness due to a dysfunction of the brain's ascending reticular activating system, or ARAS, which is responsible for the maintenance of wakefulness."

"He's going to be okay," Olive said softly.

"Yes, because if he's not, I'll climb into his coma and drag him out myself."

"I'll help."

"Misfits unite."

Olive laughed softly. "Misfits unite." It'd been their mantra since she'd moved in with her grandma at age fourteen, right next to Katie's family. Up until then, she'd been homeschooled on an off-the-grid farm several hours north of Tahoe in a remote wilderness that few ventured into. This meant she'd been able to build a fire in three minutes flat but hadn't known the first thing about kids her own age. Nor had Katie, which had made them easy targets at school. Poor Noah—not troubled, not a misfit—had been their reluctant protector.

"Are you close?" Katie asked.

Olive eyed the lake on her right. The azure blue water ran so deep, it could swallow up the entire Empire State Building. Massive groves of pine trees climbed so high in the sky they seemed to brush up against the few puffy white clouds floating by. Just taking it all in lowered her blood pressure. "I'm about to pass your work."

"The library? Great, you'll be here in ten point five minutes. Don't get lost."

Olive laughed. "It hasn't been *that* long. And I never get lost."

"Not true. Remember when you were taking your driver's license test, and the DMV guy said turn right, but you always mixed up your rights and lefts, and you turned left—"

"I've got that down now," Olive joked, hoping to ward off the whole tale. Unlikely since Katie had never met a story she wanted to stop in the middle of.

"You ended up on a one-way street going the wrong way and totally freaked out, so you rushed to make a right turn, but it wasn't a street, it was a trail, and since it was posted everywhere that no cars were allowed, you failed your test—"

"I remember."

"Your instructor got chest pains and had to be taken by ambulance to the hospital, but it turned out to be just indigestion because he'd eaten four hot dogs at that food shack at the lake, the one that had been shut down for giving dozens of people food poisoning. Do you remember that part?"

"It's ringing a bell," Olive said dryly.

"You made the front page of the local paper. It's rare to make the front page, but you managed it again a few years later when—"

"Let me save you some time, okay? I remember *all* the stupid stuff I did. I'll see you in a few—" She broke off when a guy stepped off the sidewalk without looking. Slamming on the brakes, she nearly had heart failure before her car skidded to a stop a few feet from him.

When he turned to face her, she sucked in a shocked breath.

"What?" Katie asked.

Olive's car was half in the crosswalk, slightly crooked, the smell of burnt tires assaulting her senses. The guy she'd nearly hit yanked out an earbud and lifted a hand up to shade his eyes, clearly trying and failing to see past her windshield into her rental Mini Cooper.

A whoosh of relief escaped her. Noah Turner himself. He mouthed *sorry!* and then just continued on his way, his gait uneven, clearly favoring his right leg.

"He's sorry?" she muttered. "I almost had a heart attack, and he's sorry—"

"Who are you talking to?"

"I almost ran over your brother."

"*Again?* He's not going to like that."

She resisted the urge to thunk her forehead against the steering wheel. "I'm pretty sure he couldn't see my face, and I don't plan on enlightening him. You can't either."

"No worries," Katie said. "You're the One Who Shall Not Be Named."

"What?"

"Crap," Katie muttered, accompanied by a sound like maybe she'd just smacked herself in the forehead. "Don't let Olive know that's her nickname."

"Oh my God. Seriously?"

"Don't take it personally," Katie said. "He's got a whole list of things Mom and I can't talk to him about. One is women and/or marriage—all women, not just you."

Olive choked out a laugh. "Wow."

"We're also no longer allowed to ask when he's going to settle down and have kids. But really, he should've made a rule about matchmaking, because Mom's been trying to set him up with every even vaguely single woman she meets."

Olive found her first genuine smile for the day. Here she'd been dreading coming back and having to see Noah, but it sounded as if his hands were full.

"Oh, and you'll be staying with us," Katie said.

"That's sweet," Olive said while thinking *hell no*. "But I can't put you out at a time like this. Gram's got plenty of room—"

"She's been renting her extra rooms out to supplement her social security checks."

Olive felt her heart squeeze. "*What?*"

"You didn't know?"

Guilt swamped Olive. Had she been that busy keeping her PR firm afloat that she'd neglected to make sure Gram was okay? They'd always been close, really close, even though Olive hadn't lived here since the summer she'd graduated high school. She'd gone to New York for college. After that, she'd taken a PR grunt job in London. Her boss had been an asshole, but she'd loved the city, loved how different it was from everything she'd ever known. She'd left the job a year ago but had stayed in London to start her own PR firm. She had only two regrets about that, and Katie was one of them. Her grandma was the other. "No, I didn't know she was renting out rooms."

Katie was quiet a moment, as she always was when trying to think about how to say something without being too harsh or blunt. "Maybe she didn't want to worry you," she finally said.

Gram had been a nurse for forty years. She had a pension and her house was paid off. *Why* would she rent out rooms? "You've got enough going on, I'll get a hotel—"

"No!" Katie lowered her voice. "I need you, Olive."

Katie had been there for her through thick and thin, and there'd been a lot of thin.

"Promise me."

Gah. "I promise. And I'm here," she said, turning into the shared driveway between the Turner house and Gram's.

"Your ETA was 12:32, and it's 12:38," Katie said. "But then again, you did almost hit my brother. That must've added a few minutes to your time."

Olive caught sight of Katie's face pressed up against the window. Next to her stood a shorter mini-Katie—her five-year-old son, and Olive's godson—Joey. Her heart warmed at the

sight of the house, at seeing Katie and Joey, at everything, including Holmes, the family's twelve-year-old basset hound,
snoozing on the porch, big as a hairy kindergartner and snoring
loud enough for her to hear from her car.

"Uh-oh," Katie said.

"You know I hate an uh-oh."

Katie sent her a grimace through the window. "Noah just
texted that he's almost here. He wasn't supposed to get back
from his run until 1:24, which would've given you enough time
to see me before going to visit Gram. He must've cut through
the woods even though he isn't supposed to jog on uneven turf
yet. That's going to set his recovery back."

Olive didn't want to think about how he'd gotten injured in
the first place, as it would make her sympathetic toward him.
She really needed to hold on to her self-righteous anger in order
to stay sane. As she leaped out of the car, her anger turned to
anxiety. She had learned it was important to be flexible in life
whenever necessary. "Let me know when the coast's clear and
I'll come over."

They disconnected and Olive turned to Gram's house just as
the front door opened.

"You're finally here!" Gram cried, wiping her hands on the
same floral apron she'd worn for as long as Olive could remember. In the blink of an eye, she was being hugged by arms much
frailer than they'd ever been, but no less fierce or short of love.
She held on tight, smiling because, as always, her grandma
smelled like roses and vanilla and childhood dreams.

"Oh, honey, are you a sight for sore eyes . . ." Gram's face
tightened with worry. "But about your room—"

"It's okay. Katie told me about your renters. I'll sleep at her
place, but are you okay? If you're short money, I can—"

"No, I'm good. *Really*," she promised. "The Bunco girls are planning a trip to Hawaii this winter. Renting out the extra rooms seemed like a great way to get the money. I hear about these great mai tais, and how at a luau you can watch hot men dance while they twirl firesticks every night." She smiled and gently patted Olive's cheeks. "Oh, I've missed you."

"Missed you more." The words were woefully inadequate. "Before I forget, have you talked to Mom or Dad? Yesterday was our monthly check-in call, and they didn't answer or call me back."

Gram shook her head. "They're probably traveling to some festival or craft fair to sell their wares and forgot. Remember last year when they went to Burning Man? It was two weeks before they remembered to check in." Holding on to Olive's hands, she spread their arms out. "You didn't have to dress up for me."

In her sundress, denim jacket, and wedge sandals, Olive wasn't all that dressed up. But she supposed, compared to the secondhand clothes she used to wear, she looked very different. She'd eventually learned to dress the part of the polished, elegant, self-reliant, successful woman she'd wanted to be. In her line of work, image was everything. Image and confidence. Which, let's face it, she was still working on.

"You look fantastic, but you also look worried."

"I am. For Katie."

"Of course. But it's also more."

Olive didn't bother denying this, it wouldn't work. She was a grade A plus liar when she needed to be, after all she was in public relations, but she'd never been able to fool Gram.

Proving it, she found herself being pulled through the house and out the slider to the side yard and the patio there, where she took her first true deep breath in . . . she had no idea. She hadn't realized until this very moment just how much she'd been missing the stability Gram always provided.

"Sit," her grandma said. "I'll be right back with the cure."

"Mew."

Olive looked down and found herself being stared at by a tiny gray-and-white kitten with slightly crossed blue eyes. "Well, hello." She reached for her, but the little thing hissed and backed away. "Tiny but mighty, huh? I come in peace."

"Maybe you do, but she most definitely doesn't," Gram said, coming back out. "She's a stray, just appeared out of nowhere yesterday. I'm calling her Pepper because she's so spicy."

"She's so thin."

"I know. I've been putting out food and water for her. And I'm about to do the same for you."

Olive turned to Gram and laughed because the woman had a tray of milk and cookies, just like the old days.

Gram grinned. "I do love the strays."

Olive dipped a cookie into her mug of milk, watching it carefully because it was a fine line between not enough soakage and too much soakage.

"Is it your job stressing you?" Gram asked. "I thought you loved living in the UK, running your own company."

Olive thought about that as she leaned over her mug, and yet *still* managed to dribble milk down the front of her dress. Awesome. "I do love it, both London and being my own boss."

Gram expertly lifted her perfectly soaked cookie to her mouth without getting a single drop of milk on herself. "While you're here, I could use your skills at the senior center. We're trying to expand and need funding."

"Happy to."

Gram smiled. "And the boyfriend? What's his name again? Ian? The one who gave you a pretty bracelet."

No, Ian had given her emotional whiplash and a headache with a splash of trust issues after he'd cheated on her with someone she'd thought was a friend. She'd bought herself the bracelet after she'd dumped him. "I'm . . . seeing someone new."

"Oh, that's wonderful," Gram said. "What's his name?"

"Matt." Matt was funny, sweet, kind, loyal, had a great job, great family, and . . . was pretend. Which really made him the perfect boyfriend.

"He didn't want to come with you?" Gram made a show of looking at Olive's ring finger. Her *ringless* ring finger. "I'd have loved to meet him."

Okay, so there were downsides to a pretend boyfriend. But the plus side? No fielding questions from anyone about why she was still single. Or why she still had trouble trusting people with her heart. Not to mention making her seem even more put together, and she'd take all the help she could get there. "He's been super busy lately, so—"

"Poppycock. Who's too busy for love? You deserve it, more than anyone I know."

Olive didn't want for love. She wanted for structure, which had always been missing from her life. As a result, she tended to operate in relationships like that young kid she'd once been, re-creating the chaos she'd lived with growing up.

A truck drove up the common driveway, parking at the very top, on Katie's side. The man who got out was everything she remembered: tall; leanly muscled; his dark, slightly curly hair peeking out from beneath a ballcap; his eyes hidden behind mirrored sunglasses. Once upon a time, he'd always had a smile, but not today. Today his mouth was grim. He rolled his shoulders like he was in some pain, then stilled at the sight of the Mini Coop.

The one that had nearly hit him less than half an hour ago.

Olive sucked in a breath and slouched in the porch swing. She was still holding that breath when he removed his sunglasses and peered inside the car before lifting his head, unerringly finding her gaze with his own.

CHAPTER 2

Olive slid as low as she could without falling to the floor, trying to get below the sightline of the white picket fence. "What are you doing?" Gram asked.

"Hiding. You never saw me. I'm not here—"

"Could've fooled me," a male voice said.

The unbearably familiar male voice reminded her of some of the best times of her life.

And the worst.

With a grimace, she looked up.

Noah stood there, looking better than a guy who'd once ruined her life should, even with his eyes narrowed, his mouth grim, and those muscles in his jaw all bunched.

"Olive Porter, as she lives and breathes," he said with absolutely no inflection at all. Which meant she was ticked off on top of being ticked off. Ticked Off Squared.

Except . . . he hadn't ruined her life. *She'd* ruined *his*.

"It's nice to see you," Gram told him. "Been a while since you've been home."

Noah used his most charming smile. "Adele. Looking good."

Gram, being of the female persuasion, fell victim to Noah's deliciously rugged charm, beaming. "Aren't you the one." She glanced at Olive. "Is your Matt this sweet?"

Okay, first of all, Noah had *never* been sweet a day in his life. Sharp, funny, dangerous, yes. Sweet? Not a chance. And second, why had she thought it a good idea to make up a boyfriend? Why hadn't she just said she didn't need a man in her life? Because she didn't, not even a little bit. Damn hindsight. "Matt's far sweeter."

Noah just smirked, the bastard. "I need to talk to you."

Olive took another cookie. "I'm very busy right now."

But he already had her by the hand, tugging her upright, leading her in that uneven gait, which gave her a pang straight through her heart.

Stupid heart.

She must've made some sound because he glanced back at her, caught the look on her face, and hardened his. "Feeling sorry for me?"

"Not even a little bit." She took a bite of the cookie she'd managed to hold on to.

"Nice to know the sarcasm didn't change with the new look." Out of hearing range, Noah abruptly let go of her hand and stepped back from her like maybe he was trying to avoid the temptation of strangling her.

He could join her club.

Hands on hips, he gave a single shake of his head.

So he was disappointed in her. Well, he could get in damn line, because she was disappointed in herself too. She'd left here an eighteen-year-old country bumpkin who'd taught herself to look and act like a sophisticated, elegant woman who knew what she was doing. And it'd worked, even if she'd sacrificed any sort of personal life. Truthfully, her only boyfriend's name was Loneliness. She popped the last bite of cookie into her mouth. Priorities. They were important. "So? What did you want to talk about?"

His eyes narrowed. "Are you kidding me?"

"Hey, if you wanted a cookie, you should've taken one off the tray."

He just looked at her.

Okay, so he hadn't been talking about the cookies and she knew it. But something she didn't know . . . how had he managed to get even *more* good-looking with time? Used to be his eyes would warm when she amused him, and catch fire when he was aroused, but with those mirrored sunglasses back over his eyes, she had no idea what he was thinking, much less feeling. "It was all your own fault, you know," she said.

He crossed his arms over his chest and cocked his head, ready to be enlightened.

"You didn't look both ways!"

"You didn't slow down before the crosswalk."

She tossed up her hands in the way she always did when she knew she held some of the blame but wasn't ready to admit it.

"Why are you even here?" he asked. "To drop off another Dear John letter?"

As she'd never intended to write him the first one, she sure as hell couldn't have stomached writing another. Or tell him why she'd left here in the first place. It'd only hurt him, and she'd done enough of that for this lifetime. And in any case, how upset could he have been, seeing as he'd never tried to talk to her about it. "Not everything's about you, Noah. I'm just here to help your sister."

"Good, because she needs you."

This gave her a pang of guilt. She hadn't been back much. She was lucky Katie was still her friend at all. Or that Noah was even speaking to her. "How are you doing with all this?"

Again he ran a hand down his face, like maybe he was fighting exhaustion and losing. "My brother-in-law and best friend is in a coma because of me, so how do you think I'm doing?"

"Sometimes an accident is just an accident. Mistakes happen, Noah."

He removed his sunglasses, revealing those golden-brown eyes of his, the ones that had always been able to see right through all her crap. "I remember saying that to you after . . ."

She gave him a wry look and he let out a mirthless laugh. "It doesn't help, does it?" he said. "Empty platitudes."

"Nope."

They stared at each other, the air between them filled with recriminations, hurt, and, at least in her case, regrets.

"You've changed," he said.

"If you mean I stopped wearing hand-me-down clothes, then yes. I changed."

He shook his head. "It's not what you're wearing. It never mattered to the people who cared about you what you wore. You've changed," he said again. "On the inside."

"I grew up."

"Well, you're still trying to run people over, so—"

She narrowed her eyes. "Not funny."

"Not laughing. You bring . . . 'your Matt' with you?"

"No. You bring anyone with you?"

"Don't have anyone to bring."

She nodded, then plastered a fake smile on her face. "Well, this has been a whole bunch of fun, but I've gotta go."

"Of course you do."

She turned back. "Was that supposed to mean something?"

"The going gets tough, you get going."

That this statement was one hundred percent true didn't help. She drew a deep breath for a calm that did not come. Maybe because calm was hard to obtain with a lump in your throat the size of a regulation football. The man in front of her had been such a big part of her formative years. His entire family had been. They'd taken her under their collective wing and given her a sense of belonging she'd never had. But the hardened look in his gaze reminded her she'd blown that. Still, she couldn't stop the question that escaped her. "Have you ever wondered what it'd be like between us now, as adults?"

He looked at her for a long beat. "Sometimes the past is best left in the past."

She forced a smile. "Something we can agree on."

CHAPTER 3

Fourteen years ago

Olive's stomach rumbled. She'd forgotten to bring lunch, so she got in line in the school cafeteria. But when she searched her pockets, she remembered she didn't have any money.

"Hey, loser, the line's moving, keep up."

Turning, she came face to face with Cindy, her tormenter in both sophomore math and science. Cindy liked to poke at weakness, which made Olive an easy target. Stepping out of line rather than admitting the truth, she ran smack into Noah coming into the cafeteria.

"Skipping lunch?"

He never missed much. It was self-preservation, she knew. His dad expected perfection from him, and his mom needed it, both having to focus all their concentration on getting Katie through school. Olive refused to add to his burden. "Not hungry."

"You're always hungry."

"Not today."

Something came and went in his eyes before he thrust out his own lunch.

The guy had run track early that morning and had a baseball game later, he needed the calories far more than she did. "No, really, I'm fine."

"Olive—"

"Gotta go." She hightailed it out of there, because she could handle a lot of things, but pity wasn't one of them.

An hour later, just before her last class, she opened her locker and found a turkey on wheat sandwich and an apple. For a moment she was too choked up to eat, but only for a moment because when she opened the sandwich, it had lettuce and tomatoes—gross—and no mayo. Noah didn't believe in polluting his body.

He had no idea what he was missing.

Still, she was hungry enough to inhale it all, even the apple. And the warm fuzzies he'd given her almost made up for the lack of chips or cookies.

Present day

Noah watched Olive walk toward the car she'd nearly run him over with. He considered himself the master at navigating the unexpected and unpredictable, but clearly his internal GPS was still broken around her. Or maybe it was the way her dress clung to her gorgeous, curvy bod, scrambling his brain cells.

Olive Porter had most definitely grown up.

Luckily, he needed to focus if he was going to be any help to his family, and the last thing he needed was a distraction.

But the biggest distraction he'd ever met was pulling a big duffel bag from the back of her car and . . . turning toward Katie's house? "What are you doing?"

When she didn't answer, probably because she had to stagger under the weight of her bag, he scooped it from her and shouldered it.

"I didn't ask for your help."

Right, because she'd rather keel over dead. At least that had been the old Olive. He knew nothing about New Olive. She'd vanished from his life when he'd needed her the most and he'd moved on.

They played tug-of-war over her duffel bag. "Why are you heading toward my mom's house like you're staying there?" he asked.

"Because I am." She was out of breath. "Let go."

"Why are you staying there?" he asked, letting go of her bag. She nearly fell to her ass. "Sorry."

She sent him a fulminating look. "Katie insisted."

He had no intention of sharing space with this woman. He'd already shared his heart and she'd decimated it. "Bad plan."

"Ya think?" She sighed. "Gram rented out her extra rooms. And it's Katie's house now, remember? And for the record, I offered to stay in a hotel."

With a groan, Noah tipped his head back and stared up at the sky. Once Katie had married Joe and they'd had little Joey, they'd built their mom a brand spanking new apartment above the garage. Free of the big house responsibilities, she'd been able to travel with her friends and enjoy herself. In fact, she'd been on a monthlong adventure in Portugal when Noah and Joe had been in their accident. She'd come home right away, of course, which made it the first time they'd all been in Sunrise Cove together in a long time.

But Noah had been gone the most. He had a house on the south shore and an efficiency studio apartment in Yosemite, but also spent time in D.C. at the NPS—National Park Service— headquarters. Joe, down two paygrades, worked far less hours than Noah, and either stayed on Noah's couch in Yosemite when necessary or commuted from Sunrise Cove.

Olive eyed him suspiciously. "Where are *you* staying?"

Noah caught sight of Katie plastered up against the living room picture window watching them. She winced just before she yanked the blinds closed.

At his side, Olive snorted. "Busybody."

No doubt. "Wait here a sec." He strode up the front steps.

Holmes the Hound woke with a snort, his long ears rumpled and wrinkled. Seeing Noah, he tipped his head back and let out a soulful but happy howl, tail thumping.

With a smile, Noah crouched down to love up on the old guy, named Holmes because, like Sherlock, the hound could sniff out anything. Well, mostly food, but still. He weighed in at seventy pounds, his belly scraped the floor. So did his ears. He drooled, had gas that could wipe out the entire ecosystem, and could howl until the windows rattled if left alone. He couldn't see much past his own nose anymore, but he loved his people fiercely and was loyal and devoted. So much so that he'd been depressed for months after losing his best friend when Sassy Pants, the family's fifteen-year-old cat, had passed earlier in the year.

Noah gave him a quick belly rub. "I'll be back," he promised, then rose and reached for the door handle, colliding with Olive doing the same.

He glanced over at her. "I see you still take direction well."

"And you're as bossy as ever." She sent Holmes a sweeter smile than Noah had ever gotten from her. "Hey, boy." Then, since neither of them had let go of the door handle, she went back to fighting him for it. They were still wrestling when the door suddenly opened, and they tumbled inside.

Olive leaped up so fast, she nearly fell over again. Noah took longer, refusing to acknowledge the stab of pain in his leg, or let anyone see it. His sister clapped her hands together in delight. "I've been waiting for this day for *years*."

Noah straightened. "So you admit this was planned."

Katie rolled her lips into her mouth. Everyone knew she was incapable of lying convincingly, so whenever she got cornered, she zipped her lips as if to keep the words from falling right out.

Olive stepped past Noah and pulled Katie in for a hug. As always when confronted with physical contact, she turned into a corpse with rigor mortis. Her phone and glasses fell from her hands and hit the floor. "My phone. My glasses," she said, while waiting for the hug to end.

Looking amused, Olive pulled back. "Sorry, it's been too long."

"It's never too long to *not* hug."

Olive laughed. "Okay, then, how about this." And she kissed Katie noisily on the cheek.

Katie squirmed. "Worse. Way worse."

Ignoring all of that, Noah gave his sister a long look.

"Hey," she said. "My husband's in a coma, my son's missing his dad, and I've been scrambling to keep my life together. On the surface I might be cool as a cucumber, but on the inside I'm a squirrel in traffic. So sue me for wanting my brother and my best friend here under one roof." She paused. "Don't be mad."

"We're not," Olive said, taking Katie's hand in hers.

True. Noah couldn't be mad, because he was the reason Joe was in a coma. He'd been trained in evasive driving. He should've been able to handle the car. In fact, he should've seen it coming. Instead, he'd been arguing with Joe over his choice in music. "Whatever you need," he told Katie. *Money, time, babysitting . . . my jugular.* "I'm here for you."

Olive nodded. "What he said."

"What I need," Katie said, "is for the two people I love so dearly to help me with Joey and be there for Joe."

"Done," Olive said.

"It won't be easy. Today alone I said four things I never in a million years imagined saying." She held up a finger for each point. "'Sorry I flushed your poop before you said goodbye.' 'If you're going to stick your hands down your pants, you have to wash them after—with soap.' Oh, and let's not forget 'Don't lick the dog' and 'Who ate the stick of butter I had on the counter?' Which, by the way, if Joey says he has to go potty today, I suggest you run, don't walk."

Olive had a hand over her mouth, looking both horrified and like she might laugh.

Katie pointed at her.

Olive shook her head and got herself under control.

Noah turned back to the door to get Olive's duffel bag, and not, as he'd have liked, to get into his truck and keep driving until he was in another state. On the other side of the country.

"Wait—where are you going?" Katie asked in her demanding sister voice.

"Calm down."

Katie narrowed her eyes and turned to Olive. "My brother just said 'calm down' like he wants his own *Dateline* special."

Noah rolled his eyes and dropped Olive's duffel bag at her feet. "I'm going to sit with Joe for a bit." Where he'd hold his brother-in-law's hand and try badgering him back to the land of the living.

He caught Olive staring at him, expression hooded, nothing visible except for maybe irritation at having to . . . what? See him?

Ditto, babe. He gave her a curt nod, brushed a kiss to the top of Katie's head, and then he was on the road, windows down, nearly freezing his brain with the biting spring mountain air, all so he couldn't think too much.

And yet he still managed to do just that.

Twenty minutes later, he sat at Joe's side in an uncomfortable chair that had his ass numb and his leg aching unbearably. Ignoring this, he hunched forward, eyes on Joe's face. "Hey, man."

Nothing.

He let out a breath. He'd been here every day since the accident and still it was a shock. Awake, Joe was in perpetual motion, usually smiling or laughing, always joking around. The life of the party. Seeing him like this, so damn still, shook Noah to the core. "So, uh, everything's okay at home. Joey walks around in your favorite Giants hat."

The room remained silent. Well, with the exception of the whooshing and beeping of various equipment working hard to keep Joe alive. "He won't take it off, not even to sleep. Katie's holding up in her usual stoic way. She's reorganized your closet three times and, don't hate the messenger, she threw out all your old socks, including your lucky basketball pair. I tried to save them, but the trash guys had already come." He paused. Maybe he should go with positive stuff. "On the other hand, you know how you're always after her to check the oil on her POS car that she won't let you upgrade? Well, she's finally doing that. Like daily."

He leaned back in his chair and closed his eyes. "She misses you." *I miss you . . .* "I'm doing my best to make sure they have everything they need." *Except you . . . No one can replace you . . .*

He swallowed hard, keeping a few facts back for himself. Such as how Joey kept crying for his daddy and wasn't sleeping well. But then again, none of them were. "Oh, and the good news is that you were called up for jury duty last week, but you got out of it, seeing as you're here snoozing."

Still nothing.

They'd been told not to expect reactions, not a flicker of an eyelid, not a squeeze of the hand, nothing, but hearing it was one thing, experiencing it was another. He leaned forward. "Listen, man, the truth is that I'm failing Katie. I'm failing Joey. Hell, I'm failing everyone, and I need you to wake up—" He froze. Had Joe's eyelids flickered? He stared at Joe for five long minutes but didn't see it happen again.

A nurse spoke from the doorway. "Sir? I'm sorry, but time's up."

He looked at Joe. "I'll be back tomorrow." He squeezed his best friend's hand.

Joe didn't squeeze back.

Right. Because he was in a goddamn coma.

CHAPTER 4

Noah turned off his truck in front of Katie's house, barely re-membering the drive from the hospital. Despite the chilly day, a few downstairs windows were open, which meant Katie had cranked the heater and then probably baked something, warming the house up so much that she threw herself into a hot flash, and the rest of them could freeze for all she cared.

The sounds of a full house drifted out to him: talking, the clinking of glasses and dishes, music playing in the background. Shit, he'd forgotten it was their weekly family dinner night, which, if he was in town, neither rain nor shine nor near deadly car accidents could get him out of. He really wasn't feeling like pasting on a smile and being friendly, but if he left now, the next time he saw his mom she'd give him the look that said once again he'd let her down by not being around enough.

He knew his place in this family, and that was to be the one that everyone could count on. It was a role he knew how to play, as he'd been at it since the day Katie had been born three minutes and thirty-seven seconds after him. He was to show up, never need anything, and be perfect while he was at it.

Only, he'd been far from perfect.

Still was.

But he knew how to pretend, and was good at it. He didn't even mind it, not really. He knew his mom counted on him to be the glue, especially after his dad had passed away a few years ago. But at the moment, all he wanted was a shower, a beer, and twelve hours horizontal with his eyes closed. He was so done in, he didn't even care if there wasn't a woman in the bed with him.

Just get it over with . . .

He started through the living room toward the dining room but stopped at the telltale sound of a tail thumping the floor. Holmes was on his bed near the unlit fireplace, head still down, forlorn eyes open and on Noah, who'd rescued him one day in his senior year of high school, when he'd found a very bedraggled and underfed puppy hiding beneath the school bleachers.

Holmes, who maybe should've been named Couch Potato, had been great for Noah's family, low maintenance and innately lazy. Not much had changed over the years, except for his muzzle going gray with age. "Shh," Noah whispered, hunkering down in front of the dog before he could lift his head and howl his hello. Noah laughed softly when Holmes rolled over to expose his very round belly for rubs and cuddles, which he of course obliged.

Miraculously, no one had heard him come in, he realized when he turned toward the dining room. Little Joey was sitting in Katie's lap and grinning at Olive seated next to him.

Grinning.

Since the accident, none of them had been able to get the kid to smile or eat much, but Olive was gently teasing him with food, saying, "A bite for me . . . annnnnd a bite for you."

And unbelievably, Joey ate everything she fed him.

"You're good with him," Katie said.

Olive gently touched her finger to the tip of Joey's nose. "Maybe he's good with me."

Joey laughed and so did Olive, a sound Noah hadn't remembered that he loved.

Then, as if she sensed him, she looked up. Their gazes collided and held. Everyone else turned to see what had Olive's attention, and all chatter stopped for the briefest of seconds.

"Honey," his mom said. "Why are you out there instead of eating with us?"

"He's probably making sure it's a safe place," Katie said.

His mom frowned. "What is that supposed to mean?"

His sister waved her fork in Noah's general direction. "Every time he comes home, you try to set him up like he can't find a woman. Women find *him*, Mom. And anyway, maybe he's still recovering from Molly, who after two years decided she hated his job and his hours and that he wasn't family material, and he needed to change everything about himself to keep her. Thankfully, he walked away, because who needs that kind of love?"

"You know I can speak for myself," Noah said mildly. At work, when he talked, people listened. Sometimes he forgot that wasn't the case at home, and never had been. "I can even form whole sentences on my own. And I'm not still recovering from Molly, that was a year ago."

His mom ignored him, speaking directly to Katie. "Molly wasn't The One. The One is still out there, he deserves that much."

Noah's left eye began to twitch. Hopefully it was a seizure and he'd get a nice, quiet ambulance ride out of here.

"Uncle Noah's eye is doing something weird," Joey said.

"What, is it a crime to need my only son to be happy?" his mom asked the room. "Why won't he settle down? All my friends' kids have settled down."

"Except for the ones who have single daughters, who you keep trying to fix him up with," Katie said.

Olive was looking amused. Good to know she found this funny.

His mom's laser eyes landed on him. "What happened to that cute librarian friend of Katie's that you went out with last summer?"

"She decided to go back to her ex."

"Okay," she said. "How about—"

"Mom, maybe tonight, instead of invading my privacy, we just have dinner."

"Hey," she said, pointing at him with her glass. "You came out of my privacy."

"Oh my God," Katie muttered. "Mom, no one wants to think about coming out of their mother's 'privacy.'"

"Missy, check your attitude."

"For complaints about my attitude, please contact the manufacturer. And do you remember when you made me play soccer? Even though I hate to run?"

"Made you? You begged me to sign you up, said it was a huge dream of yours. And I *always* let you both follow your dreams—unless I'd already paid the registration fee on your previous dream. Then you had to follow that one for six to eight more weeks."

Katie rolled her eyes.

"Fine, new subject. After dinner, I need someone to help me update my phone, and also I can't get to Netflix from my remote."

"I can help you now," Noah said. "For Netflix, you hit the home button. I circled it with a red Sharpie so we didn't have to do this every day. As for your phone, you just hit update."

"Also, before you ask," Katie said without missing a beat, "the Wi-Fi password is still your phone number."

"Don't you two dare use that patronizing tone with me when I have questions about tech stuff. I once had to teach you both how to use a damn spoon."

"'Damn' is a bad word," Joey said.

His grandma smiled sweetly at him. "You're right, love, but you should know, my children are rude idiots."

Joey nodded wisely.

"And will you sit already?" his mom asked Noah. "You're giving me a neck ache standing there." She loaded up a plate and pushed it toward the only empty seat.

Right next to Olive.

Joey climbed out of Katie's lap and into Olive's, and then reached for Noah, straddling one of his legs and one of Olive's, his short little legs pulling theirs together so their thighs were touching.

Oh good, and here Noah had thought things couldn't get more awkward. "Sorry," he murmured her way.

"Pass the green beans, please?"

"You used to hate all things green."

His mom shook her head. "That's not right. Olive's always loved green foods, *especially* my green bean casserole."

Noah, thinking of all the times he'd watched Olive drop anything green into a napkin rather than insult his mom, laughed.

His mom looked at Olive. "You don't?"

She grimaced and sent Noah a glare.

Katie leaned into Olive and stage-whispered, "I give you permission to run him over again."

Noah picked up his glass, holding it strategically so that he was flipping Katie off.

"I almost never run anyone over anymore," Olive muttered to no one in particular.

Amy shook her head at her daughter and looked at Olive. "All those years I served you green beans, I'm so sorry."

Olive waved that off. "My fault. I was embarrassed to tell you."

The exchange felt oddly . . . awkward, like they were strangers. The thing was, he knew Olive and Katie had remained extremely close, and he'd assumed the same for Olive and his mom. When had they stopped being close, and why?

"Don't forget about the ball game on Saturday," Katie told him.

Olive looked at Noah in surprise. "You're playing again?"

"No." He didn't realize he'd said this harshly until she flushed, making him wish he'd pregamed dinner with a glass of wine the size of his sister's.

"He hasn't played at all," Katie said. "Not since May seventh of our last year in high school, exactly one week before graduation, when on the night of our senior party, you ran him over with your Gram's old ATV, crushing his leg, requiring three surgeries and a two-week stay in the hospital, after which he ended up working for the forestry department instead of playing D1 baseball."

The sudden silence was so vast he could hear his own blood in his veins. Olive reached for her untouched wineglass. "I think I'll have some alcohol now."

Noah poured her a full glass.

Katie nudged her shoulder to Olive's. His sister's version of a hug. "I'm sorry. You don't like to talk about it. I'll put it on the list of things I'm not supposed to bring up."

"Thank you." Olive then toasted Katie, clearly forgiving. In fact, she was probably the most forgiving person he'd ever met.

"The ball game I was referring to is Joey's," Katie said. "Noah's going to step in for Joe as temporary coach, starting with this week's game. Assuming he doesn't choke, since he hasn't so much as said the word 'ball' in all these years."

Olive took a deep drink.

Katie grimaced. "I did it again. I'm sorry. Did I mention my husband's in a coma?"

Olive sighed and reached out to hug Katie, who held up a hand to stop her, which meant that hand ran right into Olive's face.

Olive raised a brow at her. "Did you just smack me?"

"Actually, your face walked right into my hand." Katie paused, then also let out a sigh. "Fine, I smacked you. I'm sorry! You know how I feel about hugs."

Olive took another deep drink of her wine.

His mom looked at Noah. "I always thought it was such a shame you gave baseball up altogether, when it was such an important part of your life. We thought you might find other ways to be involved with the sport. Instead, soon as you recovered, you went off to Yosemite Community College and to work for the National Park Service."

"Oh good. We're going to keep talking about this."

"Yosemite," his mom repeated. "A million miles away."

"Your math isn't mathing, Mom."

"Fine. But a three-hour drive is way too far."

It'd felt like the right distance to him. Close enough to help out if his family needed it. Far enough that he got to miss a whole bunch of family dinners. It'd been a shock to him, having picked Yosemite out of a hat, that he'd ended up loving it and his job.

"You could've coached," his mom said.

"Yes." He winked at Joey. "And now I am."

She sighed. It was a sighing pandemic in here tonight. He gave Olive a *gimme* gesture toward the wine bottle.

She handed it right over.

His mom was staring at him, clearly still waiting on an explanation. "Mom, baseball wasn't an important part of my life. It was an important part of Dad's life."

He caught a blink-and-miss-it wince from Olive. Guilt. He hated that, because he'd never blamed her for what had happened. Not even for a single second.

Although . . . he *did* blame her for vanishing from their lives. Well, *his*, because she'd been in constant contact with Katie. Even from a different continent, she put in the time and showed up for his sister.

But with him, she hadn't been able to get away fast enough, and that still burned. They'd seen each other here and there, like Katie's wedding to Joe, a few of Joey's birthday parties, his dad's celebration of life, and she'd been perfectly polite.

And distant.

But then again, so had he. He'd not trusted himself to push for a real conversation and reveal feelings he'd long ago buried.

Mostly.

"Now's the perfect time to give up your dangerous job and move back to Sunrise Cove," his mom said. "You could back up our manager at Turner Rents and Supply." She smiled, because *she* was their manager.

Years and years ago, she and his dad had taken over his grandpa's Turner Rents & Supply. They rented out and/or fixed snow and ranching equipment. The place had been his dad's baby. As a teenager, Noah had been under a lot of pressure to work there, and he knew his parents had expected him to take over if baseball ever failed him. Well, as it turned out, *he'd* failed baseball, by choice, but much to his parents' displeasure, he hadn't gone on to run the family business. After Olive had left, he'd taken inspiration from that and done the same, putting Sunrise Cove in his rearview.

"And if you lived here, I *know* we could find you the perfect woman to date," his mom said.

Katie snorted. "Noah doesn't date. He fornicates."

Olive choked on a sip of her wine.

"Katie!" their mom gasped.

Katie patted Olive on the back. "What? I'm not wrong." She looked at Noah. "Tell me I'm wrong."

He stared at her. "Seriously?"

"Need me to define 'fornicate' for you?"

"No, I want you to stop talking."

"Children! We have a guest."

Everyone looked at Olive. She sent them all a weak smile. Probably she was wishing she'd gotten a hotel room. In Rome.

"Mom, Olive's not a guest," Katie said. "She's family."

He wondered if he'd gone gray during this thirty-year-long dinner.

"Jessica's daughter Chloe is single now," his mom said. She'd pulled out her phone and was searching for something. "Katie, where's that text you sent me about it?"

Noah looked at his sister. "This wasn't in our family text chat."

"You should know that every family text chat has a smaller group chat without the annoying one," Katie said. "And if you think your family doesn't, I've got some bad news."

He looked at his mom. "That true?"

"Very," his sister assured him.

"Found it!" His mom looked up from her phone. "Jessica says Chloe's working at the bar and grill and gets off at eight. You can meet her for a drink and get to know her."

Jessica was his mom's longtime best friend. Chloe had been a year behind him in school. She was sweet, quiet, and shy, and though their paths occasionally crossed, she'd never said one word to him in all the years Noah had known her.

"Chloe is nice and very normal," Katie said. "But Noah doesn't like nice and very normal. He likes fun and a little wild."

Olive choked again.

Noah patted her on the back himself this time, while sending daggers to his mom and sister. "I will pay you a thousand dollars to stop talking."

"Each?" Katie wanted to know. "Because I could use a thousand bucks."

Noah drank the rest of his wine even though he hated wine. It always gave him a headache, but it didn't matter because he already had one.

"Did you know that people with siblings have better survival skills than most?" Katie asked Olive. "It's because we've had experience in physical combat, psychological warfare, and sensing suspicious activity."

"I'm just saying," his mom said to Noah. "You're thirty now, and you might want to think about settling down, giving me more grandchildren, and Joey a cousin."

"Ruff, ruff!" said Joey, who on any given day spoke both human and dog.

"Or you could just adopt a dog so he could have a sibling," Katie said.

His mom beamed in delight. "Katie! Did you just make a joke?"

"No. It's just that a dog's a lot cheaper than a kid." She ruffled Joey's hair. "Not that I'd trade you in, not even for all my money back. I'm pretty fond of you now that you're potty trained."

Joey climbed over Olive and back into his mom's lap, wrapping his arms around her neck.

"Mmm, puppy cuddles. My favorite thing." Katie hugged him tight and kissed the top of his head. "I think I'll keep you forever and ever."

"So if I was five too, you'd hug me?" Olive asked her.

"If you came out of my vagina, yes," Katie said.

"Dear God, Katie."

Katie smiled at her mom. "Oops, sorry." She looked at Olive. "If you'd come out of my *privacy*, then yes, I'd hug you."

Amy Turner rolled her eyes and turned to Olive. "I hear you stopped working for that UK public relations firm and started your own. How's that going?"

"It's early days yet."

"It's going great," Katie said. "She's been super successful for her clients."

Noah's mom, never able to ask just one question when she could ask a hundred, said, "So what's been your favorite, most successful PR campaign so far?"

Olive thought about that for a few seconds. "Maybe the one I did for a clothing designer who was scheduled to have a pop-up store in the city. Her sister's a baker, so for the opening we created an edible dress, made entirely from chocolate."

"I love chocolate!" Joey said.

"Me too," Olive said, gently booping his nose. "The plan was to have my client smash it apart and give out pieces of it to everyone in line for the opening. Only it got unseasonably hot that day, and the dress melted before we got started. It was such a huge puddle of chocolate that it slickened the entryway, and my client slipped and fell into the chocolate."

"Five-second rule!" Joey yelled, making everyone smile.

"Did you get all awkward?" Katie asked Olive. "Because you get all kinds of awkward when the attention's on you."

Olive got Joey to eat another bite off her plate and beamed at him. "I think your mommy's forgetting that the only person in this room to ever be more awkward than me is her." She looked at Katie. "But yes. Yes, I did, thank you very much. I also ended up with chocolate all over me and I definitely licked my own arm more than once."

Katie laughed.

His mom smiled at the sound and looked at Olive. "The day you moved in next door was a great day. Before you, Katie was so lonely."

"I don't like people enough to get lonely," Katie said, then paused, seeming to realize she'd inadvertently insulted everyone there. "Except for you guys, of course."

"You never had friends before Olive," Noah's mom said. "I was always so worried."

Olive looked at Katie. "You used to talk about two girls you were friends with before me. They were twins too, and had just moved away. I can't remember their names."

"Star and Candy," his mom said. "They were her made-up friends."

Olive blinked at Katie. "You lied? I didn't know you could."

"No," Katie said. "I didn't lie. You never asked if they were real."

"Misdirected then," Olive said. "Same thing."

"Look!" Katie pointed to the center of the table. "Cake!"

"Where?" Olive asked, then frowned. "Hey!"

Noah looked at his mom. "You should concentrate your efforts on setting Katie up with friend dates, instead of me with date dates."

"You think I haven't tried? Because I have. But whenever someone was due to come over, Katie would put her coat on before answering the door, like she was just leaving."

"I always do that," Katie said. "In case it's someone I don't want to see."

"And if it's someone you do want to see?" Olive asked.

"In that extremely unlikely event, I say I just got home."

"Brilliant," Olive said.

"I need to brush up on my don't-talk-to-me face for when Joey starts kindergarten in the fall."

"But wouldn't it be nice to build yourself an outside support system?" their mom asked.

Noah watched a flash of guilt cross Olive's face, probably for not being that support system.

"No. Girls suck. Remember when you made me try gymnastics, and the girls stole my clothes out of the locker room while I was in the shower?"

Her mom's face hardened. "The other girls in your class were all so awful."

"Not *all* of them," Katie said. "Sami was nice."

"Oh, you mean the one with the muddy shoes."

Katie rolled her eyes. "Good to know you remember people based on slights they committed over a decade ago, Mom."

"You know who never came into my house with muddy shoes? Olive."

This was true. In some ways, Olive had been the most adult teenager Noah had ever met. To say she'd grown up rough was an understatement. She'd been an outsider in her own home.

Or tent, as the case had often been. Her parents had been far more worried about getting to a Grateful Dead concert than the emotional stability and well-being of their own daughter. By the time she'd hitchhiked to Gram's house all those years ago, it'd taken her parents two days to notice she was gone.

"A dear friend of mine works at the zoo," Noah's mom said thoughtfully, looking at Olive. "They're trying to grow their social media. I know it's not as elegant as a clothing designer, but would you be willing to talk to her?"

Olive smiled. "Of course."

Noah knew very little about Olive's life now, but it was clear she'd changed a lot, learning to trust and believe in herself enough to run her own PR firm. It surprised him. Not that she was successful, because that he could one hundred percent believe— she'd always been one of the smartest people he knew—but that she ran a company that required her to step out of her lone-wolf attitude and be public, social, and good with people. Though he supposed her glossy, sophisticated look was all part of that.

Which meant . . . maybe he wasn't the only pretender at the table.

CHAPTER 5

Fourteen years ago

Olive headed out of school and toward the beat-up old truck Noah and Katie's grandpa had gifted them when they'd turned sixteen a few months ago. The twins were supposed to share the truck, but Katie had failed her driver's test four times and refused to try again.

Both Noah and Katie were already in the truck. Olive slid onto the bench seat and inhaled deep because something smelled like . . . "French fries?" She'd missed lunch, but this time it wasn't her fault. Earlier, Cindy and her friends had shoved Katie in the hallway. She'd fallen hard to her knees, spilling her drink and sending her books and things sprawling far and wide. Olive had shoved Cindy back, but by then several teachers had come out, catching only Olive, who'd ended up in detention. "You guys didn't have to wait for me."

Katie handed over the French fries. "Supersized."

Olive's stomach rumbled, but she didn't take them. "They're pity fries, right?"

"No, they're fury fries," Katie said, and glanced at her brother.

Olive looked at Noah too, which wasn't a hardship. She would never admit to crushing on him, never ever, but it didn't mean she couldn't admire from afar. He was in his usual jeans and a T-shirt, ballcap on backward, his hair curling around the edges, looking better than she wanted to admit. But though he flashed her a small smile, it was far from his usual trouble-filled one. His body was practically vibrating with tension. No, wait. Anger.

"I took care of it," he said.

A bad feeling came over her. "It?"

"He went to the principal and told her what really happened," Katie said.

Olive gaped at him. "What? No!"

"They can't keep getting away with all the shit they've been pulling," he said quietly.

She stared down at the fries. "So these really are pity fries."

"No," Noah said. "They're thank-you fries. For having Katie's back when I can't."

That made her chest ache. For Katie. For Noah being the kind of guy he was. For herself, because though she wanted to be a part of this family, what she wanted even more would never happen because Noah had friend-zoned her. Instead of crying, she stuffed more fries in her mouth, closing her eyes to fully appreciate the trans fats hitting her system.

"In science today we learned that eating foods like French fries might be linked to depression," Katie said.

Olive kept shoveling in the fries. "Maybe it's just that when people have a crap day, they need French fries—which means it's the cure for depression, not the cause. And who cares if they're fattening." She sank a little against the seat and kept eating. "We can't all have rockin' abs."

Since Noah was the only one in the truck with rockin' abs, Katie gave a snort.

Noah just slid Olive a sideways glance.

Damn, her mouth had a big mouth. "I mean, not that I've noticed or anything."

Katie snorted again.

"I haven't!" But if she'd been Pinocchio, her nose would've just grown long enough to shatter the windshield.

Present day

After Olive helped Katie handle Joey's bedtime routine—bath, potty, stories, water, another trip to the potty, etc.—the two of them sat at the kitchen table eating a whole rack of cookies between them.

Like old times.

And just like old times, Katie doodled in a notebook because the repetitive motion of writing soothed her brain, which she'd once described as similar to having thirty TVs on in the same room, all on different channels, all at full blast.

Olive eyed the page Katie's notebook was opened to. It was filled, and even though every line said the exact same thing, each had been written in a different font. Not a surprise, since for as long as Olive could remember, Katie'd had all the fonts memorized.

"'The mountains are calling, and I must go,'" Olive read, knowing it was Katie's favorite line by John Muir. "What font is this one?" She pointed to a line halfway down the page.

Katie, in the act of dipping a cookie into her mug of milk, glanced over. "Kefa. Are we going to play the name the font game?"

"Sure. Unless you want to tell me how you're really holding up."

Katie shrugged. "Physically, I'm here and fine. Mentally, I'm in a pool in Hawaii with Joe, ordering our third mojito."

Joey appeared at their side in dinosaur pj's, hair adorably tousled. "Cookies!"

Katie sighed but pulled Joey onto her lap. "One," she said.

He studied the open package of cookies and very carefully made his choice, then he just as carefully dipped it into the milk before stuffing it into his mouth.

"You're supposed to take bites, not shove the whole thing in," Katie said.

He grinned at her, his mouth rimmed in chocolate.

"This is an interesting font, what is it?" Olive asked, pointing to another line in the notebook.

"Wingdings three," Joey said.

Olive smiled at him. "Like mommy, like son."

"Okay," Katie said. "Kisses and then back to bed."

Joey kissed his mom, then hopped like a bunny out of the room.

"Ribbit, ribbit!" he yelled from the hallway.

Okay, not a bunny then, but a frog . . . "He's pretty amazing."

Katie smiled. "I know. And I made him. Well, okay, his dad helped."

"How was Joe today?"

"The doctors say they expect him to start showing signs of waking up any day now. All his scans look better and the brain swelling has gone way down." She paused. "I'm scared, Olive. I love him too much. I'm trying to be strong for Joey, but it's hard."

"You're the strongest person I know," Olive said softly, hurting for Katie. "But it's okay not to be okay."

"It's just that I'm on sensory overload all the time, and because of what happened to Joe, everyone wants to hover over me, and I don't know how to explain I don't want anyone in my space bubble because I can hear the dog snoring, the freezer dropping ice, and there are clothes in the wrong places, dirty dishes in the sink, and I can feel my toes too much."

"You don't have to explain, because your family knows and gets you, and so do I."

Katie looked at her. "*You're* a part of this family, you idiot. So is your grandma. She's so sweet. You know Noah's been helping her out around the house, fixing whatever she needs fixing, sending her texts to remind her to check her blood sugar. Today, she dropped off a tray of lasagna for him. Don't worry, I plan to make sure he shares with us."

Olive had only heard one thing. "Why does she have to check her blood sugar?"

"To make sure her borderline diabetes stays borderline."

Olive blinked, and Katie winced. "You didn't know?"

Olive shook her head. "No, but it's my fault. I call and check in, but she hates to worry me. The distance is hard."

Katie was quiet a beat, the way she got when she was thinking about saying something very serious. "Your grandma once told me that sometimes you've got to hug someone even when you don't want to, so you know how big to dig the hole."

Olive snorted. "A second joke in a week? Look at you, making a funny to ease my mind. Does this mean you'll hug me goodnight?"

"Only if you want to be buried after."

It was too late to check in with Gram—the woman liked to go to sleep early. But later, when Olive finally climbed into bed, she dragged her laptop in with her and put in two hours to, one, research diabetes and, two, catch up on work.

When she finished, she realized her shoulders were at her ears, she was tense as hell, and . . . in a bad mood. Running her own PR firm was a dream come true, but if she was being honest, it wasn't always what she'd thought it would be. Being the boss, being in charge of literally every single decision all day long every day, was hard, but she was good at hard.

The loneliness, not so much.

Now, being back in Sunrise Cove, she realized something even more unsettling—and humbling. Katie, the person she'd flown halfway across the planet to help, was less in need of help than Olive herself was.

And . . . Noah was "fornicating" like it was his job?

Aha, *now* she was getting somewhere with her bad mood. But tired of thinking too hard, she closed her eyes, then jerked awake at the blaring of a foghorn that nearly put her into V-fib. Her cell phone.

It was morning.

Heart pounding in her ears, she reached out, accidentally knocking the phone to the floor, where it continued having its seizure. "Ugh." Leaning over the edge of the bed, she stretched to grab it and . . .

Fell.

Right next to a sleeping Holmes. He opened his bloodshot eyes and she kissed his snout. She could see a streak of dawn's light peeking in through the slats of the shades on the window, and wished she was still sleeping. Her caller was Evan McAlister, a client whose company operated a handful of hockey arenas around the globe.

"Olive," he said with obvious relief when she finally answered. "I've left some messages. It's so unlike you not to answer at any time day or night. You okay?"

Was she?

Honestly, she had no idea. And yes, she tended to spoil her clients by always being available, needing their repeat business. "I'm in the States. I sent out an email a few days ago to everyone that I'd be in a different time zone for a few weeks. I'm working as always, just different hours of the day than you're used to."

"Oh, right. I remember now. And . . . I woke you. I'm sorry. I just wanted to go over the campaign one more time."

They were planning an auction with some high-profile athletes who would spend a day with the winning bidders, teaching them how to ice-skate. "Sure," she said.

Holmes licked her hand and she cupped his adorably baggy, wrinkly face. She got a sweet little lick in return that melted her, making her wish she could get off the roller coaster long enough to rescue an animal in need . . . or start a family of her own. She realized having a baby was quite a leap from a dog, but the heart wanted what the heart wanted.

Only, seeing as what her heart wanted probably required actually going on a date, she wasn't going to get there any time soon. With a sigh, she reached for her laptop, because even though she and Evan had been through their campaign a bunch of times already, some clients needed more hand-holding than others. "Hold on a sec . . ." Where had she left her glasses? Maybe on the counter in the bathroom where she'd removed her makeup last night? Rising to her feet, she pulled the bathroom door open, strode in, and bounced off something hard.

Noah, wearing a towel and nothing else besides the sexy.

He had his toothbrush in his mouth, stubble that was at least two days past a five-o'clock shadow on his jaw, and . . . she lost every thought in her head. Along with her phone, which slipped out of her fingers and hit the floor, from which she could hear the tinny sound of Evan's voice. "Olive? Olive, are you still there?"

Noah raised a brow at her, then scooped up the phone and held it out. When she took it, he headed back to his sink and dropped his towel.

She'd like to say she stared at his broad shoulders and back, but she wasn't that noble. Plus, he had the best ass on the planet, though it was fairly quickly covered up as he pulled on a pair of running shorts. He also tugged a T-shirt over his head, finger-combed his hair, and stuck on a ballcap.

Must be nice to spend two seconds getting ready . . . "Gotta go," she told Evan, torn between throwing herself at Noah or running for the hills. Damn, her emotions were really giving her whiplash today. "Family emergency."

"Family emergency," Noah repeated when she disconnected her call, leaning against the sink casual as you please. "Interesting choice of BS excuses since you took yourself out of this *family* years ago."

Yes. Yes, she had, for reasons she could never, ever share with him. "Let me know when you're done in here," she said with as much dignity as she could, which wasn't much since, unlike him, she stood there in an oversized T-shirt, baggy sweat bottoms, and hair from hell. "I've got a video call in a bit and it takes a while to fix the whole hot mess thing I've got going on."

That got her an almost smile. "You got the hot part right," he murmured, voice low and morning husky. "Unlike last night at the shit show we'll call dinner," he said, "you actually look exactly how you used to."

Since he didn't seem happy about that, she let the annoyance in, since hopefully it would get her through being in such close quarters.

"Why are you working this early?" he asked. "You hate mornings."

She did hate mornings, but was surprised he even remembered that about her. She was also struck by the odd trick he had of making a person want to talk to him, to tell him stuff he wanted to know. It was something in that open, direct golden-brown gaze of his. She had no doubt it made him uniquely successful at interrogating felons.

And women. Let's not forget that, and unfortunately, she wasn't nearly as immune as she wanted to be. "The time zone necessitates mornings. But also, my parents missed our monthly call, and I've learned if I call them once their day gets going, they forget to answer their phone. I need to try them before my meeting and arrange a time to go to the farm and see them while I'm here."

He looked surprised. "Do you do that often?"

"Rarely," she admitted. "We usually meet somewhere on their travels. I actually haven't been back to the farm since I left it. I'm not even positive I could find it." And she was only halfway kidding.

He paused, something he didn't do often, so she figured she wasn't going to like what he said next.

"I could take you."

She was right. She didn't like it. His offer felt like pity, and they both knew she'd always been allergic to that particular emotion. "Thanks, but I'm fine."

Noah laughed ruefully. "How many times have I heard that?"

Right. "Look, maybe we need to call some sort of a truce while I'm here. It'd help if you'd stop baiting me."

"*I'm* baiting *you?*" he asked incredulously.

"Aren't you?"

He studied her a beat. "The only way a truce is going to happen is if we stay away from each other."

"Exactly. So you stay on your half of the bathroom and I'll stay on mine."

He snorted. "How exactly is that going to work when it comes to the shower and the toilet?"

"It's called knocking."

"Which you didn't do," he pointed out. "Two minutes earlier and you'd have caught me in the shower."

Her gaze, independent of her brain, slid down his body and back up again.

He was smirking. "See something you like?"

"*No!*"

He smiled. "You used to have a crush on me."

No use denying what everyone had known. "Past tense, trust me."

His mouth curved in a half smile. "I had a crush on you too."

That made her laugh. "Right."

"I did."

She stared at him and realized he was serious. "Okay, first of all, and not that I believe you, but nice job on pretending you didn't. I certainly bought it."

"And second?" he asked.

"And second . . . you had your chance with me and you passed."

"You didn't want me that night," he said. "Not really."

"Oh, do tell."

"You wanted an escape," he said. "Which doesn't count."

Hell if she was going to correct him. She'd already embarrassed herself enough. Gathering her dignity, or what was left of it anyway, she turned to go. "Fine. Whatever."

"Olive."

She glanced back, finding him watching her with a pensive gaze. "If you need an escape while you're here, don't come knocking. I'm still not your guy."

"Don't worry." He would be the very *last* guy on the planet she'd go to. For *anything*. "I've got a boyfriend." Fantasy boyfriend, but whatever.

"So where is he?"

"What do you mean?"

"You're here to support your longtime best friend and to see your grandma. Two very important people in your life. Why isn't he here with you?"

"He's busy."

"Too busy to support his woman?"

She walked out rather than respond, because she had no good response. Then she called her client back. After, she tried her parents again. No answer. By this time, the bathroom was empty, so she claimed it as her own by locking both doors. See? How hard was that? She showered, dressed, and headed into the main part of the house to see about some desperately needed caffeine.

Then stopped short in the living room.

Noah was on the floor doing push-ups, with Joey on his back helping him count.

"One, two, three, four, five, thirteen, twenty!" Joey yelled.

Noah laughed. "Thanks, Bud."

Joey beamed.

Seriously? The man had to be cute on top of hot? Good thing he was also an asshole.

CHAPTER 6

The following morning, Noah woke up to the sun stabbing through the window and right into his eyeballs. The stitches at his hairline itched like crazy, and his head pounded. Probably because he hadn't slept well since the accident over a week ago now.

With a groan, he sat up and shoved his fingers through his hair to hold his head on to his neck.

On the floor lay Holmes. He didn't lift his head, but watched Noah with forlorn eyes. Noah's heart ached for the old guy. The death of Sassy Pants had been a blow to the whole family, but Holmes had taken it the hardest. "How about breakfast?" Noah asked. "Scrambled eggs? Sorry I can't add bacon. The vet told Katie it was bad for you. He also said you have to stop begging the neighbors for treats, which we know you're still doing since you haven't lost weight."

Holmes huffed out a sigh and closed his eyes.

Noah's heart cracked. "Okay, fine, if you promise not to tell anyone, I'll use the fake butter spray in the egg pan."

Holmes didn't budge.

Noah squatted low and hugged his favorite old man. "I'm sorry." He caught a glimpse of the time and sucked in a breath. "What the—*ten a.m.*?" He'd never slept past seven a day in his entire life, and even as he thought it, his phone buzzed an incoming call from his mom.

"*Where are you?*" she asked.

Oh shit. He'd promised to go by the shop and pitch in today. Just the thought made him feel as trapped and claustrophobic as the time he'd gotten stuck in an elevator for six hours, but he knew his place in this family—back up his sister as needed, back up his mom as needed, while having no needs of his own.

How was it that no matter how far he took his life away from here, it still came back to him like a boomerang? "I'm sorry, I overslept. I'm getting ready now."

"You never sleep in." Her voice softened. "Are you not feeling okay? Is it your head? The doctor said you'd be fine."

"Yes, and you agreed, because I, and let me quote you, 'have the hardest head on the planet.'"

"Well, not the hardest," she said, affection creeping into her voice. "That honor belonged to your father. You take after him, you know."

He hated to believe he was like his old man, but the truth was, the apple never fell far from the tree, no matter how much he'd like to think otherwise. After three years, one would think it'd make the heart grow fonder, but the truth was, his dad had never forgiven him for even the smallest of transgressions, which was hard to forget. Aaaaaand it was far too early in the day to be dealing with emotional shit. "Give me twenty," he said, and staggered into a very hot shower.

He dressed in two seconds, his most immediate need being caffeine, and lots of it. Stepping out of the bathroom, he promptly tripped over Holmes. "Come on, buddy," he said. "I'll let you ride shotgun." And then, in a hurry, Noah scooped him up—and nearly staggered under the weight, which he didn't mention. Halfway down the stairs, he heard Olive on a call.

"It's not about the beer," she was saying. "It's about getting the locals into your bar and grill for the food and the beer, but wanting them to stay because they feel like they're part of the establishment. You do that by, one, buying better chairs and, two, teaching them the ins and outs of brewing. You can hold competitions for homegrown, then have a party at the end where you name the winners. You can even offer a deal to sell first place's beer for a limited run. Sell tickets to a lottery to give someone the chance to create a specialized beer that you put on your menu— Yes, I know it all sounds expensive, but if we do it right, with some press and social media blasts, you'll have everyone in town showing up to be a part of things."

Smart, Noah thought, turning the corner into the living room, stopping short at the sight of Olive sitting on the floor, using the coffee table as her desk while on a video call.

Without taking her eyes off the screen or stopping talking, she waved a hand at him out of view of the camera.

Message received. She'd like him to go far, far away.

So of course he didn't. He couldn't help it; she brought out the contrary in him. Always had.

"Name me one person in all your entire providence who doesn't like beer or competing," she said. "Go ahead, I'll wait."

Noah grinned.

This earned him a second go-away wave.

Since he couldn't think of a single time she'd ever done as *he'd* asked, he stayed where he was, still cradling Holmes like a baby. Mostly because, while being amused, Noah was also fascinated at the image she made. She'd always been a contradiction of terms. Cluelessly sexy and smart as hell. Silly and serious. Timid and stubborn.

And same as back then, he loved to watch her.

Holmes licked his chin, and Noah gently set the dog on the couch before turning back to Olive.

She'd created a whole setup behind her. Dragged some potted plants to frame the wall, all the lamps in the house placed in a semicircle at her sides for lighting, and presumably not in view of the laptop she was speaking to.

And that wasn't the only smoke and mirrors she was pulling off. She'd done her hair and makeup and wore a silky forest green top, from the waist up looking so elegant and sophisticated, she could've walked right off a TV set. It was almost intimidating how good and put together she looked.

Almost.

Because as he walked by, carefully avoiding the camera, he caught sight of her baggy sweat bottoms and bare feet—although her sparkly deep blue pedicure and the delicate little silver ring around her second toe definitely belonged with her top half.

Business on top, party down under.

Laughing to himself, he moved toward the kitchen, winking at her when she glared at him. He filled Holmes's bowl, then poured a coffee, added enough sugar and cream to turn the concoction into a dessert, and set it on Olive's makeshift desk while still staying out of camera range.

She drank from it gratefully, or so he assumed since she never took her gaze off the laptop. He glanced at Holmes and stilled.

First of all, the old man was . . . smiling? And second of all, just between the dog's front paws sat the tiniest gray-and-white kitten Noah had ever seen. The little thing had its eyes closed in ecstasy as Holmes cuddled it close. Noah couldn't be positive at this distance, but he was pretty sure he could hear a very light rumble of a purr. "What the—"

Olive waved him away. On par. He headed back into the kitchen for a straight black coffee, then leaned in the doorway to stay for the rest of the *Olive Show* as he drank, taking a moment to text the family thread.

> Either one of you got a kitten, or I'm seeing things.

Katie got back to him first.

> Just how hard did you hit your head?

A moment later, his mom texted.

> If she's gray and white and precious, then it's the stray Adele and I have been feeding. She's been going back and forth between our houses. We're calling her Pepper because she's feisty. Don't let her up on the furniture. Katie hates fur on the furniture. And WHAT'S TAKING YOU SO LONG TO GET HERE?

Noah looked at the kitten, indeed on the furniture, being cuddled by Holmes, who'd taken an interest in exactly nothing for months. The dog rubbed his huge head gently against Pepper's cheek, while the kitten sat there, eyes closed, looking joyous. He texted his mom back.

> Sure. No furniture. Got it.

His mom called him. "Seriously. Hurry up!"

"I'm hurrying."

"Good. Oh, and I know I said I wouldn't, but a woman named Misty is going to call you. I met her at the library. She's single and sweet. Take her out. And before I forget, don't touch the cookies I made last night. They're for a bake sale and I don't want to have to make another batch."

Oh, he was going to eat the cookies. Every last one of them. And then possibly change his number and not tell a single soul. He took another look at Olive, who was smiling at her screen. Once upon a time, he'd considered her one of his closest friends. He'd cared about her, far more than had been good for either of them.

Now here they were all these years later and he couldn't seem to tear his gaze off her, looking and sounding a million miles away from the woman he'd known.

And yet still a million miles from who he was and what he wanted, which was no strings and, most especially, not love.

His phone vibrated an incoming call from a number he didn't know. This happened occasionally, it was probably a work call. "Turner."

"Uh, is this Noah?" an unfamiliar woman's voice asked.

"Yes."

"Oh, hi. I'm Misty."

Well, hell.

"Your mom suggested I give you a call. She said you were in town for a bit and looking for things to do . . ."

He turned to face the doorjamb he'd been leaning on and lightly banged his forehead against it a few times. "I'm so sorry, Misty. But I'm actually super busy with . . ." With what, genius? "Work."

"Your mom said that you're off work, at least for the next few weeks . . ."

For good measure, he hit his head a few more times. *Thanks, Mom.* "Listen, she means well, and I'm sure you're amazing, but the truth is, I'm not interested in dating right now. I'm sorry."

"It's okay." She sounded amused, thankfully. "My mom insisted I call you as a favor to her friend. But if you don't mind, it'd be great if you took the fall for the lack of a date happening."

With a sigh, he went into the kitchen, grabbed the tin of cookies on the counter, and moved back to the doorway to dig in.

"Sounds good," Olive said, eyes on Noah. "But something's come up and I've got to go— Yes, thank you." She disconnected and pulled out her earphones. "Do you happen to have a home remedy for Slow Death by Work Annoyance?"

He offered her the tin of cookies, chuckling when she took one for each hand, but waited until she'd eaten them both before asking, "Better?"

She nodded and gave him her fake smile. "Sure. Thanks."

He lifted his free hand in a surrender gesture and turned to go.

"It's just that this client . . . they're Gen Z. I told them I was older than Google and they thought I was joking. And when I said I was serious, that *anyone* born before 1998 was older than Google, they were horrified at how old I must be."

He turned back. "Well, you are thirty now, so—"

"Ha." She gestured for another cookie. "They said they didn't want cheugy or high key. And I have zero idea what either of those things are."

"Did you admit that?"

"Hell no."

He let out a short laugh. "Cheugy's something not on trend. And high key is the opposite of low key."

"And you know this how?"

"You're not the only one dealing with Gen Zers," he said. "I'm one of the oldest on my team."

She laughed, and the sound did something to him. While he was still trying to understand what the hell that meant, she stood and stretched.

"Nice work uniform," he said.

She looked down at herself and shrugged unapologetically. Another thing that was new. She used to worry about what people thought of her. Especially him. That wasn't ego, it was just truth. He'd cared what she thought too. A whole hell of a lot.

"I got Joey to school for Katie, who's at the hospital," Olive said, finishing her second cookie. "I thought I was alone in the house. In all the years I knew you, you never slept in. And did I just hear you turn down a date with a woman named . . . Misty?"

He grimaced. "My mom's relentless."

She snorted. "Poor Noah Turner, having to chase them off, just like in high school."

"Hey, remember when I was your fake boyfriend? Maybe you could be my fake girlfriend. I mean, you do owe me."

She rolled her eyes. "You're way past the statute of limitations." She looked him over. "You look terrible."

"Aw, thanks."

"No," she said. "You're squinting, you're pale. What's going on?"

"I'm fine."

Every time she'd seen him, he'd had a ballcap on. Well, with the exception of when she'd caught him getting out of the shower, but she'd not been looking at his forehead then . . . In any case, he wasn't wearing a ballcap now, just bedhead, and he knew his mistake the minute she headed right for him, not stopping until they were toe to toe. In her bare feet, she had to tilt her head back to see his face.

"It's nothing—" he started to say but lost all the air in his lungs when she reached up and ran a finger just beneath the line of stitches high on his forehead.

Her eyes, accusatory, flew to his. "Katie told me you were fine, but you're favoring your leg, and you have stitches."

He shrugged. "The head's just a minor thing. I did sort of reinjure the leg, but it's nothing." He held out the tin again. "More?"

She took another two cookies but couldn't be sidetracked. "What else?"

"What else what?"

"What else is injured?"

When he didn't answer right away, she let the silence stand. It was a tactic he'd used often on the job, a weighted silence designed to make the other person fill the empty air. He was absolutely not going to fall prey to it. Not even a little bit. "I'm fine," he said, and wanted to kick himself.

Her eyes, those stunning deep green eyes, never left his. "You never used to lie," she said. "About anything."

"I'm fine."

"Say it one more time and maybe I'll believe you."

He sighed. "It's true. I'm not cleared for work yet, but I'm—" He broke off when she raised a brow. "Getting there. Everything is healing on schedule."

"And here?" She put her hand on his chest, over his heart.

The genuine concern in her eyes brought him back to that long ago summer before the accident, when they'd been so close, and he forced a smile. "Worried about me, Oli?"

She stilled for a beat, while he did his best not to kick his own ass for using his old, affectionate nickname for her. His only excuse was that he was even more tired than he thought.

"Just because we're . . . whatever we are, doesn't mean I've ever stopped worrying about you," she said quietly.

He looked into her eyes, letting them tell him what she was really feeling. Wistfulness. Sorrow. Neither of which made sense. "You've got a funny way of showing it."

Her eyes skittered away. "What happened to leaving the past in the past?"

"Hard to do when the past is standing right here in front of me." And she wasn't just standing there, she still had her hand on his chest. Plus, she smelled good, which was killing him. *She* was killing him. "What would your boyfriend think of you touching me?"

She yanked her hand back but didn't speak.

Apparently, sometimes a silence could speak for itself.

CHAPTER 7

Thirteen years ago

As she did every day after school, Olive climbed into Noah's truck. Katie had left early for a doctor's appointment, so it was just Olive and Noah today, and her pulse kicked up a notch at the sight of him in his faded-to-a-buttery-softness jeans, battered running shoes, and a T-shirt that showed off all the work his coach had been forcing on him in the gym.

His gaze was on his side mirror, studying the traffic. "You're late" was all he said, his tone holding zero recrimination, calm as always.

"Sorry."

He turned to look at her and his easy expression turned to surprise. "What happened?"

"Nothing."

"Your clothes are torn and . . ." He leaned in and her heart stopped because he was going to kiss her. God, please don't let her have bad breath from that bag of nacho chips she'd eaten—

He pulled something from her hair. A leaf.

She was an idiot. "It's nothing."

"You're bleeding."

She eyed the rips in her jeans and her equally torn skin. Damn.

Noah took her hands and flipped them over, eyeing her bloody palms. "Did you fall?"

More like she was pushed.

Noah put the truck back into park and unbuckled his seat belt. "Who?"

"No."

He stared at her. People didn't say no to Noah Turner.

Just then Olive and Katie's numero uno nemesis, Cindy, came out of the school and crossed the street in front of the truck. She also had sticks and leaves in her hair, her sweater was torn, and she had the beginnings of a black eye.

Noah turned to Olive, brows up.

"Hey, it's not like I started it." She couldn't quite keep the satisfaction out of her voice. "I just finished it."

He grinned. "Proud of you."

Present day

The first half of Olive's day consisted of working with Holmes lying at her feet. Between his front legs sat Pepper, barely the size of his paws. The two had become inseparable. Holmes had been downright cheerful, and the kitten seemed to think the dog was her mama.

It was the cutest thing Olive had ever seen, and she enjoyed their company as she and Stephanie, her administrative assistant and the closest thing she had to a BFF in the UK, spent several hours on the phone, discussing their current clients and their campaigns one by one.

And as always when business was finished, Stephanie tried to turn it personal. "So . . ." There was a smile in her voice. "How's dating in the States treating you?"

"I've barely been here a week," Olive said.

"And?"

Olive laughed. "Give it a rest."

"I would, if you'd put yourself out there even a little, tiny bit. You do know that your parts are in danger of shriveling and dying, right?"

"That's not a thing."

"You sure?"

Olive disconnected and then looked down at her . . . parts. "Don't give up on me yet, okay?"

Her parts pleaded the Fifth.

She called her parents again and had to leave yet another message. Why hadn't they called her back? She'd talked to Gram about it—daily—but her grandma insisted this was on brand for them.

Olive knew that to be true, but it didn't erase the worry.

When it was time, she picked up Joey from pre-K. Once back home, they went into the kitchen to make him a snack. "What would you like? PB&J? Cheese and crackers? Grilled cheese?" she asked, listing the top three things in her cooking repertoire.

"Carrots with hummus."

She blinked. "Are you five or fifty?"

He smiled. "Veggies are good for you."

"Did your mommy put you up to saying that?"

"You're funny, Auntie Olive. Even Holmes loves carrots and hummus, and he doesn't like much."

Olive looked at Holmes. His tail thumped on the wood floor. Pepper looked up at her with equal expectation.

"See? They want to share our snack," Joey said.

So they all ate carrots and hummus. Well, not Pepper, who watched, fascinated, as the humans played cards. It was then that Olive learned that Joey had inherited Katie's memory after he handily beat her at a matching game.

Three times in a row.

"So you're cute *and* smart?" she asked, smiling at him.

He beamed. "Mommy says I get it from my daddy."

She laughed. "*And* your mommy."

He nodded. "She says you just gotta concentrate. I'll help you," he said, reminding her so much of Katie that her eyes stung.

With his help, she won two out of five, but she was pretty sure he let her win. The house was quiet around them. She knew Amy was on an overnight girls' trip and Katie was still at the hospital, but she had no idea where Noah was and he didn't show up. She told herself she was relieved.

"Uncle Noah's at the hospital with Mommy," Joey said.

Which meant on top of his mommy's memory, he also had her uncanny ability to read people's thoughts. She sure hoped he couldn't read the X-rated ones she'd been having about his uncle . . . "You hungry for dinner?"

Joey roared like a lion.

"I'm going to take that as a yes. Let's go to Gram's for dinner." They were followed by Holmes and Pepper, who watched as they made their own personal pizzas, layering on cheese and pepperoni.

Joey also added spinach leaves and pineapple to his, but Olive and Gram preferred their pizza as pizza-y as possible.

When Joey fell asleep on the couch, Olive covered him up with a throw blanket and then she and Gram tiptoed into the kitchen to catch up with each other. She was trying to figure out how to ask why Gram hadn't mentioned Noah helping her out around the house, not to mention the borderline diabetes diagnosis, when her grandma distracted her.

"My friend Phyllis, she owns the Sunrise Cove Diner. She asked me to have you call her. She's been trying to find someone to help raise the diner's profile. When she heard you were in town, she got so excited. Can you call her?"

"Of course."

"Thanks, honey. I owe her because she set me up with her older brother. We had an okay time, but he's eighty, which is too old."

"Aren't you eighty-seven?"

"Yes, but I'm a young eighty-seven." Gram sighed. "I miss sexy men. I miss men who still have their own teeth. And I really miss having a good butt to stare at. Old men don't have butts. Their back goes straight into their legs."

She couldn't find fault with that argument. She liked good butts too. Just that morning she'd tried valiantly to fight the urge to stare at Noah's and failed. She'd definitely spent a few seconds staring. Okay, a minute tops. She probably deserved some sort of medal. "Still nothing from Mom or Dad?" she asked, needing a subject change.

"No, but you know them. They'll call back when they call back."

Olive understood that, understood them, but she couldn't say that it didn't hurt, not crossing their minds enough to remember her. And now her gram was hiding things from her.

"What's on your mind, honey? Something's bothering you."

"Why didn't you tell me you had diabetes? Or that you needed help around the house?"

Gram stirred her tea for a beat. "I guess I didn't want to worry you."

"But I worry anyway."

Gram sighed, then reached for her hand. "If Noah's in town, he comes over and handles my honey-do list. It's the stuff I can't do for myself, like climb up a ladder to change a lightbulb. If he's gone for a long time, which is often the case, he sends Joe if he's home, or Katie if Joe's not. Sometimes he pays a high school kid to help. It's sweet of him to look after me. And I think he does it because he cares so much about you."

Well, she was wrong there. "The diabetes—"

"I'm diet controlled, so it's not too serious. I'm careful, and I've been educating myself. As for not telling you . . ." She smiled ruefully. "It goes back to the not wanting you to worry thing."

"Gram . . ."

"I know"—she squeezed Olive's hand—"I'm sorry."

"Sorry enough to tell me what goes on with you from here on out?"

"Scout's honor," Gram said.

They streamed an episode of *Survivor*, and it felt just like the old days, like nothing had changed, and it made Olive feel like things were under control.

It was a nice delusion that ended when she carried Joey across the shared driveway and tucked him into bed, because *every-thing* had changed. She'd left here with her tail between her legs, walking away from the only people who'd ever made her feel like she meant something.

And now she was struggling to find her way back into those relationships. Well, with the exception of Noah, who'd made it abundantly clear that wasn't an option, which she was relieved about.

Liar, liar, pants on fire . . .

She'd planned to go straight to bed, but veered to the kitchen and made herself a bag of popcorn. She was pulling it from the microwave when Katie came in the back door, face pale, eyes suspiciously red.

Olive put a hand to her heart. *Joe.* "What happened?"

"Besides the love of my life being in a coma? Nothing. Nothing at all."

"Oh, Katie. I'm so sorry."

"I don't want you to be sorry. I want my damn husband to wake up and smile at me. I want him to tell me one of his dumb dad jokes. I want him to attempt to make me breakfast and burn water. I want him to annoy the crap out of me by leaving the toilet seat up. I want him to send me a hundred dumb reels while he's in the bathroom for a year." Her voice cracked and broke Olive's heart. "I want him back, Olive."

She moved close, but Katie, correctly interpreting that Olive meant to hug her, shook her head. "Don't! I'll break."

So Olive simply, gently, bumped her shoulder to Katie's.

Katie closed her eyes. "Thank you," she whispered.

"For the affection?"

"For not hugging me."

Olive snorted and Katie gave a very small smile. Then, very slowly, she dropped her head to Olive's shoulder. "I'm tired of holding it together all by myself," she whispered.

"Then it's a good thing you're not by yourself," Olive said. "You've got your family, and me. We'll hold it together for you until he wakes up."

"*You're* my family too, you wonderful idiot." Katie pushed free. "One of these days you're going to go back to believing that again. And hopefully, you're also going to tell me why you even left here in the first place."

She made a sound that could have been interpreted as agreement, while thinking *not likely* . . .

Katie drew a deep breath. "I really don't think I could do this
without you."

"Are you kidding? You're the bravest person I've ever met.
You used to shrug off the mean girls in school. You never cared
about fitting in. You managed to find a way to learn, even when
your teachers didn't understand you, or even try. You've always
embraced being exactly who you are, and you went out and got
yourself a beautiful life, one that suits you. You've made more of
yourself than I could ever hope to do."

As always, uncomfortable with praise, Katie looked around.
"Joey being good?"

"Yes, though his allergies might be acting up. He told me his
ear hurt. I asked him inside or outside. He walked outside and
came back in and said both."

Katie smiled. "I might be saving too much for college." She
snatched the bag of popcorn. "What, are you a Neanderthal?"
She poured it into a bowl, grabbed a gallon of ice cream out
of the freezer and two big spoons, and met Olive at the table.
"What?" she asked when Olive just stared at her.

"Well, for one, you never eat empty calories," she said. "And
two, you're lactose intolerant."

"The ice cream's dairy free, and I gave up denying myself a
luxury the day Joe landed in the hospital. Life's too short."

"Here, here," Olive said, and they dug in, eating in compan-
ionable silence until she realized Katie was staring at her. "Do I
have something in my teeth?"

"Did something happen between you and my brother?"

"Uh . . ." Were they talking about the past, or—

"Because he was at the hospital tonight and seemed pretty grumpy."

"How can you tell?"

Katie chortled. "Let me guess. He was an idiot."

"Again, how can you tell?"

Katie studied Olive. "Words, please."

Right. But how to explain her and Noah? "To be honest, I kinda need someone to explain to me first. Even the CliffsNotes version would be great."

Katie's gaze went thoughtful. "There's something about you that's always sort of smoothed him out and de-stressed him. It's like he can be his true self with you. He doesn't seem to give that power to anyone else."

Feeling a little gutted by that, Olive let out a long breath. "Thanks, Yoda. I'll be careful with the Force. But really, there's nothing going on between us."

Katie raised a brow.

Olive stuffed a huge bite of ice cream in her mouth to keep from spilling her guts, but gave herself a brain freeze. Dropping the spoon onto the table, she cupped her own head and sucked in air.

"Press your tongue to the roof of your mouth," Katie said casually. "And that was such a rookie move. Now I *know* something's happened between you two."

"The only thing that happened is that he's kind of a jerk."

"Ouch," Noah said as he came into the kitchen.

"But true," Katie said.

Noah ruffled his twin's hair. "Most definitely."

He didn't ruffle Olive's. Just gave her a hooded look she couldn't begin to interpret.

Holmes wandered into the room and moved straight for Noah, who loved up on the old man. His new shadow, Pepper, proceeded to wind herself in and out and around Noah's legs, purring so loudly it sounded like an engine rumbling. She made sure to look at Olive often, and it didn't take a cat translator to know what the kitten was saying—*back off my man*.

If Olive could speak Cat, she'd have assured Pepper that she could have Noah.

The man himself moved to a cabinet, opened a small pack of cat food, and poured it into a bowl.

The kitten attacked it like she'd never eaten before.

"Aw," Olive said, heart melting. "She was starving."

"She's always starving." He looked around. "Where did Holmes go?"

"Not far," Katie said. "Not without his baby."

They found him in the pantry, his food bag opened and spilled, the dog sleeping on top of the whole mess, in a clear food coma.

Noah smiled. "I guess if you can't hide the crime scene, just pretend you're the victim."

They all moved back to the kitchen.

"Oh and hey," Katie said to her brother. "Guess what Joey said early this morning when he dropped his lunch box on his toe. He said, 'Truck me.'"

Noah winced. "Uh . . ."

"Seriously?" Katie asked.

"Hey, he was helping me change the oil in my truck and I dropped a heavy wrench on my foot."

"What's wrong with 'truck me'?" Olive wanted to know.

Noah bit his lower lip, looking as if he was trying to hide a laugh.

"Well," Katie said, jabbing the spoon at Noah again, this time connecting with his chest, leaving a chocolate stain on his T-shirt. "Joey has trouble making the *F* sound." She looked at Olive. "So you do the math."

Olive laughed. "Oh my God."

"Not funny." Katie narrowed her eyes at her brother. "When his principal calls to tell me the kid dropped the f-bomb, I'm going to forward the call to you."

"Look, I'm sorry, okay? I'll talk to him. I've just been gone so much, I forget to watch my language."

"You know he worships the ground you walk on," Katie said. "He wants to be like you."

Noah looked pained. "I'm not exactly the best role model."

"Then try harder."

Olive, enjoying Noah being in the hot seat, jumped in surprise when Katie suddenly whirled on Olive with her big spoon. "And you. You're no better. You stay away because . . . well, I have no idea why, you've been mum on that subject for years. I'm over it. The both of you need to make a real effort or . . ." Katie tightened her lips together. A massive sign of emotion from the woman who didn't often reveal herself. "Oh, forget it. You'll both do whatever you want anyway." She tossed the spoon into the sink and turned to leave. "I seriously can't believe *I'm* the mature one in this room."

Noah caught her hand. "Hey."

"Hey yourself."

"I'll do better. I promise."

"*We'll* do better," Olive said, glancing over at Noah just as he slid incredulous eyes at her, his brows lifting.

Katie nodded and left the room.

"We've hurt her," he murmured, gaze pensive. "I'm a lot of things, not all of them good. But at least I can accept blame."

She stared at him incredulously. "You think I can't?" Was he serious? She'd walked away from everyone and everything she'd ever loved *because* she'd accepted blame for what had happened to him.

Her phone, sitting on the counter between them, suddenly buzzed with an incoming call. They both looked at the screen.

It's Max So Answer Me was calling.

"Sorry, I've got to take this," she said, and answered to her graphic designer. "What's up?"

"Sorry it's so late there for you, but I'm getting an early start over here. Just wanted to let you know we got all the info on the new client. Love that you took on a zoo. Loved your draft ideas. We'll all add to it ASAP. When do you plan to be back? We miss you."

"Miss you too," she said. "And I don't know yet." She disconnected and turned back to Noah.

"Thought your boyfriend's name was Matt."

There was something in his tone, but it couldn't be jealousy. Noah Turner didn't do pointless emotions. "Max is my graphic designer."

He opened his mouth, but before he could say anything, a set of tiny footsteps padded down the stairs, and then Joey burst into the kitchen, hair wild, his little *PAW Patrol* pj's crooked and wrinkled.

"I heard her, I heard her!"

Noah caught the little guy up in his arms. "Whoa. Heard who?"

"The tooth fairy!" He put his hands on Noah's cheeks. "Did you hear her?"

"Not sure," Noah said. "What does the tooth fairy sound like?"

"You don't know?"

"Well . . ." He exchanged a quick look with Olive. "It's been a long time since, uh, the tooth fairy came to visit me. Also, why would she come by tonight? No one's lost a tooth."

"My friend Sarah did. But she and her mommy don't have a place to live, and she was afraid the tooth fairy wouldn't be able to find her in their car."

"Why do I get the feeling you've done something about that?" Noah asked.

"I put her tooth under my pillow for her and promised I'd bring her the money I got. But the tooth fairy never came."

Again, Noah glanced at Olive. "How many nights has it been?"

"Three."

While Olive's heart ached, Noah looked Joey in the eyes. "Bud, sometimes the tooth fairy's super busy. I mean, she's got a lot of little kids across the whole world to look after, right? So it can take a few nights to get to everyone. Keep the faith, I'm sure she'll still come."

"You think?"

Noah nodded solemnly. "I know."

Joey looked hugely relieved. "'Kay." He put his hands over his belly. "I gotta tummy ache." He scrunched up his face and then came an unmistakable sound. "I farted," he announced.

Noah smiled. "That always makes me feel better too."

Dammit, why did the man have to be gorgeous, smart, *and* sweet too? It really wasn't fair. This would be so much easier if he indeed was the jerk she'd told Katie he was.

Joey sighed. "I want my daddy to come home."

A look of pain crossed Noah's face. "I know. So do I."

At that, Joey looked up. "You do?"

"Very much."

Joey looked to Olive, and she nodded. "All of us do," she said softly.

"Maybe we could google how to help him wake up," Joey said hopefully.

"Hey, did you know that Olive is older than Google?" Noah asked the boy, who gasped in horror.

Olive smiled sweetly. "And did you know Noah is even older than me?"

"Only by two months," Noah said.

"Which is the definition of older."

Joey took in this new information about his uncle being ancient. Or at least that's what Olive assumed he was doing, but his next words proved her wrong.

"Are you and Uncle Noah going to get married and have babies so I can haz cousins?"

Olive, who'd just popped the last piece of popcorn into her mouth, promptly choked hard enough that it almost came out her nose.

Noah reached over and patted her on the back.

"My daddy hugs my mommy when she's coughing," Joey said.

Noah snorted, and then to Olive's shock, he stood up, dropped Joey into his chair, and moved toward her. He stopped in front of her and then waited.

For her to give him permission, she realized. She wanted to smile, but couldn't. Instead, she stood too, put both arms around his waist, and set her chin on his chest, looking up at him.

He drew in a surprised breath and then his arms closed around her, pulling her the rest of the way against him. She almost closed her eyes to enjoy the feeling of him holding her so close, but kept them open because he was looking at her, like *really* looking at her. They stood like that, staring at each other, only moving apart when Joey clapped his hands in amusement.

"Okay, Trouble," Noah said, then scooped him up, hanging him off his back, to the kid's utter delight, before carrying him out of the kitchen and presumably back to bed.

Olive stood in the middle of the kitchen with an odd ache in her chest and wasn't even sure why. Maybe it was because she thought Joey was the best kid on the planet, not that she was biased or anything.

But maybe it was also, at least partly, the way Noah was with him. Funny and playful, but also sweet and gentle and loving, which was a whole new side of the man who claimed not to want a family of his own. A side she hadn't been privy to, all thanks to a promise she'd made.

It always came down to her choices, didn't it. She didn't like regrets, but the truth was, she had plenty.

She startled when she realized at some point he'd come back into the kitchen and was watching her.

"You okay?" he asked quietly.

His concern only intensified her ache. "It's you guys I'm worried about," she said, just as quietly. "Not me."

"Because you're fine."

"Yes."

He shook his head. "Still always fine. Still never needing anyone. Must be nice."

"So are you the pot or the kettle here?" She shook her head. "You know what? Never mind. It doesn't matter." And she took herself off to bed.

CHAPTER 8

A few days later, after dropping Joey at school, Olive took Gram out to breakfast at the diner—her new client.

"You didn't have to take me out, honey."

"If I wanted to see you, I did," Olive said on a laugh. "You're a busy woman, running the social activities at the senior center."

Gram beamed. "And I love it. I'll be gone a lot this week too. Today we're going to read to the animals at the shelter, and then tomorrow we'll be at the preschool teaching the kids how to dance." She leaned in. "I'm so grateful for what you're doing for the diner. Your idea was a stroke of genius. Phyllis is ecstatic."

Not a stroke of genius, but rather a marriage made in heaven. Phyllis had been having trouble with her outdated menus, as well as keeping a chef, both of which were costing her repeat business. Olive had merely suggested hiring grandmas from the senior center population who had honed their cooking skills over decades feeding their own families. Each "chef" would create a menu based off their heritage. The ones who were able-bodied enough to actually cook on-site at the diner were each assigned one night a week to run the kitchen and make their beloved family recipes. The ones not mobile enough could still get involved by allowing Phyllis's kitchen staff to use their tried-and-true recipes.

So far, Phyllis had enough unique dinner menus to go a full month without repeating, and they were putting it all into motion starting this week. Best yet, local social media was abuzz about it. "I'm so glad it's all working out."

Gram pointed at Olive with her blueberry muffin in hand. "You're too modest. Just like I know you won't brag about your work, you also don't brag about how great you are with Joey, or how much of a lifesaver you've been for Katie."

Olive shook her head. "Joey's a great kid, which makes it easy, but as for Katie, I haven't been all that much of a help. She also has her mom and brother here."

"*You're* Katie's preferred moral support, don't you ever doubt it. Noah said that if Joe wasn't in a coma, Katie would literally be over the moon to be spending time in person with you—"

"Noah said that? Gram, tell me you aren't talking to Noah about me."

"Oh, shoot, was that my phone?" Her grandma started patting down her pockets. "I think I've got a call—"

"What you have is you've-been-caught-itis."

"Fine. Yesterday, he came over and fixed that spot on my roof above the kitchen door where it leaks. That's how I found out you're doing a campaign for the zoo, at Amy's request."

Olive narrowed her eyes. "Noah told you that."

"Yes, which was when I noticed he was smiling more than I'd seen in a while. I asked him if it was because of you—"

"Gram, oh my God. You didn't."

"Well, it's not like you're going to tell me what's happening between you two. You're always so touchy about it."

"Because Noah is in my past. I . . . I've got a boyfriend."

"Do you? Do you really?"

"Yes!" But the lie burned her cheeks. "Fine. I don't."

"I knew it."

"How?" Olive asked. "How did you know?"

Gram shrugged. "You never glow when you talk about him—unlike when you talk about Noah."

"That's because he drives me crazy! The glow is sheer irritation!" Only fifty percent of a lie . . .

"Honey, listen," Gram said. "I think you're still punishing yourself for things that everyone else let go of a long time ago." She leaned forward and took Olive's hands. "It's your turn to let go."

She didn't have time for this today. Or maybe ever. "I have to go. I need to work." She rose and pointed at her grandma. "I love you, but stop talking about me to Noah." Realizing she'd left a loophole, she turned back. "Or anyone. Okay?"

"You're late for work, remember? And love you too!"

Having promised Katie that she'd pick up Joey from school, Olive cut a video meeting with a client short and ran out of the house, not wanting to be late for the little guy.

But she skidded to a stop on the porch at the sight of Noah on his knees in front of Holmes's bed. "Is he okay?"

"More okay than I've seen him since he lost Sassy." He shifted aside, letting her see for herself.

Holmes was sleeping on his bed, his long ears brushing his front paws. Under his left ear sat the still teeny, tiny Pepper, not sleeping, looking rumpled and grumpy at the rude awakening.

Olive dropped to her knees beside Noah. "Aw. Happiness looks good on him."

Holmes opened his eyes and gave Pepper a long, wet lick up the side of her face. The rough rumbling began from deep in her throat and made Olive feel warm and fuzzy on the inside. Although, if she was being honest, some of that came from being shoulder to shoulder with Noah, who smelled so delicious she nearly licked him like Holmes had Pepper.

Noah sat back on his heels. "Katie suggested I take these guys home with me for a while when I go. Said she could use some time worrying only about Joe and Joey."

"Makes sense. Holmes loves you best anyway."

"I'm gone a lot."

"Maybe you could hire a dog walker."

"And now there's Pepper too," he said.

"Cats are easy."

He didn't say anything.

"Let me guess," she said. "In the same way you don't do relationships, because you're happy on your own island, you don't want any pets either. It threatens your need for freedom from roots and ties. How am I doing?"

"Shockingly well actually. But don't forget you left too."

How could she, when he kept reminding her? "I was always leaving for college. All I actually did was leave before summer started, instead of after." She got to her feet. "I've got to go get Joey."

Noah got to his feet too and caught her hand.

She yanked free. "I'm going to be late."

"Not if I drive."

"Wow. That's so sexist."

"It has nothing to do with you being female." He nudged her off the porch and opened the passenger door of his truck for her. "You drive like a turtle."

"Excuse me, if I was a turtle I wouldn't be able to drive. And don't look now, but you've got a shadow. Well, two shadows."

Holmes had gotten up to follow after the first love of his life—Noah, with Pepper in his wake.

"Aw, look at them," she said, and when he did, she snatched the keys from his hand, then climbed into the passenger seat and over the console to sit behind the wheel. She cranked the engine and met his irritated gaze. "Either get in or shut the door."

The dumbfounded expression on his face almost erased her own irritation. Almost. Even if his "don't forget you left too" comment was true.

Finally, he gave a small shake of his head, like he couldn't believe he was going to do this, and scooped up Holmes, setting him on the backseat.

"Mew!"

"Yeah, yeah, I hear you." He dumped Pepper in next, and she immediately snuggled into Holmes, who smiled and licked the top of her little head.

Noah got in, muttering something to himself about how and where he might've lost his man card.

Hiding her smug smile, Olive drove to Joey's school. Noah went inside and Holmes sat up, whining as he walked away.

"He's coming right back."

Holmes didn't relax until Noah came out, hand in hand with Joey. At the sight, the dog tipped his head back and let out a *woo-woo-woo* of delight before sitting down again and apologizing to a dislodged Pepper with a full face lick.

Noah opened the back door and buckled Joey into his booster seat as the kid clapped in delight at finding Holmes and Pepper.

"How was your day, kiddo?" Noah asked as Olive drove away from the school.

"I got a smiley face from my teacher for my paper." He thrust the paper toward the front seat.

Noah took it and smiled wide at whatever he saw. When he caught Olive glancing over at him, he said only, "Wait."

After Olive pulled up at Katie's, Noah handed her the paper. The teacher had asked the kids three questions, beneath which were Joey's answers.

Who is your hero?

My dad

Why is this person your hero?

He is brave

Is there anything your hero is afraid of?

My mom

Olive was still laughing to herself when they let Holmes and Pepper inside the house, and then drove onward to the hospital. A few minutes later, they were sitting in a hospital hallway on unbelievably hard chairs, watching in disbelief as Joey drew a map of the interior of the entire hospital, which he'd memorized from his few visits.

Katie suddenly rushed out of Joe's room, tears pouring down her face. Olive's heart stopped, until she realized Katie was crying and laughing at the same time.

"He squeezed my hand!" she cried, then turned to Noah and flung herself in his arms. "He did it every time I asked him a question!"

Noah pulled back, his hands on Katie's arms, his eyes very serious on hers. "Honey, remember the doctor told us those were just reflexive motions—"

"No, this is different, it's real! I need you to go in there and talk to him and see if it happens for you too."

Noah practically ran into the room.

Katie picked up Joey and hugged him tight before turning to Olive, beaming, tears still streaming. "It's going to be okay. He's going to be okay. The nurse paged the doctor, but I'm sure of it."

Olive wanted that more than anything, and held her arms out for Joey. "I've got him. Go back in, stay as long as you want, we'll be fine."

Ten minutes later, the doctor came down the hall and headed straight into Joe's room, and two minutes after that, Noah and Katie came out. Katie smiled at Joey. "Hungry?"

"Yeah!"

They headed off to the cafeteria.

Noah braced a hand on the wall, head bowed.

Olive moved close. "You okay?"

When he didn't say anything, didn't move a single muscle or even breathe, she put a hand on his back. At her touch, his arms snaked out and wrapped her in a crushing hug. She froze for a surprised beat, then hugged him back.

He shuddered, then lifted his head. His eyes were wet. "He's waking up," he said, voice hoarse. Then he smiled. His real smile, the one she hadn't seen since she'd been a teenager.

She sucked in a breath. "I'm so glad," she whispered back, feeling relief and joy, along with something else that she had no business feeling in an ICU hallway.

THE NEXT MORNING, Olive dressed for success and stared at herself in the mirror. It seemed weird to wear business clothes to a zoo, but this wasn't a social visit. She'd made a promise to Amy that she'd meet with her friend, and there was no way she'd break a promise to the woman who'd given her the very first taste of unconditional acceptance.

She studied herself critically. She looked how she always did for work: professional, elegant, polished. Normally, that gave her a boost of confidence, but for some reason, being perfectly put together today didn't feel the same. Instead of making her feel safe, it just made her feel silly.

Shaking her head at herself, she grabbed her messenger bag that held her laptop and turned to go. Her eyes landed on the closed bathroom door, and before she could stop herself, she knocked. When Noah didn't answer, she opened the door and walked through the bathroom to peer inside his opened bedroom.

The bed was neatly made. She hadn't seen or heard from him since they'd gotten home from the hospital last night. Maybe he'd gone out and ended up spending the night with someone. Not that it mattered. Whatever—or whomever—he was doing was absolutely none of her business.

Not even a little bit.

Rolling her eyes at herself, she headed for the kitchen seeking caffeine. She grabbed a to-go mug and was just adding a little coffee to her creamer when she heard something. Turning, she watched Noah pad barefoot into the kitchen, wearing black sleep pants and nothing else. They were low-slung enough to reveal those incredibly sexy V lines that some guys had between their hips and abs. She didn't know what they were called, all she knew was that they caused an annoying flutter in parts south, parts that had been severely neglected this year.

And how demoralizing was it to find herself wanting him. Seemed she'd grown up, but hadn't gotten much smarter. It reminded her of the time she'd been six and had climbed up onto the rounded top of the center post of a merry-go-round. She'd

sat there watching the world go around. She hadn't been partici-
pating in making things happen, but from where she'd sat, she'd
been in the middle of everything.

She had that same feeling now. She only hoped she didn't
throw up like she had back then. She studied his profile. Sharp
angles, sculpted jaw, straight nose. Eyes that, when he chose,
could reveal his thoughts. He could be hard or soft. Funny or
serious. He had a lot to offer someone but chose to be alone. He
had his reasons, she knew. Good reasons. But it still made her
ache.

Noah's brow raised. "You might wanna . . ." He gestured to
what she was doing.

She turned back to find her cup overflowing onto the counter,
dripping down the cabinets and onto the floor. "Shit. Damn.
Hell." She grabbed the closest thing to her, a small kitchen
towel, and squatted low to clean up the floor.

She heard his uneven gait come close and then those long
legs came into view as he crouched beside her, his bare torso up
front and personal. The view froze her—until she realized it was
shaking.

The jackass was laughing as he used paper towels to wipe up
her mess. Angry at her reaction to him even now, she snatched
the paper towels. "I've got this."

"You should pour yourself another cup," he said. "I think you
need the caffeine."

"You drove home like that?" she asked, gesturing to his lack
of clothing.

He tilted his head to the side. "Drove home from where?"

"Whoever you spent the night with," she snapped.

That annoying almost smile slid onto his face. "You think I
scored last night?"

"I don't know. I don't care."

That got her a full-out grin. "You sure?"

"Very!" If he kept grinning, she wasn't going to be held accountable for her actions.

"I fell asleep on Joey's floor telling him bedtime stories," he said.

Feeling incredibly stupid, not to mention like a complete shrew, she covered her face. But when she heard him chuckle, she dropped her hands and glared at him. "How is this funny, me being a perpetual idiot around you? You drive me crazy!"

"Ditto, babe."

With a sigh, she opened her mouth—to say what, she had zero idea—but she realized he was holding his right leg out, like it hurt him to be hunkered down. "What are you doing? You're going to hurt yourself."

Having efficiently cleaned up the mess in a blink of an eye, he rose to standing, and if she hadn't been staring at him, she'd have missed his grimace. "You okay?"

Not answering, he tossed the mess into the trash. Then he leaned insolently against the counter. "You still like me."

"Well, a whole bunch less at the moment."

He laughed.

Shaking her head, she doctored up a new coffee. "Are you going to put on a shirt or what?"

He moved into the laundry room and she heard the sound of a dryer opening and closing. Then he was back, pulling a T-shirt over his head before pouring his own cup of caffeine.

Black.

He might be sexy as hell, but he didn't know the first thing about the small pleasures in life.

"Better?" he asked as she sipped her breakfast.

Deciding that ignoring him was the best way to go, she pulled on a blazer over her jersey dress and slipped into a pair of boots that had seriously cut into her food budget for the next month.

"So you're wearing the *whole* enchilada today," he said. "Not just the top half." His gaze slowly slid down her body and back up again. "You know, sometimes I catch glimpses of the old Oli, but other times, I don't even recognize you."

"Did you imagine me doing my job dressed as I used to?"

That put a small smile on his lips. "I liked how you looked back then."

He was sending mixed signals that messed with her head and heart, and she didn't like it. "People change," she said quietly. "Life happens and they grow up. Not that it matters, since as you pointed out the other night, this is a temporary situation and we're not going there anyway."

He didn't take the bait, just held her gaze. "What happened to you?"

You, she wanted to say. But there was no use in looking back. It wasn't as if she could explain anyway. As always, the only road was straight ahead. She turned to the door, stared at it, and realized she couldn't hold her tongue after all. "You seem to like giving me crap about how different I am, but you've changed too."

"Yeah? How?"

She slowly faced him again. "You used to be accepting, non-judgmental, *kind* . . ."

"I think you just described a golden retriever," he said dryly.

She tossed up her hands. She had more important things to worry about than verbally sparring with the first man who'd broken her heart. "I've got to get to work."

"The zoo." He met her gaze. "Kick ass, Oli. You'll be great."

The sincerity caught her off guard. "How do you know?"

He shrugged. "Because that London campaign you did to raise awareness for emergency preparedness week, where you gave out foam ducks printed with the city's logo and website to every kid who completed their passport at the emergency preparedness event, was a massive hit." He smiled. "Oh, and when you were hired to increase attendance at a Texas rodeo, you involved local politicians, getting them to chase bulls on national TV . . ." Still smiling, he shook his head. "The pics alone spread the word far and wide. But my favorite might've been when you hosted a frozen turkey curling tournament inside a new building to raise the money needed to bring the summer fair inside, keeping people safe from a historic heat wave."

She blinked in shock.

He gave a small grimace. "I couldn't sleep on the floor of Joey's room, so I did some googling."

"Thought I was the one who shall not be named."

"Things change."

"Do they?"

"Yes." He ran a hand down his face. "Having you here, it's . . ."

She inhaled, preparing herself for a mental blow.

"Not what I expected," he admitted quietly. "When you left and didn't look back—"

"We both know I looked back. That I also came back when I could." She paused. "One of those times being when we . . ."

His intense gaze held hers utterly captive as she shut her mouth rather than open that massive can of churning, writhing worms. "Well. There's really no reason to go there, right?"

Nothing. He said nothing.

Right, then. She nodded, mostly to herself. He didn't want to discuss that visit five years ago, fine. Neither did she.

There was a small muscle ticking in his jaw as he seemed to struggle with words. "I'm talking about our friendship. What we meant to each other."

She laughed sharply, hating the sound. "Don't do that. Don't put this all on me. We both avoided each other, and we *both* did a great job of it." Which was all she intended to say, because no matter what they'd done to each other, she was unwilling to hurt him with what his dad had asked of her, not to mention her agreeing to it. "I've gotta go."

He gestured at the door with his mug. "By all means. You certainly know how."

Closing her eyes for a beat, she drew a deep breath and walked out.

CHAPTER 9

Twelve years ago

Noah finished mowing the front lawn of his parents' house, and then turned to do Olive's grandma's as well. Olive sat on the grass beneath a tree, pretending to read. He knew she was pretending because she hadn't turned a page in the half hour he'd been watching her. Worse, he could feel her sadness, and it slayed him. "What's wrong?"

She lifted a shoulder.

"Olive."

"You don't want to hear it."

"I do," he said.

"You don't."

Snatching her book, he held it behind his back.

"Hey!"

"Is it someone from school? Cindy again?"

"Give me back my book."

"So that's a yes." He crouched at her side, studying her thankfully bruise-free face. Her untamed hair flew around her face.

He knew she hated it, but he loved the wild chaos. "Why didn't you tell me you need help?"

"Because I don't!"

He stared at her, willing her to talk. It always worked. Always. Olive had never met a silence she liked.

She sighed. "I need a boyfriend."

"What?"

"See, I told you that you didn't want to hear it." Her ears were red and so were her cheeks. "I don't want to go off to college still a . . . virgin." She closed her eyes. "But I'm not exactly seen as datable."

Shit, maybe he should just bash his head in with her book, it might be less painful. "Oli, you're . . ." Don't say it, just don't. It'll open a door you won't be able to resist stepping through . . . "one hundred percent datable."

She snorted, and the sound broke his heart. She didn't believe it. "You are."

"Okay."

He tried to hold his tongue, and failed. Spectacularly. "What if people thought we were going out?"

Her head came up and she stared at him.

"Then, after a week or two you could tell everyone you dumped me," he said. "Guys will be lining up for you after that." He'd have to resist killing them all, but that would be tomorrow's problem.

She was wide-eyed. "You'd do that for me?"

He'd do anything for her. "Consider it done. As of this moment, we're a . . . we."

"A pretend we," she said softly. "Right?"

"Right. A pretend we."

Present day

After leaving Noah in the kitchen, Olive headed out, stopping short on the porch.

Holmes lay on his back on his bed, legs in the air, tongue lolling, grinning upside down at Pepper. The kitten, barely the size of one of the dog's massive paws, was pretending to be vicious, growling and pouncing on Holmes.

Heart melted, she got behind the wheel of her rental car, leaned her head back, and closed her eyes for a beat. If old man Holmes could drag himself out of the depths of despair and find a way to open his heart up again, certainly she could.

And maybe if she kept telling herself that, she might learn to believe it—

She nearly jumped out of her skin when her back passenger door opened and Katie leaned in to install a booster seat and then buckled Joey in before hopping into the front seat. "Hey."

Olive stared at her. "What are you doing?"

"Coming with you."

"To the zoo!" Joey yelled, his legs bouncing in excitement.

"But . . . Joe," Olive said.

Katie smiled. "I sneaked in early. The nurses promised me if he wakes up, I'll be the first to know. The zoo will be fun, and we could all use some of that, right, Joey?"

Joey roared. "To the lions!"

At the zoo's front gate, they were given free passes and told a Janie Smithson would meet them at the petting zoo in a few minutes.

"Can I feed them?" Joey asked when they got to the petting zoo, pointing to a little hut where you could buy pellets. "Please!?"

"Um . . ." Katie said, probably because she hated to get dirty.

We'll do better. That had been Olive's promise to Katie. And maybe she hadn't pictured this particular scenario when she'd made that vow, but it certainly fell under the purview. She didn't have to glance down at herself to be reminded that she was wearing one of her favorite outfits, because it didn't matter. A promise was a promise. "I've got you," she said.

Katie looked hugely relieved. "Thank you. And when we get into the meeting, I've got you. I'll be your assistant, whatever you need. I know you're only doing this as a favor to my mom. Just like I know you two are keeping a secret from me."

Olive's heart skipped a beat. "What? I . . ."

Katie rolled her eyes. "Your voice just went up two octaves and only dogs can hear you now. Don't panic. When you're finally ready, you'll tell me. I'm guessing it's related to why you rarely come home, which makes no sense. My brother doesn't blame you for what happened to him. It's time for you to let go of the guilt and forgive yourself."

"Some things are unforgivable."

"Yeah, maybe if you're a murderer," Katie said. "Which you're not."

She found a smile at that. "How do you know?"

"Because you can't even kill a spider." Katie reached for her hand. "Sometimes the person who won't let go is the one person who needs to."

Olive raised a brow. "Is that why you maneuvered me and your brother into both staying at your place?"

"Duh."

Olive narrowed her eyes. "More words."

"Look, two of the most important people in my life have avoided each other for years. Which, BTW, doesn't just affect you guys, it affects the whole family. Christmas, Easter, everything."

"Hey, we do fine."

"Yeah," Katie said drolly. "If fine is barely making eye contact. I miss you, is that so weird? FaceTime isn't the same as having you here."

She thought they'd done remarkably well with FaceTime, having movie nights in a blanket fort, Katie taking her along into Joey's first day of preschool . . . but yeah, okay, she could admit it wasn't the same as being there in person.

"I worry about you," Katie said softly.

"Well, I'm okay, so you can stop."

"Never," Katie said. "We have each other's backs, always. Misfits unite, remember?" She took Olive's hand. "I want you back in my life. You've left me no choice but to use the absolute worst thing that's ever happened to me to get you here."

"So you don't need me here? It was a ploy?"

Katie's gaze softened. "I *always* need you."

Olive smiled at her. "Good to know."

"Mommy! I want to feed the babies!"

Olive turned to Joey. "Let's do it." She bought him some feed, which came in little paper trays like the ones fast-food stores used to serve French fries—and what she wouldn't give to be at a fast-food joint getting fries instead of pellets right now . . .

Joey ran around like a madman, chasing the baby goats, piglets, and lambs to his heart's content. As for Olive, a baby cow locked eyes with her, then nuzzled her in the stomach, snorting, searching her for food.

"Um, yeah," Olive said. "I don't have any."

The baby gave a forlorn *mooooo* and nuzzled her again.

"She thinks you're her mama," Katie said from the other side of the fence.

"Ha-ha."

The baby cow continued to nudge her with that wet, goopy nose and lots of green boogers that would probably give her nightmares for a week. "No, but really, I don't have anything—"

Another baby cow joined them and promptly started sucking on the hem of Olive's dress, pulling it between her teeth and gently tugging.

And then not so gently.

"She likes you!" Joey said. "Maybe we can get one for our house!"

Olive didn't look down, not wanting to see what was happening. Instead, she took a small handful of feed from Joey's paper tray and held it out.

The calf snorted up the food with such enthusiasm that Olive staggered backward. Her boots didn't have any traction in the mud spots and for a moment, she was like a cat on slippery linoleum in an old-timey cartoon . . .

And then she was on her ass in the mud.

She looked up in time to see Katie bent over with uncontrollable laughter. It was a rare sight, but she couldn't even enjoy it because the calf was still snuffling all around, looking for food.

Then Katie whistled and Olive looked up. Next to her stood a woman holding a snake that had wrapped itself around her hands and arms.

Janie, the zoo lady, she presumed.

"Oh my God," the woman said when Olive and Joey left the pen. "Are you okay? Are you hurt?"

"Just my dignity."

Katie was still chuckling and trying to get a hold of herself when she made the introductions.

Janie smiled at Olive. "I see you met Betsy, our newest calf. She's the sweetest."

Not exactly the word Olive would've chosen.

"Why don't you all follow me," Janie said. "We have a sink behind the feed hut where you can wash up."

Five minutes later, Olive's hands were clean again. The same could not be said of her outfit.

"And how rude of me not to introduce you to Sally," Janie said of the snake around her neck.

"Janie told me she's a Sierra garter snake," Katie said. "Or more officially, a *Thamnophis couchii*. She's young. She'll grow to be anywhere from one and a half to four feet long. They've got narrow heads, only slightly wider than their necks, narrow snouts, small eyes, and keeled dorsals."

Janie smiled. "Nice memory."

"They also come in different colors," Katie went on. "Olive green, dark brown, and black, and their backs and tops consist of dark blotches."

Janie seemed surprised. "Wow. *Really* nice memory."

Olive bit back a smile, because she knew Katie wasn't done and wouldn't be until she finished reciting everything she'd learned.

"They're active during the day and live in the water," Katie said. "They feed on fish, amphibians, frogs, and salamanders."

Janie laughed. "I feel like I should offer you a job. Would you all like to go to my office now? Some of my staff will be at our meeting, so we can discuss—"

"They also eat the larvae of those fish and amphibians," Katie added.

"Cool!" Joey said. "Are they poisonous?"

"No," Janie and Katie said at the same time.

Katie glanced at Olive, biting her lower lip like she always did when trying to figure out if she'd overstepped the socially accepted boundaries to a situation. Olive smiled at her, and Katie smiled back, looking relieved.

"Can we get one, Mommy?"

Katie's smile dropped away. "Uh . . ."

"It's almost my birthday, you know!"

A nearly inaudible sound came from Katie's throat. Facts, she loved. Snakes, not so much.

Janie looked at Olive like maybe she needed help navigating the group.

"Your office would be great," Olive said.

Sally came with them. Which was how Olive found herself sitting at a round conference table with some of Janie's staff while covered in mud and a bunch of other questionable things she didn't want to think about. Oh, and Sally, right at home on the table, making her way from staff member to staff member.

"She's looking for treats," Janie said when Sally slithered her way to Olive.

Olive lifted her hands. "Sorry, ma'am, I've got nothing for you." This didn't stop the snake as she slithered up Olive's arm. She froze, a little surprised to find Sally cool to the touch, and smooth.

Across the table from her, Katie's eyes were wide. "Are you okay?" she whispered.

"Pending," she whispered back.

"Sally, come on back," Janie said indulgently, then spoke to Olive. "Most zoos in the country are struggling financially, and we're no exception. Attendance is down. As you know, we need a campaign to get people interested in visiting us, but also to raise awareness and funds to continue our animal rescue efforts. We're at a loss on how to do that. When Amy told me about you, Olive, and what you do for a living and how good you are at it, I knew we had to hire you."

Olive hadn't blushed in years, but she felt her face heat with pleasure. But that might have been just an impending stroke thanks to Sally, who hadn't gone back to Janie, but instead was making her way toward Olive's neck.

Thankfully, the guy sitting next to her gently coaxed the snake into his arms, allowing Olive to take a deep breath. "I've been thinking about this ever since Amy brought it up. One thing we could do is create a spring event. With the snow in our rearview, people will be looking for something fun to do. How about a fundraiser dinner?"

"I guess we could rent out a ballroom in one of the Tahoe hotels," Janie said. "And hope we take in enough money to recoup the costs?"

"What about holding it right here at the zoo?" Olive asked.

Janie blinked. "Huh. I never thought about that. We've never done anything like that before."

"Which is what makes it so perfect," Olive said. "If it's at night, and you close the zoo to the general public, that would make the tickets a hot item. You've got so many wonderful animals here to see."

"Not as many as most zoos, since we're so small."

"It would still be a huge attraction. You have roaches on hand for a food source, yes?"

Janie nodded, looking confused.

Olive looked around the table. "Has anyone here ever been heartbroken?"

Several hands went up, including Janie's. "My ratfink boyfriend just dumped me for a friend of mine, so yes."

"What a roach," Olive said, and smiled. "You should name a roach after this ex and feed it to Sally."

Everyone, including Janie, grinned at the thought.

"A lot of fundraisers focus their marketing on a couples' night out at a dressy event," Olive said. "Instead, we could put the focus on singles, people who want to meet other animal lovers with a shared interest."

Janie gaped at her. "That's brilliant. But how do we get people's attention? How to get the media to report on it? Because that's been our problem in the past, getting the word out to make the event worthwhile."

"We offer an additional ticket—at an extra cost, of course—to our singles who want to name a cockroach after an ex. An ex-partner, an ex-friend, an ex-coworker, it doesn't matter. They name their cockroach, and then . . . we feed them to your snakes, or Komodo dragons, or whatever else you have here who eats roaches. We put that in the press release, and trust me, the word will get out."

Janie was practically bouncing up and down in her seat. "Oh my God. It's perfect. Amy told me you were brilliant, and she wasn't kidding."

High praise, coming from Amy. Also, surprising, but she pushed that aside for now. "This kind of fundraising doesn't have to end with the dinner either."

Janie smiled. "You mean like add it as an option to our entrance fee? For people who want a little extra fun to their day? *Yes*."

"Definitely that," Olive said. "But I was thinking even bigger. If we leave it on the zoo's website, people from all over the country could continue to purchase the option online, and they could get a video of the feeding."

"Gruesome," Janie said. "I love it." She stood up and offered Olive a handshake. "You're amazing. *And* you're hired."

CHAPTER 10

Olive didn't sleep that night, both excited and unsettled. Excited because she had another new client. Unsettled because she still hadn't heard from her parents, and even though no one else seemed worried, she was.

But also . . . she couldn't stop thinking about Noah's parting shot about her leaving . . .

You certainly know how.

True, by the way. Yes, in a way, he'd left her too when he hadn't even tried to track her down himself. But this wasn't about him, it was about her. She'd gotten really good at leaving over the years. She'd left her parents as a teenager. She'd left Noah, good reason or not. She'd left Katie, who hadn't deserved it. She'd also left one of only two semiserious relationships with men.

She was a Leaver.

But actually, that was a lie she told herself. The truth was, she didn't know how to handle love. The girl who'd fallen in love with her fake boyfriend at age sixteen hadn't known how to deal with it, and she still didn't know, because somehow, no matter how much she tried to do things differently, deep down she still felt like that weird, off-the-grid kid who no one knew how to relate to.

Just before dawn, her alarm went off. Groggy, she showered, dressed, and tiptoed downstairs to the living room, going still at the sight of Noah sprawled out on the couch, fast asleep.

On top of him lay an also-sleeping Holmes.

And curled against the dog's chest sat Pepper. The little kitten was wide awake, eyes narrowed on Olive.

The cutie pie was on the job, guarding her two men.

Olive pulled on a jacket and stepped quietly outside, where the cold air had her breath turning into little puffy clouds. Since she was allergic to mornings, she didn't often see a sunrise, but she'd been missing out because the sky was a gorgeous wash of pinks and purples, illuminating the landscape with a vibrant, almost surreal glow.

Today was the town's monthly farmer's market, something her parents never missed. Once a month, they sold their wares there: her mom's soaps, candles, and jewelry, and her dad's plants—at least the legal ones.

If all was okay with them, they'd be there.

The event was hugely popular, and already parking was scarce, which made her doubly glad for the Mini Cooper. She could park it anywhere, including the sidewalk if she had to, which she'd done at least three times since being back in Sunrise Cove.

One of those times was even on purpose.

"Olive? Olive Turner?"

Turning, she came face to face with Henry Milson. They'd gone to school together; he'd been on the varsity baseball team with Noah.

"Wow, it is you," he said, still tall, still handsome, still annoying. "The girl who ran over the town hero."

She managed a smile. "And it's you, the boy who thought he was God's gift."

He tipped his head back and laughed. "Still not afraid to speak your mind. And look at you, you turned out great. We should go out sometime."

Her first thought was that he was messing with her, but he was smiling, looking friendly. "Sure you want to risk it?" she asked. "I might run you over."

He grinned. "I'll drive."

She snorted. "Thanks, but I'm going to pass."

He handed her a business card, which said he ran a local bike shop. "If you change your mind, look me up."

"Sure," she said, waiting until he'd walked on to drop his card in the trash. She made her way through the aisles, experiencing a déjà vu. Or maybe it was just memories. How many Saturday mornings had she and Katie spent here, admiring all the different things for sale, eating their weight in churros and street corn and whatever else they could afford, pooling their resources from chores and babysitting.

For as long as she could remember, her parents had rented their space on the far south side, last aisle, in the middle.

But when she got there, all she saw was an empty booth.

"Olive! Yoohoo, Olive!"

Turning, she found her high school English teacher waving to her from the booth across the way. Mrs. Carlyle was selling her infamous knit goods: scarfs, blankets, stuffed animals, hats, and, Olive's favorite, "man mitts," and no, they didn't go on a man's hands. The woman was somewhere between sixty and immortal, and was wearing a T-shirt that read *I knit because stabbing people is frowned upon*. She'd always been incredibly kind to Olive, so she smiled and waved. "Yep, it's me. The girl who ran over the town hero."

Mrs. Carlyle blinked. "Well, I'm sure it was an accident, dear. And how lovely to see you. Where are your parents today?"

"I was wondering the same thing. I thought they'd be here."

"They're here every second Saturday of the month without fail," Mrs. Carlyle said. "I don't think they've ever missed one. Well, except for the occasional Grateful Dead concert or musical festival."

Not good news. Olive turned at the sound of footsteps. Amy stood there, holding a tote bag full of fresh veggies and fruit. She eyed the empty booth, then Olive. "This doesn't necessarily mean anything," she said gently. "Your mom loves a good time above all else, so if something came up that called to her, it's very likely she chose that over being here today."

Surprise filled Olive. "I didn't realize you two knew each other that well."

Amy shrugged. "We went to school together."

Since neither Amy nor Olive's mom had ever mentioned being friends, Olive hadn't had any idea. "Were you close?"

"No. But I'll ask around here today for you, see if anyone's heard from them."

"I'd appreciate that, thanks," Olive said, but Amy had already walked off.

"I bet you didn't know I was also your mom's English teacher back in the day," Mrs. Carlyle said.

And the surprises kept coming. "I had no idea."

"Amy's too." Mrs. Carlyle tilted her head. "You don't know, do you?"

Uh-oh. "Know what?"

"That they were mortal enemies in school."

Olive felt her jaw hit the floor. "*What?*"

"Oh, honey, the stories I could tell you."

"I'm listening."

Mrs. Carlyle smiled. "I adored your mom. Violet was such a shy one. Not the sharpest in her year, but she did the best she could under the circumstances."

Olive's mom had told her very little about her growing up years, just that her own mom had walked away, leaving only her dad to raise her. They'd lived paycheck to paycheck, and Olive's mom had spent a lot of time alone or unsupervised because her dad had worked long hours at a lumberyard.

"She was at a disadvantage being that she didn't have anyone at home really looking after her," Mrs. Carlyle said. "Poor thing was scrappy, though. And . . ."

"And what?"

"Well, she didn't fit in, not really. Honestly, she didn't seem to want to. As a result, she was frequently bullied. Not that we used that word back in those days. Mostly, teachers and admin turned a blind eye to such things, letting the kids work out their problems on their own."

The story was uncomfortably similar to Olive's own, and it made her realize she had some more things in common with her mom than she'd even known. "Do you remember who bullied her?"

Mrs. Carlyle's gaze looked beyond Olive, so she turned to see who the woman was looking at.

Amy, who'd stopped a few booths away and was picking out some vegetables.

Olive turned back to Mrs. Carlyle, a thousand questions on her tongue, but a group of people stopped at the woman's booth.

How was it that neither her mom nor Amy had ever mentioned their past? But come to think of it, she'd never seen the two interact, mostly because her own mom had rarely if ever come to Sunrise Cove.

Her phone buzzed an incoming call from Katie. "Joe?" Olive asked quickly.

"Nothing yet. Did you find your parents at the farmer's market?"

"No."

"I'm sorry, but I was thinking. Isn't this around the time of year they go hiking with that nudist colony they love?"

Things you don't want to picture . . . "That was last month."

"There's still a chance they've just lost track of time."

True enough. She tried to shrug it off. "They'll show up."

"They will."

Olive found a smile. "Look at you being all positive. I don't think I've told you how happy I am to be back in Sunrise Cove with you. I know I don't tell you enough how much you mean to me, mostly because you hate mushy stuff, but—"

"Mushy stuff isn't allowed. It's in our rules."

Olive snorted. "I just wanted to make sure you know how much I love you—" Olive pulled the phone from her ear and looked at the screen. "Aaaand she's gone." With a short laugh, she headed out. Five minutes later she was getting back into her car while munching on her third churro—because why have one when you could have three *and* a gut ache to boot?

Back at home, she checked in on Gram, then worked for several hours until her alarm went off, reminding her to get to Joey's game. After parking at the fields, she walked to the stands, where she found herself grinning because . . .

T-ball.

Big, badass Noah Turner was coaching *T-ball.*

He stood near home base wearing jeans, jersey, baseball cap, and a pained expression, watching as his team bounced around the field like a bunch of tumbleweeds in the wind. When he sharply blew his whistle, the pandemonium came to an immediate halt.

"Bring it in," he said with calm authority. Which, damn, was really annoyingly hot.

He gestured the kids in closer. Whatever was said in the huddle, she had no idea, but they all clapped, yelled "*Cubs!*" in semiunison, and then scattered back to the outfield.

The first kid up from the other team was so short, he had to swing up to reach the ball—which flew about three feet and died.

No one in the field moved toward the ball.

"Teddy," Noah called out. "That's you."

"Oh!" Teddy ran from the mound to pick up the ball and dropped it. Twice.

Olive was pretty sure she could hear Noah grinding his back teeth to powder.

Someone behind her on the stands leaned in. "Isn't it good to see him out there again?"

Olive took a peek. It was Gina Davies, who'd dated Noah briefly in high school. Since she was wearing a big fat diamond ring on *that* finger, it was safe to say she'd moved on. Olive smiled noncommittally.

"After you ran him over," Gina said, "none of us thought we'd see him back on the field ever again."

"Actually," Olive said, "he's not on the field. He's on the sidelines. Coaching."

"Well, the boys are lucky to have him." Gina cupped her perfectly manicured hands around her perfectly glossed lips and went category-five stage mom as she yelled, "Sammy! Look alive out there, baby! This is your calling!" She sat back and lowered her voice. "Assuming his future girlfriend doesn't take it all away from him, that is."

A woman on the other side of Olive patted her knee. "Honey, don't listen to her. Hardly anyone still blames you."

Olive had no idea who the woman was, but she searched her brain for something to say. "Great day for this."

A man behind her snorted. "Yeah, if you're on the other team."

The Cubs' right fielder was sitting on the grass, facing away from the game, pulling daisies. Their first baseman appeared to be singing a song to himself and dancing like no one was watching. And their third baseman was working on his somersault game.

Noah stood on the sidelines, hands on hips, staring down at his shoes, whether to hide his smile, or just so he didn't have to watch the calamity, was anyone's guess.

When it was the Cubs' turn at bat, Noah's day didn't improve any. The first batter kept missing the ball entirely, probably because his eyes were closed.

Noah swiped a hand down his face. "Carlos," he said with what looked like remarkable restraint. "Eyes on the ball. Which means your eyes have to be open."

A few more batters came and went, all fouling out. Noah appeared to have gained an eye tic.

When the teams took a brief break between innings, Olive walked over to the fence, only a few feet away from where Noah was giving a pep talk. Well, maybe not exactly a pep talk.

"We're not the Bad News Bears, here, guys. We got this."

"Who are the Bad News Bears?" a couple kids wanted to know.

Noah gave a rare sigh.

Olive laughed.

He craned his neck and leveled a look her way. "Having a good time?"

"I mean, it's not a bad time." She smiled at the look on his face. "Come on, it's T-ball. What did you expect?"

"I've got no idea." He lowered his voice. "This might surprise you, but I suck at this."

"At what, being motivating? Gentle? Understanding?"

"Yes," he said, and made her laugh again. He gave a small head shake, but he also almost smiled on the inside, she could tell.

One of the kids ran up to Noah and wrapped their arms around Noah's long legs. "Coach! There's a snake in the dugout! A big, scary snake!"

Noah patted the kid on the back, then disentangled himself as a panicked murmur grew among the parents in the stands. Kids were running around, screaming like they were in a horror flick as Noah headed toward the snake sighting.

Was his limp less noticeable today? Olive hoped he felt good enough to run from the snake if need be, but then, in less than a minute, he came back out . . . *carrying* a black snake, which was at least a mile long. Okay, three feet, but still.

"Just a garter snake," he called out to everyone. "Harmless." He then headed to the end of the outfield. Beyond the fence was open land covered in hip-high wild grass. Noah let the snake loose there and then stood a beat, his back to the stands, hands on hips as he presumably watched the snake slither off. Apparently satisfied the snake wouldn't return, he came back.

"Damn, he's the hottest thing on two legs," a woman whispered somewhere to the right of Olive.

"He's the hottest thing on the entire planet, two legs or other-wise," another woman whispered.

"You do realize I'm sitting right next to you, Cheryl," a man sitting at the woman's side said.

"Yes, Bob, I do realize. I also realize that if we'd found a snake in our yard, you'd run right over the top of me to get away."

"Well, that's just survival instincts," Bob said.

Olive was dealing with her own survival instincts, and they were screaming at her that she was feeling things that she shouldn't be feeling, especially since once upon a time, those particular feelings had nearly destroyed her.

CHAPTER 11

Twelve years ago

Two days after Olive and Noah started Fake-Dating-Gate, she knew she'd screwed up. Sure, suddenly the entire school looked at her differently, plus people were talking to her, including her—which to be honest, pissed her off—but . . . she was no closer to meeting her goal.

Her Lose-Her-Virginity goal.

Hell, she'd never even been kissed.

And worse, there was only one guy on the entire planet she wanted to take the job. Except Noah didn't want it, not for real.

She waited for him after his game, the one he'd won by hitting a home run in the last inning, landing the team in the state playoffs. Half the town had come, and finally the players started to trickle out, much to the crowd's pleasure.

Noah somehow managed to slip out unseen by everyone but her, and she made her move, closing in, grabbing his hand, and pulling him around the side of building and out of sight. Caught off guard, he said her name in surprise when she pushed him up against the wall. "Congratulations," *she murmured, her heart thumping so loud she could hardly hear herself think. She went up on tiptoe and pressed her lips to his.*

He went still as stone, but didn't push her away.

Taking that as a good sign, she pressed closer, but though she'd googled "how to kiss," *it all fled her brain at the warmth of his body, the silky heat of his lips, and the way his hands had slid to her hips, holding her tight. Pulling back a fraction, she whispered,* "Show me how to do this right—"

He groaned and dropped his forehead to hers. "Olive—"

"Just this, okay? Just a kiss. Please, Noah."

As if the sound of his name on her lips galvanized him, his features softened and he leaned into her. "Don't ever beg a guy for anything, okay? We don't deserve it. You, on the other hand, deserve everything."

Her belly fluttered.

"Just a kiss," *he said gruffly.*

He might as well have offered her a night of hot, sweaty sex given how everything in her body pulled tight like an overstretched bow at just the sound of his voice. She nodded, afraid to speak. God had granted her one full sentence. She didn't dare hope for a second.

Then she couldn't think anymore because he hauled her up against him and kissed her. Really kissed her, and it was better than she'd imagined. But then she was weaving unsteadily on her feet because he'd stopped, nudging her away from him, holding her up with his hands on her arms.

"More," *she whispered, staring at his mouth.*

With a groan, he dropped his head to her shoulder.

So she turned her face into him and pressed her lips to his neck.

Making another of those very male sounds deep in his throat, he tightened his grip on her. And thanks to her hands flat on his chest, she could feel his heart pounding beneath her palm. It was the first time she knew it wasn't just her under his spell, but that he was caught up in it too.

"I'm a really bad idea, Oli."

"Brand-new information," she said, trying to lighten the mood by teasing, but still not opening her eyes. Even without looking, she felt his smile.

After a moment, he sighed. "I've tried to steer clear."

And now on to the gut-wrenching portion of the evening . . . "How's that working out for you?"

"Not great . . ." He paused, hesitating. "You know we can't do this, right?"

"But—"

"We can't," he whispered, voice tinged with regret. "Please don't make this harder than it already is."

She held on to that, his regret, telling herself he'd change his mind.

But he didn't.

Present day

Olive worked hard to keep control of her own runaway thoughts, but watching Noah coach the kids was sexy as hell. Even worse, watching him handle the snake situation, running toward the potential danger instead of away, had been even sexier. Dammit. She knew he worked hard to stay fit. Even recovering from the accident, he'd done some sort of exercise every day rather than take a break. Personally, she thought taking rest days was very important to a fitness regimen. She was currently on rest day four hundred and something, and she felt great.

When the game was called and both sides declared winners, Joey ran up to Olive. "Did you see me hit the ball?"

He hadn't actually hit the ball—he'd hit the tee and the ball had fallen off. "I did," she said, and hugged him. "You were great."

"Can I play with Mikey on the playground for a few minutes?"

"Sure, as long as I can see you."

"Mikey has hermit crabs!"

"That sounds . . ." *Kinda icky . . .* "Wonderful." She playfully tugged on the bill of his baseball cap. "Have fun."

He and Mikey raced to the playground near the stands.

Olive's gaze tracked to Noah, sitting on the players' bench, making notes with one hand, his other absentmindedly rubbing his injured leg. As she headed toward him, he was staring down at his clipboard, looking . . . well, not thrilled. And it hit her, how hard this must be for him, back in a world he'd had to give up. Having to relive the dream that could have been. She knew what he'd told his mom, that the dream had been his dad's, but Olive didn't know if that was really true, or if he just hadn't wanted his mom to worry. Either way, she quietly sat next to him on the bench.

He looked up, and she didn't have to read minds to know what he was thinking. She was the last person he'd want to see. "Is this the first game of Joey's that you've been to?" she asked.

"No, but it's the first time I coached."

"I imagine that's not easy for you."

She saw the surprise in his eyes, like she was the first person to get it, although he didn't say anything. But she needed to. So she drew a deep breath and pulled up her metaphoric big girl undies. "You know, I still think about that night, and how—"

"Olive. Don't."

Right. Of course he wouldn't want to talk about it. Dumb. She was so dumb. Embarrassed, she stood and started to walk away.

"I don't blame you, you know."

He said this to her back with a quiet certainty, and she turned around. Hard to guess at his feelings since he wore those dark sunglasses, but *she* felt . . . well, everything. The breath had left her chest. Her heart pounded in her ears. But this wasn't about her. As much guilt as she carried for what had happened to him, she knew he carried the same for what happened to his brother-in-law. "And Joe wouldn't blame you either."

It'd been a shot in the dark, a wild guess, but she knew she was right when he scoffed.

"He should," he said. "He should absolutely blame me. I was distracted and he paid the price."

"I see." She put some humor in her voice, hoping to defuse his guilt and tension. "So you should've known that you were going to get shot at? Are you a superhero now? Because nobody's perfect, Noah."

He let out a rough laugh, and his shoulders lowered. "Katie told me you didn't find your parents at the farmer's market."

She remembered what Mrs. Carlyle had said about her mom and Amy, but decided there was no reason to open that can of worms.

The past was best left in the past.

Noah was watching her, not saying anything, patient, steady, and, as always, someone she could count on and trust. Maybe not with her heart, but with everything else, including her life. "Apparently it happens." When she'd seen their empty booth, she'd been at DEFCON 1, but now, just from being in his calm presence, she was at DEFCON 3, rounding the bases to DEFCON 4. "No one seems worried."

"But you still are."

She sighed. "I can't shake the bad feeling."

"When was the last time you saw them?" he asked.

She appreciated, more than he could know, that he didn't offer empty platitudes or a sympathy that she didn't want. "A year ago. The last time I was back in the States."

There was no judgment in his voice when he said, "Still, that's a long time. They didn't come to see you?"

"No." She slid him a look. "Sometimes distance makes the heart grow fonder."

His smile was brief, his eyes still intense. "I can't help but feel like I'm missing a piece to the puzzle that is Olive Porter."

Because he was. His family had been her family. She'd have done anything for them. So when his dad had come to her the day after their horrific accident saying that Noah needed time and space to figure out his life *without* her influence—she hadn't even realized she *had* influence—she'd believed every word. And because Noah's dad had been somewhat of an authority figure in her life, she hadn't even questioned it.

Maybe because at the end of the day, love had never done her any favors. Worse, she didn't believe Noah could or would ever love her, and with his dad asking her to go, she also didn't believe his family could love her either.

Except Katie. She knew Katie loved her. But Katie also had loved her dad very much, which meant Olive couldn't, wouldn't, drag her best friend into it. She owed the Turner family that much, to not further divide them. Instead, she'd kept it all to herself and left, all while knowing they were better off without her there anyway. As for herself, she'd been on her own again, but she was used to that.

Once she'd grown up a bit, she did have regrets about how she'd handled everything. Or, more accurately, how she hadn't handled everything. She wasn't sure what the statute of limitations was on requests made by a dead man. Even now, she was still trying to figure that part out without derailing her life, Noah's life, and everyone else's as well.

Joey ran over and hissed at them.

Noah blinked.

"He's a snake," Olive said. "We met one at the zoo."

Joey smiled, jumped into Olive's arms, and cuddled in. "Is it ice cream time yet?" he asked.

Noah smiled and ruffled his hair. "Snakes can't eat ice cream."

"I'm back to being a boy."

"Perfect," Noah said.

Twenty minutes later, Olive sat at the ice cream bar in the local creamery. Not too far away, Noah and Joey shared a huge ice cream sundae, their heads bent together, laughing at something on Noah's phone.

Katie slid onto the stool next to her. "Joe squeezed my hand again. Twice. The doctor said he really does expect him to wake up any day." She looked across the table and smiled. "Doesn't that cuteness overload make your ovaries yearn?"

Olive's ovaries weren't yearning. They were exploding. Watching Noah interact with Joey had something moving inside of her, but hopefully it was indigestion.

Katie sighed at her lack of response.

"What do you want me to say?"

"I want you to say you're into him. For real, not pretend."

Olive slid her a look. "You knew it was all for show back then?"

"I knew a lot of stuff."

Olive hesitated. "You know that once Joe wakes up—and he will—I'm going back to London and Noah's going back to Yosemite. I'm trying not to disappoint or hurt anyone this time."

"You're already hurting," Katie said. "I can tell."

"No, you can't. You can recall conversations verbatim that I can't even remember having, you're the best mom on the planet, and your skills as a research librarian are unprecedented. You're really great at a lot of things, but reading people's emotions isn't one of them."

"Okay, true, but I know *some* things."

"Such as?"

"That while you might like your life overseas, I can tell you don't love it."

"Based on what?"

"The way you don't like to talk about your life over there, or when you do, your smile doesn't meet your eyes, and there's something off in your voice. Come back to us, Olive. You can love it here. I know it."

It was a ridiculous notion, so she was stunned at the pang of longing that settled in her gut. Because it was true, she didn't enjoy living so far away. She loved her job, and the people she did that job with, but there were other kinds of love that were missing.

They both looked over at the sound of Noah and Joey laughing. Joey had a dollop of ice cream on his nose.

Katie shook her head. "I can't believe my brother thinks he wouldn't be a good dad."

"What? He'd make a *great* dad," Olive said, trying to leave the wistfulness out of her voice.

"I agree, but Molly, his ex, really did a number on him. She'd been talking about their future, and he was slowly coming around to the idea, and then suddenly she just couldn't deal with his long hours and the danger of his job. Told him he had to choose: her or the job. And when he chose, she then made sure he knew the breakup was all on him, not her."

Olive shook her head. Why did people hurt those they supposedly loved? "Her loss because Noah knows how to balance responsibilities, not to mention pressure, like no one else."

Katie nodded. "True, and we both know exactly how much pressure he's been under for most of his life. He wasn't about to let that continue, but it still hurt him. And now he's blaming himself for Joe being in a coma . . . And let's not forget how it all started. With me. How he always had to be okay because I wasn't." She said this in her usual matter-of-fact way, without emotion, but it hurt Olive for her.

"Katie, it wasn't your fault either."

She shrugged, then pasted on a smile when Joey ran over, grabbed her hand, and dragged her to a table with his friends and their moms.

Olive turned her head and found her gaze locked with Noah's. Something passed between them, something nameless but . . . easy.

It felt a whole bunch like the affection they used to share.

He shifted to a closer stool and she used her professional smile. "Do you always come here after Joey's games?"

"Joe started the tradition." He let out a breath. "Half the time, I'm not sure how to be a help here, so I do whatever he'd do."

Amy came and sat with them, looking at Noah. "Some of the dads want to talk to you." She gestured with her chin to a table across the room.

Amy watched him go, but was probably not staring at how good his ass looked in his jeans like Olive was.

"It's still there, isn't it?" his mom asked quietly. "That pull between you and my son."

Olive's heart skipped a beat. "It was all a long time ago. We were just silly kids."

Amy gave a small smile and nodded. Then shook her head. "When it comes to this kind of a connection, time doesn't matter." She paused. "I've never said this before, because I was too ashamed. But . . ." This pause was longer. Finally she grimaced, and when she spoke, her voice was low, an agonized whisper really. "I'm so very sorry for the role I played in you leaving town."

Olive's mouth fell open. As far as she'd understood, no one had ever known of the promise she'd made, except for Noah's dad and herself. "You knew?"

Apparently, she hadn't masked her hurt because Amy's eyes were remorseful. "I did."

And she'd done nothing. Now Olive's heart didn't just skip a beat, it hardened.

Amy watched her, probably taking in the emotions she was having a hard time fighting: anger, betrayal . . .

"When Chuck told me what he'd asked of you," Amy said quietly, "I told him to undo it."

Olive looked away, trying hard to absorb the blow without letting anyone see that she was upset. "He didn't."

"I know."

"Nor did you reach out to me. Not even after Chuck was gone."

Amy closed her eyes for a beat. "No. And I'm sorrier for that than I can say. I should have, but after all this time, I wasn't sure what to say."

Just keep breathing. Slow and easy. Do not cry, not here.

Amy opened her eyes. "Believe me, I hear myself. In hindsight, I know how unfair this was to you. Especially since we cared for you, we really did. But at the time, there were things in play that you didn't understand." She drew a breath. "Chuck's tumor was already pushing in on his brain and causing mood swings. So what he asked of you . . . it had nothing to do with his feelings for you. But he knew Noah's love for baseball was waning. He got it in his head that if you weren't around, Noah wouldn't give up on the dream."

Olive wasn't sure what to do with that. She'd felt so bad for the entire Turner family when they'd lost Chuck. Katie had been particularly gutted—which was a big part of why Olive had never told her what her dad had asked of her. Instead, she'd let Katie think that she and Noah had lost touch because they'd had a fight they couldn't resolve. Katie had spent several years trying to talk Olive into meeting Noah to fix things, but she'd eventually given up.

And if Olive was being honest with herself, even knowing what she knew now, about Chuck being sicker than anyone had known, about Amy not protecting Olive, she still didn't hold what happened against any of them. "I've never blamed you," she said to Amy now. "Or Chuck for that matter." She blamed herself, because it hadn't mattered what he'd said to her, she should have pushed back. "I just felt so guilty about my role in ending Noah's career that I turned into a coward. It wasn't your husband's fault I stayed away, it was mine."

Amy's eyes went shiny with unshed tears. "That's . . . incredibly generous of you. I'm not sure if you know this, but I think Noah mourned the loss of you more than baseball." She paused. "Are you two . . . ?"

Olive let out a mirthless laugh. "Noah and I don't agree on much, but we align on one thing—we're not going to revisit the past. We're just . . . friends. We want different things in life."

Amy put her hand on Olive's arm. "Where does this leave you when our hell is over and Joe wakes up?"

Honestly? Olive had no idea. Living the life she'd dreamed about, but was feeling unfulfilled with, she supposed. Since that was a depressing thought, she smiled grimly and got up to get some more toppings for her ice cream.

Noah was on the other side of the toppings station. His eyes took her in. "You okay?"

"Yep," she said, snapping the *P*. She added her weight in chocolate syrup to her bowl. And then crushed peanuts. That should help.

"You're allergic."

"It's more of a sensitivity," she said defensively. Would her throat get all scratchy? Was she going to wheeze? Was she going to break out in a rash? Most definitely. Did she care? Nope. Not in that moment, not even a little bit.

CHAPTER 12

Twenty minutes later, Noah was back at Katie's house, trying to find a corner of the house to claim as his own. He desperately needed a few minutes alone with his thoughts, but this was the problem with his family, he was *never* left alone, with his thoughts or otherwise.

Joey had fallen asleep on Noah's bed, Katie was visiting Joe, his mom would be coming back in a bit with dinner, Holmes and Pepper had claimed the porch swing and were also napping, and the house seemed to be overcome by clothes in what was probably-most-definitely a passive-aggressive love note from his sister that she wanted someone to do her and Joey's laundry.

It should probably be his mom, not him. Years and years ago, when they'd been in high school, he'd been grounded for something, probably for being a dick, and his punishment had been laundry. He'd thrown everything into one load, including his red jersey with everyone's whites. Then he'd compounded his error by drying everything on high.

His dad had bitched for a week about his tighty-whities being pink and how his pants had shrunk. When Noah had suggested maybe it wasn't that the pants had shrunk, but that his dad had been eating too much pizza, he'd been grounded again.

Good mems . . .

Thinking maybe the kitchen might be empty, he made his way there via the living room, and nearly stepped on Olive. Sitting on the floor, her back to him, she was folding Clean Clothes Mountain.

He opened his mouth to tell her that Katie wouldn't expect her to do laundry, wouldn't expect her to do any of the extremely thoughtful things she'd taken on, like ordering dinner in so no one would have to cook, taking care of Joey—something she did with surprising ease—or just in general doing whatever had to be done, but before he could speak, he realized her breathing sounded off. Each inhale was a wheeze, then a rough, strained cough.

Hoping he was wrong, he quickly moved around the couch to see her face. She was indeed struggling to drag air into her lungs. "You okay?"

She nodded, but it took her several agonizing seconds to get a word out. "Yep."

Bullshit. Her throat was beet red, and as he watched, she reached up and scratched at it. "Oli." He dropped to his knees in front of her. "Do you need the hospital?"

"No. This just . . . happens sometimes. I'm fine."

"You're not fine. It was the peanuts."

"I only had a few."

"Your ice cream was covered in them. What do we do?"

"There is no we. I'm a me. A me, myself, and I."

"Oh good, you're not going to be stubborn about accepting help at all, then."

"I . . . don't . . . need . . . help."

He took the shirt she was folding from her hands and tossed it aside. "Has no one ever taken care of you?"

"Yeah." She looked away. "You and your family."

Damn, now *his* throat felt tight. "Where's your EpiPen?"

"Don't need it. Benadryl would work if I'd packed it. But it knocks me out while also giving me weird nightmares that I can't wake myself up from."

"Is it better than being dead?"

She rolled her eyes. "Dramatic much?"

Apparently air wasn't required for sarcasm. He accessed the camera app on his phone and held it up so she could see her face and neck.

"Oh crap," she breathed-slash-wheezed.

He had more descriptive words but kept them to himself as he pulled her upright and led her into the kitchen. Katie was allergic to many different foods and always kept Benadryl on hand. He pulled a bottle from an upper cabinet, but Olive was shaking her head, even as she continued to scratch and wheeze and cough. "I'm okay."

"You will be." He shook out two pills and filled a glass with water.

With a sigh, she downed the Benadryl. "I hate you a little bit."

"Yeah, I know. Let's go."

"Where?"

"Bed."

Somehow she managed to choke out a laugh, even as he tugged her down the hall. "Interesting," she said. "But to recap, you turned me down."

"That was a lifetime ago. We should be able to laugh it off by now." One would think . . . In her bedroom, he yanked down the bedding and gestured for her to get in.

She was sucking some serious wind now and bent over at the waist, hands on her knees. "Hold . . . on."

She had sixty seconds to start breathing easier or he'd search her purse for her EpiPen himself, stab her with it, then haul her ass to the hospital—

"Are you going to help me or stand there?"

That's when he realized she wasn't bent over trying to breathe, she was trying to get her boots off. He stared at the sexy-as-hell knee-high boots.

"There's a zipper—"

"I see it," he said. The problem was that the hem of her dress fell over the top of the boots. This meant sticking his hands under her dress. Trying to be impassive, he quickly unzipped and pulled off the boots, then went from hot and bothered to amused because her socks were Hello Kitty.

"They have to go too," she said. "I can't sleep in socks."

Of course not. This time his fingers brushed bare, warm skin as he slid the socks down. He was sweating by the time he rose to his feet again. "Can you pull a deep breath yet?"

She tried and yawned wide. "Anyone ever tell you that you need to get a grip?"

"Yes. You, many times." He gestured to the bed. "Get in."

"I can't sleep in this dress," she said. "It's new."

He had no idea what it being new had to do with anything, and it wasn't often that he needed his mom or sister, but he wished like hell one of them was home. "Okay, I'll just . . ." He gestured vaguely to the door.

Before he could turn away, she grabbed his arm. "Just un-zip me. Jeez, it's not like you've never undressed a woman before."

"Not this woman."

"Well whose fault is that?" Turning her back to him, she lifted her hair.

The zipper went from the nape of her neck to . . . God help him . . . an inch past a strip of black silk very, very, *very* low on her back. So low he could see twin dimples on either side of the teasing glimpse of her sweet ass. Her bra was a matching thin black silk across her back, with crisscrossing straps that had him swallowing hard.

"You okay back there?" she asked.

He had to clear his throat to talk, like a damn rookie. "Yeah."

Stepping out of her dress, she kicked it aside. Then she nearly killed him dead when she climbed onto the bed on her hands and knees in those sexy undies—

"Noah?"

He realized he'd lost a little chunk of time because she was lying down. Drawing a deep breath, he yanked the covers up to her chin.

She snorted.

Ignoring that, he pointed at her. "Stay."

She yawned again. "Like I have a choice. You've just sentenced me to a very shitty twelve hours . . ."

Why did she have the power to bring him to his knees with just a few words? "If you need anything, call out. You won't be alone." He flipped off the light and started to close the door.

"Don't" came her soft, disembodied voice in the dark. "Please don't shut it all the way . . ."

Something in the plea stopped him cold. Olive never showed her fear. Or at least the Olive he'd known. Slowly, he turned back, but the room was too dark to see. He opened the bathroom door to let the nightlight's glow beat back some of the darkness. "Better?" he asked quietly.

No answer, just the sound of her soft breathing, which was much easier now than it had been a few minutes ago. This allowed him to take a deep breath of his own.

Leaving the bedroom, he was surprised to find Joey waiting in the hallway. "What's wrong?" the kid asked.

"Olive's taking a nap."

"Oh."

Man and boy stared at each other. Noah wasn't often alone with him and he had to search his brain for something for them to do. "Want to watch TV?"

"Mom said only an hour a day, and I already had my hour. I wanna play a game."

Which was how Noah found himself playing Go Fish. At first, he'd been worried. Was he supposed to let the kid win, or teach him about competition? In the end, it hadn't mattered. Joey had just handily trounced him when Noah's mom came in with a casserole. She kissed Joey.

"Kiss Noah too!" Joey demanded.

His mom smiled and Noah sighed, because she grabbed his face, and to Joey's delight, kissed it all over.

"Seriously?" he asked her.

She just laughed. "If you'd go out with . . . well, anyone, I wouldn't have to kiss you. You'd have a girlfriend to do it for you."

"Noah needs a girlfriend!" Joey yelled.

Noah pointed at his mom, but she was too busy laughing to be any help at all. "I've got some computer work to catch up on." He was halfway down the hall when he heard it.

A whimper.

Shit. He stepped into Olive's bedroom, where he found her fighting a war with the blanket and losing. "Hey," he said quietly. "It's okay. You're okay."

"Blood . . . too much blood."

His heart stopped. "Oli."

"Don't you dare die on me."

Those had been her words to him that night in the woods beneath a hellish storm after his leg had been crushed beneath the ATV. Hitting the switch on the lamp by her bed, he sat on the edge of the mattress and put a hand on her shoulder, rubbing it up and down her arm. "I'm too stubborn to die. Wake up, Olive, and see for yourself."

"Noah?"

Her voice sounded tortured, devastated, and shame hit him like a one-two punch. What did it say about him that he'd never imagined what that long ago night had looked like from her point of view? It said he was *still* an asshole. "I'm right here with you, and I promise I'm okay. Open your eyes, Oli."

Her eyes flew open and she blinked, then launched herself at him.

Catching her saved both of them from tumbling to the floor but didn't help his heart any because she wrapped herself around him and held on tight, trembling. He ran a hand up and down her back before attempting to disentangle himself. "It was just a dream."

Giving a vehement head shake, she burrowed in, her voice thin, shaky. "No, it all really happened. You and me on the ATV when that crazy storm hit, knocking a huge branch down right in front of us, blocking the trail. Me climbing into the driver's seat while you got out to try and drag the branch aside, my foot slipping off the brake—" A strangled sound escaped her throat. "I rolled down the hill right at you. You tried to help me stop before I got hurt, but you got caught under the wheel—"

"Ancient history. I'm okay, Olive."

Lifting her head from where she'd had her face pressed in the crook of his neck, she stared at him from wet eyes. "Are you really?"

"Yes," he said firmly, still holding on to her because . . . well, he didn't have a good reason for that other than she was in his lap, straddling him, and felt so good, so damn good, that he couldn't make himself let go. "It's you I'm worried about at the moment. Are *you* okay?"

"No." Her face was once again pressed against him. "I can't keep kissing men and pretending they're you."

He froze. "What?"

Now she froze too. "Nothing. I'm still dreaming. Ignore me."

"You pretend they're me?"

"This is your fault. I told you I didn't want to take the stupid pink pills."

"Without them, you'd be in the hospital."

She drew a deep breath, reminding him they were plastered together as they both looked down to see if her rash was gone.

It was. Her smooth skin taunted him. As did her lack of clothing. His hand still made slow sweeps up and down her back, his fingers itching to slip beneath that silk. "You pretend they're me?" he repeated softly.

"Maybe I used to." She sighed, her lips brushing his throat. "But luckily, time heals all wounds. I'm hungry." Pushing away from him, she pulled on a pair of jeans and a sweater, covering up those delicious curves.

When they got downstairs, the lights were off. His mom had put Joey to bed and apparently had gone to bed as well.

He and Olive went in search of sustenance and found Pepper sitting in the middle of the kitchen table looking quite at home.

Noah shook his head at her. "Off the table, cat. You know the rules."

Pepper looked offended.

Olive laughed. "Doesn't listen very well, does she."

Noah snorted. "Currently, none of the women in my life listen worth a damn."

"Are you comparing me to your cat?"

"She's not mine, but she does remind me of you."

"Because I don't listen?"

He met her gaze. "Because you have the same arresting eyes that show me only enough to know I'm in trouble." He stroked a hand down the kitten's back and she arched into his fingers, purring, eyes closed in ecstasy. After a moment, he scooped her up, saying "go find your dog," and nudged her out of the kitchen. He turned to the other female in the room. "What would you like to eat?"

"Anything."

Most women didn't mean that, which he'd learned the hard way. But Olive wasn't like most women. Which he'd also learned the hard way. "Nachos?"

"Mmm, yes!"

So he made them a plate of nachos to go along with the brandy they'd pilfered from the pantry.

Olive sat on the countertop watching him watch her. "Let's play a game."

His mind tried to veer into the gutter, but he reined it in. "Like Trivial Pursuit or something?"

"Or something."

He leaned against the opposite counter and tried to interpret her mysterious smile.

"Two truths and a lie," she said.

Yep, he should have run when he had the chance. Clearly there was something she wanted to know, but didn't want to come right out and ask. Fine with him, he had things he wanted to know too. "Rules?"

Her smile deepened, maybe pleased he was going along with this, or, more likely, he'd just stepped into her web.

"Whoever's first gives their two truths and a lie," she said. "Then they take a shot while the other has to guess the lie." She held out the bottle of brandy.

"Ladies first."

"One," she said, without missing a beat, "my ex is dating a former close friend of mine. Two, my former close friend told me this in a voicemail. And three . . . my boyfriend Matt is a really great guy." She chased that with a healthy pull from the bottle.

Pushing away from the counter, he stepped forward until he bumped into her knees. When she shifted so that her thighs cradled him, he nearly groaned out loud. "If number one is true," he murmured, "I'm available to rearrange your ex's face if you'd like."

That got him an almost smile, until he realized her eyes held more than a hint of sadness.

"Let me confess something," he said softly, his hands going to her waist, "I've been hoping that Matt doesn't exist, that he's a fake boyfriend."

"Like you once were?"

He gave a wry laugh, even though it wasn't funny. It'd never been funny.

She was quiet for a moment, and during the space of several slow breaths, her gaze dragged over him from head to toe. It felt like a physical caress.

"The first one is true," she said. "So is the second."

He felt outraged on her behalf, and knew that he'd finally gotten the answer to the shadows in her eyes. But he also knew that if he expressed sympathy, she might slug him. So he went for levity. "So. Matt *is* pretend."

As he hoped, she relaxed her shoulders from where they'd been up at her ears and let out a rough laugh. "Yes, he's one hundred percent made up, from his great smile to his eight-pack abs to his not-hairy toes."

He shook his head. "Why?"

"Because hairy toes wig me out."

He gave her a can-we-get-real look.

She blew out a breath. "Look, Matt might not be real, but my ex—Ian—is. When he cheated on me, I felt . . ." She waved the brandy as she searched for the right word. "Betrayed. It took me a long time to get over it, but I did. I've even dated since then, but nothing serious. When I knew I was coming here, I made up a boyfriend because, believe it or not, coming back, knowing you'd be here, that you'd *all* be here, felt . . . intimidating."

"Oli," he said, pained that she'd feel that way.

She looked away. "The first time I showed up in Sunrise Cove, I had the clothes on my back and not much else, with absolutely zero idea who Olive Porter even was. I didn't want to do that again. This time I wanted to be someone successful, both personally and professionally."

She'd tucked her hair behind her ears, tamed for the moment, though a tendril of hair had fallen across her cheekbone. Her arresting eyes set off the forest green of her sweater, which barely met the waistband of her jeans. He wanted to touch her. Hell, who was he kidding? He wanted a lot more than that.

"Your turn," she said, handing him the brandy. "And no cheaping out either, I want good stuff. *Deep* stuff."

He rarely had a case of nerves, but they jangled around in his gut now. "Okay . . . deep stuff . . ." Shit. Why had he agreed to this again? "One, I tease my mom, but I really don't mind getting set up on blind dates. Two, I got dumped by my ex via voicemail, same as you. And three . . . once, a long time ago, the girl of my dreams left me a Dear John letter and then ghosted me." He took his shot and felt it burn going down, but at least the alcohol killed his nerves.

"You got dumped by voicemail too?" she asked.

He shrugged. "She didn't like that my lifestyle doesn't lend itself to relationships."

Her eyes flared with anger. For him, he realized.

"And the girl of your dreams?" she whispered. "That was . . . me?"

He just looked at her.

Her gaze dropped to his mouth. His body reacted predictably, which, given his position standing between her thighs, she couldn't possibly miss.

"It was," she breathed, sliding her hands into his hair, pulling him even closer. "It was me."

And then she kissed him.

In a million years, he couldn't have described what it felt like to hold her, to have her mouth on his, to feel her hands tighten in his hair, holding him where she wanted him.

As if he'd move away. Hell, he was afraid to breathe for fear this would turn out to be a dream. When their tongues touched, she let out a low, barely audible moan and tried to get even closer. One of her hands left his hair to slide inside the back of his shirt at the small of his back to hold him close as she slowly rocked against him, nearly driving him right out of his mind.

When he pulled back, her eyes slowly opened. "You don't want this?"

In spite of his brain being scrambled, he found a smile. "I'm pretty sure you know exactly how much I want this."

Holding him prisoner with those eyes, she slowly, purposefully, rocked her hips to his again, yanking a rough groan from deep in his throat. "Mean," he managed.

She laughed and pressed her forehead to his. "I want another kiss, Noah."

The way she said his name . . . "Take whatever you want." My body, my life . . .

She kissed him again, melting against him in a way that tore another groan from deep in his throat. One of his hands slid down the back of her jeans and beneath the silk, cupping a bare cheek, squeezing—

"Whatcha guys doing?" Joey asked.

Shit. Turning, pulling his hand from Olive's jeans, Noah came up with a smile. Well, it might've been more a grimace, but he couldn't help it, he didn't have any blood left in his brain. "Just making sure Olive's okay."

Olive nodded like a bobblehead. "Yep. And I am. I'm one hundred percent okay."

"What was wrong?" Joey asked.

"Um . . ." Olive blinked. "Cramp. A really bad cramp."

"On your bottom?"

Olive covered her horrified laugh by coughing.

In a stroke of great luck, Noah's cell phone buzzed in his pocket.

"Joe's awake!" Katie yelled in his ear. "He's watching me with a smile. He hasn't spoken, but the doctor says he's going to be okay. Get down here. And bring Mom and Joey!"

Some sisters cried when they were feeling too many emotions. His sister, the master of the monotone, spoke at a high decibel when she felt too much. But none of that mattered once the meaning of her words sank in. "Joe's awake?" he asked, afraid to believe.

"Yes!"

Noah disconnected and picked up Joey, hugging him close and spinning them around. "Your dad's awake!"

"*Finally*," Joey said. "That was the longest nap ever!"

Noah set him down. "Go get your backpack and put a few snacks and whatever toys you want in it. You can stay in your pj's. I'll be ready to go in a minute."

Joey whooped and raced out of the room.

Noah stood there for a few seconds, eyes closed, taking his first deep breath since the accident.

"Joe's awake?" Olive asked softly.

She was staring up at him with painful hope. Unable to form words, he nodded.

"Oh," she breathed, and stepped into him. "Oh, what a relief!"

Chest tight, he wrapped her up in his arms, an inch from losing it. But losing it would have to wait. "I'm going to take Joey and my mom to the hospital to see him."

"They might only let two of you in there with him at a time. I'll go with and help keep an eye on Joey."

Grateful, he nodded. "That was a close call."

She looked up. "For Joe? Well, yeah."

He gave a slow head shake. "For us."

"For us," she repeated, as if trying to get the words to compute. "You mean . . . because of Joey?"

"That too."

She paused. "You regret the kiss."

"I try very hard not to do things I regret."

Turning away, she stuck her feet into a pair of battered sneakers. "Nice nonanswer."

"I actually don't regret a thing when it comes to you."

She twisted to look at him. "What then?"

"We said the past is best left in the past."

The sound she made said he was an idiot, and for the record, he agreed.

She pulled her hair up and knotted it on top of her head, exposing her neck and collarbone. He was always so unprepared for his visceral reaction to her. Nowhere was safe to look, every part of her soft and tempting. And with the memory of their hot-as-hell kiss on his brain, he was having a hard time recalling why he'd tried so hard to resist her in the first place. All his hard-won self-control, every single drop, had taken leave. "Oli—"

She started out of the room. "This is Joe's moment, not yours, not mine. Let's just move on." And with that, she headed into the living room. He could hear her talking to Joey, sounding perfectly normal.

But nothing was normal. He was feeling things he didn't want to feel. And for the first time in his life, his hard-learned logic and reasoning seemed to escape him at every turn when it came to one sexy, sweet Olive Porter.

And he had no idea what to do about it.

CHAPTER 13

Olive wasn't sure why she'd butted in and insisted she go to the hospital, but the way Joey held her hand as they walked through the double glass doors made her glad she had.

Joey's other hand was in Noah's, and she glanced at his face. She'd seen him run the gamut of emotions in the past hour. Happy when he learned about Pretend Matt. Relief at hearing Joe had woken. Surprise, hunger, and desire after their kiss.

He hadn't been alone in that. The memory of his mouth on hers, the feeling of him standing between her thighs, his eyes dark and focused only on her.

And then his blank expression as he reminded her the past was best left in the past—which, no kidding.

When they arrived at the ICU wing, Katie came out of Joe's room, beaming as she crouched in front of Joey. "I'm going to take you in to see your daddy, but you can't stay long, okay?"

"Why?"

"Because he's still very tired."

"But he's been sleeping forever. How come he's still tired?"

Katie kissed his forehead. "It's complicated, baby."

"That's what grown-ups always say when they don't want to tell you stuff."

"How about we concentrate on what I *can* tell you, and that's that your daddy is awake right now and can't wait to get his eyeballs on you."

"'Kay. Oh, and Mommy, guess what? Olive and Noah kissed!"

Noah grimaced.

Amy probably gave herself whiplash with how quickly her head spun around to look at them.

Katie just grinned as she went brows up at Olive. "Eventful evening."

A nurse came out of Joe's room. "Only a few minutes," she said firmly but kindly. "He needs to rest."

Katie took Joey in first. Noah, Olive, and Amy stepped up to the doorway, watching Joe track his wife and son as they moved toward him. Katie pulled a chair close to the bed and sat with Joey in her lap. He immediately leaned over and kissed his daddy's cheek. "For your owie."

Olive's heart ached and she pressed a hand to it, watching Joe slowly reach out, his arm trembling with the effort as he took Joey's hand, his gaze turning back to Katie with an enviably easy love in his eyes, the three of them a tight little unit.

Amy sniffled, and Noah wrapped an arm around his mom's shoulders. He'd been standing there stoically, giving nothing away, but at the sound of his mom crying softly, he closed his eyes and let the relief and emotion show on his face. It was so real, so intimate and vulnerable, that Olive felt like an intruder.

A few minutes later, Katie waved them in, but Olive hung back.

Katie crooked a finger at her. "You too."

So in she went.

The corners of Joe's mouth turned up at his audience. "Yo."

"Yo," everyone echoed back.

There was a brief silence, probably because all of them, Olive included, were nearly choking on their relief and joy.

Joe looked at Noah. "You okay?"

Noah closed his eyes for a beat, then opened them. "I am now."

Joe gave him a crooked smile and attempted a fist bump, but couldn't hold out his hand. Noah wrapped his fingers around Joe's wrist and guided the fist to his.

Amy kissed Joe on the cheek. "Soon as you're upright, you and Katie need a getaway. I'll plan it for you. If you guys could go anywhere, where would you pick?"

Joe's eyes were on Katie. "If we're together, it doesn't matter."

"Oh, good answer," his wife said. "I was going to say out for donuts."

Everyone laughed and a good amount of the tension drained away as Joe's eyes tracked to Olive. "Hey, stranger."

"Daddy, Olive gotta cramp," Joey volunteered. "On her butt! That's why Uncle Noah's hand was there, to make her feel better. He also kissed her!"

Katie snorted. "Nothing gets by my kid."

"Olive told Uncle Noah she wanted another kiss," Joey said. "And then he told her to take whatever she wanted, and she kissed him. That's when Uncle Noah had his hand on Auntie Olive's bottom. What?" he asked when everyone stared at him. "That's where her cramp was, right, Uncle Noah?"

Everyone looked at Noah.

Except Olive, who craned her neck to look at the nurses' station right outside the door. Because seriously, where were the ICU nurses when you needed them? Surely this many people in a room was a violation, right? In fact, she'd just head out there and—

Katie snagged her hand. It took her a moment to speak because she was laughing so hard. "Want to tell me again there's nothing going on between you two?"

"There isn't," Noah said.

Insulting. But . . . "He's right," Olive said.

Joe was smiling. "Nice. It's even almost believable. You just didn't practice the fib enough. It's got to roll right off your tongue."

Noah raised a brow. "You've never fibbed to me."

"Not true." Joe looked at Olive. "I fib to him all the time."

"Hey," Noah said.

"Sorry, man." Joe smiled at Olive. "See?"

Noah rolled his head on his shoulders, like his neck was tense.

Joe just grinned and pointed first at Noah, then Olive. "I approve."

Olive smacked her forehead with the palm of her hand. This wasn't going well. "I'm not available."

"Right," Noah said. "She's not available."

"Is this because of her made-up boyfriend named Matt?" Katie asked.

Olive gaped at her. "You know?"

"Of course I know. I know everything. Why does no one ever believe that?" She looked at Olive. "You have a tell when you lie. You repeat a question instead of answering right away, so you have more time to think. You also squeak."

Everyone's head swiveled back to Olive, who glared at a laughing Noah. "You think this is funny?"

Amy smacked Noah upside the back of his head.

"Ow!"

"Then behave."

Noah ran a hand down his face. He started to say something, but stopped because Joe was cracking up, and it was the sweetest sound. Given the look of love on Katie's face, she agreed.

"Maybe you should make up a girlfriend," Katie told her brother. "That way you don't have to keep pretending it's your job that keeps you single, instead of the truth, which is that you think it keeps your life less chaotic. And also because you like your freedom. Which is dumb. Being with someone enhances your life, it doesn't take away from it." At the silence, she looked around and winced. "Uh-oh. Did I do it again?"

"Say too much?" Noah nodded. "Yep." He looked at his mom. "Why don't you ever smack her upside the head?"

"Oh!" Katie raised her hand. "I know this one. She loves me more than you."

Amy sighed. "Sometimes, I swear, I have no idea why I had children."

"I'm a children," Joey said. "Right?"

Noah scooped him up and slung him over his back, hanging him upside down, to Joey's squealing delight. "Trust me, kid," he said. "If I could guarantee a kid exactly like you, I'd have a bunch."

"Aw." Amy pressed her hands to her chest. "Really?"

"Yes," Noah said, while shaking his head in the negative then mouthing *no*.

So she smacked him upside the back of his head again.

CHAPTER 14

Olive turned off the two-lane highway onto a dirt road that she hoped was the right dirt road. The early-morning sun slanted through the windshield and directly into her eyes so she couldn't see the map app on her phone. Unsure, she pulled over and eyed the screen again. Good news: she'd remembered the exit to her parents' farm just fine. Bad news: she still wasn't ready for this.

She probably should've asked someone to come along with her instead of leaving the house at dawn on her own. But Gram was in charge at the senior center today. Katie would've come, no questions asked, but Olive refused to ask her to take a day away from Joe's side.

Noah would've dropped everything as well. She knew it. But she also knew he had to Zoom into a work meeting, and he too should be free to go to the hospital today.

So she'd left a note on the coffee maker—the one place she knew everyone would see it—and had gone alone.

When Olive was growing up, Gram always preached about believing in yourself. She'd told a young Olive many times that if she stated her intentions, and if she believed them, like *truly* believed, then those intentions would come true.

Olive had disproved that theory many times, but that was probably because she'd never quite believed that she deserved what it was she wanted.

She was working on that. Take two days ago, for instance. When she'd had the nightmare and been awoken by Noah, who'd so sweetly taken care of her, holding her against his very fine, very hard body. It'd taken her less than two seconds to wish for a kiss. And hell, maybe she'd finally lined up her intentions with truly believing, because she'd gotten what she'd wanted . . . at least for those few minutes.

She stopped at a crossroads and was pretty sure she needed to go right, but she stopped again to make sure, just as her phone buzzed with an incoming text.

KATIE: Seriously? You can run but you can't hide.

OLIVE: What am I hiding from?

KATIE: You know what. And I know that you know that I know.

OLIVE: Points for the *Friends* reference. Still have no idea what you're talking about.

KATIE: You and Noah. Go.

OLIVE: Again, there is no me and Noah.

KATIE: But if you marry him, we can be sisters for life.

OLIVE: I thought we were already sisters for life.

KATIE: Well, duh. But I want to go to your wedding. I want to babysit your babies. Our kids will be cousins. I mean, sure, my brother's super bossy and annoying and stubborn, and living with a man isn't always what it's cracked up to be. They use one soap product for everything. One! Can you imagine using the same soap on your booty that you use for your face? Gross. Also, they make a lot of weird noises, and then there's the issue of sharing a bathroom. Don't get me started on that.

OLIVE: Gee, you make it sound so great.

KATIE: Does it help to know I wouldn't trade it for anything?

OLIVE: Sorry, we've got a bad connection, you're breaking up, I gotta go.

KATIE: It's a ducking text!

KATIE: Dear autocorrect, it's NEVER ducking!

KATIE: Hello?

KATIE: Dammit.

Olive started driving again. She'd definitely be losing internet soon. In some areas of the wild Sierra mountains, things were just about as remote as one could get in the continental U.S. The road in and out of the farm had never had internet, and though there'd be some efforts to change that, she was pretty sure it hadn't happened yet.

So when Stephanie called, Olive was surprised she could get through. "What's up?"

"Just wanted to let you know I'm sending you a file with everything you wanted for the zoo campaign."

"Great, thanks. I'll look it over later today and get back to you with any changes."

"Trust me, you won't have any," Stephanie said. "So . . . you getting lucky yet?"

"Ha, and none of your business."

"That means no."

Olive sighed. "Gotta go." When her phone buzzed again two minutes later, she answered with "Still not getting lucky."

"That's not what I hear."

Olive grimaced at Gram's voice. "Hey."

"Don't 'hey' me. You kissed Noah and do you say anything to me about it? No."

Oh dear God. "How did you—"

"Because, Olive Summer Porter, I know everything. Now spill."

"It's not what you think. And I thought you had an event today."

"I do. But I'd have dropped everything like a hot potato to drive out to the farm with you rather than see you go alone."

"And I'd have loved that," Olive admitted. "But we both know this road is terribly bumpy and it would've hurt your back."

"Damn old age. Damn old bones. Damn stupid, annoying doctors."

Olive smiled. "Those 'damn stupid, annoying doctors' have finally gotten your pain under control and we're going to keep it that way."

Gram sighed. "Don't ever get old."

"I'll try real hard," Olive said wryly.

"And honey? You're doing the right thing. I know you won't sleep well until you find out your mom and dad are okay. You always were such a good girl. I love you."

"Love you too, Gram."

"Call me the minute you get there, just so I know."

"If there's service. I'm probably going to lose you any second now. I'll call you on my way back, soon as I'm able."

She'd barely disconnected when her cell rang again. "*Still* not getting any."

Dead silence.

She glanced at her screen and sucked in a breath. *Noah.*

"Olive."

And damn if her heart didn't skip a beat at the sound of his low, husky voice saying nothing but her name. *No,* she told herself. *Stop it. Don't remember the kiss. Remember what he'd made clear to everyone at the hospital.*

They weren't a thing.

The fact that it was true, and also that she'd implied it first, didn't matter. What *did* matter was how he seemed so absolutely one hundred percent certain.

"Olive? You there?"

She drew a deep breath. "Thanks for calling, but I can't come to the phone right now. Leave a message at the beep and I'll be sure to *not* get back to you. Beeeeeeep."

"The beep needs some work," he said dryly.

She sighed. "What do you want? I'm about to lose service."

"Why did you go alone?"

"Because."

He didn't say anything. Had she gotten lucky enough to have lost service already?

"I thought we agreed that someone should go with you," he said.

In case she found something bad, he meant. She sighed. "I have someone with me."

"Who?"

"You, on speaker." Then, sensing the conversation was about to deteriorate, she put a chipper smile into her voice. "Welp, this has been fun, but I gotta go—"

"Wait." He drew an audible breath. "I get it, what you're doing. I'd be doing the same thing."

She swallowed past the sudden lump in her throat. "Thank you," she said softly.

"And Olive? If someone I cared about was missing, I'd want you to be the one looking for them."

This was what she'd always gotten from him. Unconditional acceptance.

"You're going to be safe," he said.

"Safe is my middle name."

"I mean it, Olive. There's been a run of campsite thefts in the entire Tahoe area all season. People have reported two men in their twenties showing up with guns and taking whatever they want from terrified campers. Stay vigilant and be careful."

She drew a deep breath. "I will. And Noah?"

Nothing.

"Noah?" She stared at her phone. Great. *Now* the service punked out.

Luckily it took concentration on the gravel road or she'd probably have gotten more anxious the closer she got. Okay, who was she kidding? She was already at maximum anxious capacity.

After a few more moments, the gravel road turned to dirt. She'd been both anticipating and dreading this part. On the one hand, it meant she was only a few miles from the farm. On the other hand, the Mini wasn't meant for off-roading. She'd known it would come to this. She parked and began walking.

Two miles and a few wasp scares and filthy shoes later, she stopped at the gate to her parents' property—thirty acres of land that her dad had inherited a long time ago. Back then, it'd been overgrown, rocky, and completely undesirable. But as he'd told her when she'd been little, free was free. He wasn't big on hard work, but he'd always had a green thumb. So he and Olive's mom had gone with their strengths. They'd parked a trailer on the property, a home that had never really felt like one.

At least not to Olive.

Just looking at it, all her insecurities and fears of not knowing where she belonged came rushing back, knocking the wind out of her. At the same time, her heart began pounding because— her parents' truck wasn't in the makeshift driveway.

Just a sprinter van she'd never seen before.

Maybe they'd come into a windfall and traded in the old truck. She looked around, feeling unexpectedly, shockingly nostalgic. All her life, her parents had worked just enough to eke by, spending most of their time going from fair to fair, or festival to festival, loving their life.

It really wasn't their fault that Olive hadn't loved it as well.

The trailer looked dark and vacant, but the greenhouse her dad had so lovingly built had sounds coming from it, and she caught sight of a person moving around inside. A man. A tall one.

Her dad! Probably tending to his plant babies. She could even hear the distant thumping base of "I Will Survive" by Gloria Gaynor—his favorite song for the stevia section of his greenhouse. And if she strained, she could also hear Bach, which he played for the indica section. "I'm going to kill him," she told the gray clouds gathering overhead, having no idea why she'd spent so much energy worrying, or taken the day off to come up here, for that matter.

Heading straight for the greenhouse door, she yanked it open. Lush greenery filled every inch of the space, making it difficult to see from one end to the other. "*Dad?*"

A few plants rustled, and from the mix a man appeared, making her gasp and take a step back. Because nope, not her dad, but a stranger in a Metallica T-shirt.

"What the hell?" they said in unison.

"Who are you?" Olive demanded.

A small dog had run toward her, no discernible lineage, just a super cute scruffy brown mutt with sweet brown eyes, wearing a matching Metallica T-shirt, his entire body vibrating with happiness.

"Well, the little fellow there is Buddy," the man said. He also had scruffy brown hair and brown eyes. And though he looked friendly enough for a giant of a man, he wasn't broadcasting his thoughts.

"And you are?" she asked, staying at the door.

"Oh, I'm Buddy too. See, same T-shirts, same name, get it?"

She squatted down and slowly reached out to Buddy.

The dog plopped to the floor and rolled over to expose his belly.

Obliging, Olive gave him a rubdown. "I can't help but notice that Buddy isn't a boy, but a girl."

The human Buddy shrugged. "I'd never assume someone's gender. Buddy likes 'they/them' pronouns."

Olive nodded. Then shook her head. "What are you doing here?"

"We live here. I rent the driveway," Buddy said. "I work the greenhouses with the owner of the property."

"That's my dad. He and my mom aren't here?"

Buddy scratched his head. "No."

"Do you know where they are?"

Buddy gave another shrug. At this point, Olive was going to start a drinking game, a shot for her every time he lifted his bony shoulders up and down. "You have no idea where they went?"

Buddy looked around, like maybe they were in the greenhouse and he hadn't noticed. "They were on a walkabout. That's what they said the last time they called to check in on the plants."

"They call you to check in?" Olive asked. "When was the last time you heard from them?"

"Um, it's been"—he scratched his head again—"maybe a week? Or two? They did say they'd be calling again soonish to check in and make sure everything was going okay with the next, erm, harvest, but that it might be tricky, what with spotty internet and possibly running out of data."

Yep, that was her parents. "So you think they're okay?"

Buddy laughed. "I'm sure of it. The jar of ayahuasca tea is gone."

Great. Terrific. "And you have no idea where this walkabout was taking place?"

"They went somewhere new with another couple. It involved a spiritual awakening and reconnecting with their inner child."

Their inner child? They'd never *disconnected* with their inner child! She drew a deep breath. "And you don't know where they started this trek?"

"Walkabout, and no. I just take care of the plants, that's it."

Olive was pretty sure there was no new info to be had from Buddy, but she wasn't ready to give up. "This couple they went with. Have you ever seen them before?"

"Nope. They met on Craigslist. They were all going to share a yurt rental somewhere." He scratched his head again. "Maybe near Mount Eagle? Not sure."

She let out a controlled exhale. It didn't help. "Thank you. I'm going to check out the trailer."

Buddy gave her a go-for-it sweeping gesture.

She walked through the wild grass to her childhood home. She didn't have a key, but was pretty sure she wouldn't need one. And true enough, it was unlocked. Open for anyone who came by and needed the space.

With a sigh, she stepped inside. The trailer was probably from the eighties. Maybe even the seventies, but while old and faded, it was spotless.

That was her mom's doing. Her mom loved clean. Her dad not so much. When Olive had still lived here, her bed had been the pulldown couch along the wall opposite the pull-down dinette table. The couch's cushions were the same, as were the crochet pillows and blanket folded at one end.

She sat there, leaned her head back, and hugged the pillow she'd watched her mom make when Olive had been, what, maybe five? "Where are you guys?" she whispered. "Are you okay?"

But if the trailer knew, it kept their secrets.

Buddy stuck his head in the door she'd left open. "You okay, miss?"

"Olive." And nope, she wasn't okay. "If I leave you my number, can you call me when you hear from them again?"

"Sure."

She nodded, wishing she could convince herself that none of this was necessary, that her parents were okay, but she couldn't.

CHAPTER 15

Twelve years ago

One week into Fake-Dating Noah, Olive jumped when some-one pounded on Gram's back door.

It was Katie, looking unusually ruffled. "What's wrong?" Olive asked. "Are you okay—"

Katie pushed past her, into the kitchen, and went straight for the ice cream in the freezer. "We're going out on a date."

Olive grabbed two spoons and they sat at the table to eat right out of the gallon container. "Who? You and me? I've got homework—"

"Joe finally agreed to go out with me."

Olive stared at her in surprise. "But he said because he was your brother's best friend, you two could never, ever, ever go out."

"Yes, but I sort of forced—" She stopped to grimace. "Okay, blackmailed, Noah into telling Joe it was okay with him. So now we're going out. And you and Noah have to come with."

Olive's mouth dropped open. "But . . . but—"

"Listen, I've never been on a real date. I need you guys there so I can copy whatever you do. Joe said it was up to me where we go, and since we're all poor, I've got this idea, and you have to back me up."

"I'm not going skinny-dipping just because you've been dying to see Joe naked since middle school."

"Fine, whatever, no skinny-dipping. What we're going to do is go to that thrift store near the hospital—"

"Wow, you really don't know how the whole dating thing works—"

"And," Katie said, starting to sound annoyed, "we're going to walk the aisles until one of us says 'stop,' and whatever piece of clothing we're the closest to, we have to buy and wear to the diner for burgers and fries."

Olive laughed, but Katie just stared at her. "Oh, wait, you're actually not kidding."

"Your latest Cosmo mag swears it'll be a good time," Katie said stiffly.

"Well, then, what could possibly go wrong."

Katie, missing the sarcasm, smiled. "Right?"

Present day

Hell. Noah was in hell. Mentally, that is. Physically, he was at the family shop, working to help out his mom. So same same, really. "I hear you," he said into the phone for the twentieth time.

"Do you, boy?" Mrs. Garrison asked. "Do you hear me? Because I need my tractor back before the next storm so I'll be able to move snow."

It'd been a long time since someone called him boy. The woman was somewhere between seventy and two hundred years old, and mean as a snake. He should know. He and Joe, who, granted, had been a pair of troublemakers, had once climbed the water tower adjacent to her property to drink a six-pack they'd pilfered from Joe's dad. Mrs. Garrison had come out with her husband's shotgun and threatened to "put a cap in their ass" if they didn't go home.

She'd never forgiven them.

"I understand, but your tractor needs a part that hasn't come in yet." He was staring at the tractor in question, doing his best to imitate his mom's soothing the-customer-is-always-right tone. "As you were told when you brought the tractor in, the part we need is still weeks out."

"In my day, you'd improvise. Make your own part."

He put a finger to his eye, which was twitching again. But before he could formulate a response, she disconnected.

Katie was standing in front of him. She held out the iPad they used for inventory management. "I just updated this thing, so why isn't it working?"

He didn't take the tablet because his hands were filthy. "Cuz you're doing it wrong? I don't know."

"Wow," his mom said, coming up to them. "That's the most brotherly thing I ever heard you say. Why are you such a grumpy bear this morning?"

He ignored them both and thankfully, they left him alone. This was really shaping up to be a shit day. First, Olive had gone off to the farm on her own, and though he'd tried to reach her again once or twice or a thousand times, she'd remained out of range, and he was worried.

Second, he was here. He looked around the shop that his dad had occupied for as far back as Noah could remember. This place hadn't been his dad's dream, at least not at first. Nope, that honor had gone to baseball. Unfortunately, the man had never made the cut. So he'd come home to take over *his* dad's shop, doing his best to compartmentalize the disappointment.

Right now, Noah had never understood his dad more.

After his dad's death, his mom had run the shop herself. But she'd gotten restless and had wanted to be free to travel with her friends and enjoy life. She'd hired a few people and had given their longtime mechanic a raise to manage the shop when she wasn't around. Joe kept the books for her. He also backed up the mechanic whenever needed, which was how Noah had learned his best friend loved wrenching more than his day job.

Unfortunately, their mechanic was on a long overdue vacation, and with Joe still in the hospital, Noah was up at bat. And now, on top of wrenching, he also had a mountain of bookkeeping to get through. Noah hated paperwork with the power of ten thousand suns, but he couldn't leave his mom to handle it all. So he got to work on repairing a damn tractor without the right parts.

An hour later, he was standing on the tractor's front bumper, bent over the engine, a wrench in one hand, his hammer in the other, just in case he decided to bash his own head in. When he heard footsteps, he ignored them, thinking it was his mom checking on him.

"I know I'm probably the last person you wanted to see today."

Olive. Jerking upright, he smacked the top of his head on the hood of the tractor's engine compartment, lost his balance, and fell off the bumper to his ass.

"Oh my God!" Olive rushed to his side. "Are you okay?"

"Only if I'm dead." Holding the top of his head, he looked up past a pair of beat-up red sneaks, jean-covered legs longer than the legal limit, a snug red sweater, and the pretty face of the woman who'd haunted his dreams too many nights to admit out loud.

She dropped to her knees, pushing his hand from the top of his head so she could get a look. This left him eye level with her torso. The V-neck of her sweater gaped out a little, revealing today's lingerie choice. Not black silk, but the heart-stopping lacy pink revved his own engine just the same. That was when he realized her clothes were dirty and a little stiff, like they'd air-dried after being wet. And her hair had frizzed and gotten . . . big. She was a mess. A hot mess. And he loved it because it was a glimmer of the girl she'd once been. A girl he'd missed with his whole heart. "Did you go through a car wash without a car?"

She rolled her eyes. "No."

"What happened?"

She tossed up her hands. "Life."

Well, she sure as hell wore life well, because even in her current state, he wanted to eat her up. "Did you find your parents?"

"No."

Using one-word answers was his thing, not hers, and he frowned. "Do you want to talk about it?"

"You're bleeding." She rose up, pulling him with her. Apparently, she remembered her way around because she led him inside the shop to the staff room, nudging him into one of the chairs at the small table. "First aid kit?"

"I don't need one."

"Uh-huh." She kept looking through cabinets, muttering under her breath about stubborn-ass men who don't know enough to take care of themselves. "Aha!" She pulled the first aid box from beneath the sink and washed her hands.

"Really, I'm fine."

"Debatable, but you could be right given that your head is as hard as a rock."

"Ha-ha—" He broke off with a hiss when she dabbed at the top of his head with gauze that came away red. When she put antiseptic on the cut, he sucked in a breath, but that might be because she was standing between his legs, leaning over him, concentrating on what she was doing. He was concentrating too, on not looking down her sweater again.

"How you doing, you okay?" she asked.

"That's a broad question."

She tilted her head to meet his gaze, then shifted hers southbound to where his hands had taken hold of her hips, bringing her close. He dropped them like she was a hot potato.

"I don't think you need stitches," she said.

"I definitely don't. Tell me what happened at the farm."

She hesitated.

"What?"

"Are we still friends?"

Her tentative tone made him ache. Or maybe it was the question itself. "Olive—"

Her phone rang and she looked at the screen. "I'm sorry, it's the zoo's assistant director, I have to take this."

"I get it. Work comes first."

Her expression said she'd like to disagree, but she stepped away and answered.

Noah turned to the fridge to see what he could scrounge up, going still when he realized Olive was talking about . . . cockroaches? Turning back, he caught her staring at his ass. He raised a brow.

She bit her lower lip and blushed a little, but didn't break eye

contact as she kept talking, something about zoo patrons nam-
ing their sponsored cockroaches after an ex, then getting a video
of it being fed to one of the zoo's amphibians or small mammals
such as mice and shrews.

He grinned at the ingenuity of it. Damn, she was amazing,
and as he listened to her laugh over something, he thought, *And
so was her laugh.*

When she disconnected and turned to him, he didn't even try
to hide his amusement. "You're going to make the zoo famous."

"A girl can hope."

"Are you going to tell me what happened to you at the farm?"

She looked down at herself, then turned to the sink to wash
her hands again like her life depended on it. "The Mini couldn't
take me all the way in—I knew that. I walked the last two miles
and got caught by rain on the way back out."

He thought of her alone on that deserted road, with no cell
service, and ground his back teeth. "You should have let one of
us go with you. And by us, I mean me."

"I didn't want to take you away from anything."

She still, even now, didn't know how important she was to
them. Him. He could tell her, but she wasn't going to hear him.
She didn't trust words, she only trusted actions. He'd always
known that, and he'd done his best to make sure to show her,
but they'd been so young.

And dumb. "Are you okay?"

She let out a breath. "That's . . . a broad question."

He felt his lips twitch. "Do your best."

She then told him about Buddy, both of them, and finally
said, "I don't know what to do next. What if something's
happened and the last time I talked to them, we parted on an
argument?"

If there'd been one thing she could say to make him understand, it was that. He moved to her, taking her hand in his. "What did you fight about?"

"I was angry because they'd let their medical insurance lapse and haven't seen a doctor in years. It was like fighting with a brick wall." She sighed. "You know what I mean."

He gave a mirthless smile. "The brick wall? Oh yeah. My family always means well, but they've never understood some of the decisions I've made or how I choose to live my life." He cupped her jaw, letting his thumb gently stroke her cheek. "What did Buddy know about their whereabouts?"

"He said they were with some couple they met on Craigslist. *Craigslist.*" She tossed up her hands. "The last time a friend of mine met someone on Craigslist, the guy showed up with handcuffs!"

"Just so you know," he teased, "I've got a work-issued pair. In case you're interested."

"I'm being serious!" But she blushed and bit her lower lip.

Oh, she was interested . . . He took her hands again and squeezed them. "Do you have a plan?"

"No! I've never even seen a pair of handcuffs in person!"

He laughed again. "About your parents."

"Oh my God." She covered her face and took a deep breath. "You turn me inside out." She dropped her hands. "No, I don't have a plan. Well, not exactly, but you have to promise to listen before you throw it back in my face—"

"I always listen. And I'd never throw anything back in your face."

"Oh really?" she asked. "Because the first conversation we had in *years*, you brought up my Dear John letter. And the last conversation we had, you told everyone there was nothing going on between us—approximately thirty minutes after you kissed me stupid."

She was right. And he was still an ass. "I panicked."

"Right," she scoffed. "You never panic. You've got nerves of steel."

"Not when it comes to you. Never when it comes to you."

She stared at him, then shook her head. "Look, let's just keep this about my parents, okay? My only plan is to give Buddy a few days and see if he hears from them, and if not, then I start looking at yurt rentals."

"Why wait?"

"Because I'm hoping Buddy comes through. Do you have any idea how many yurt rentals there are near Mount Eagle? Hundreds. I googled it." She blew out a breath. "If this was your mom and it'd been two weeks, what would you do?"

"My mom's allergic to irresponsible to the point of obsession." And though his mom drove him crazy, he hated how Olive's parents had always left her feeling unimportant to them. What kind of a parent chose their lifestyle over the happiness of their only child?

Not that he was much better. At least according to his ex. He'd always assumed he could have the job and a family, but Molly had proven otherwise.

While he was thinking too hard, Olive turned to go. "All right, well, I'll get out of your hair."

"Wait."

She turned back, her expression telling him she was braced for rejection, but the chin tilt told him she'd go it alone if she had to. Because she was used to that. Which he also hated. "I've got access to better search programs than you do. Let me do some digging. Let me see if I can narrow the field."

There was a beat of surprise in her eyes, then a gratitude he didn't deserve. "Don't spend the time yet," she said. "I'm willing to give it a few more days. But thank you." Her eyes went suspiciously shiny. "Really." Again, she turned to go, quickly this time, but just as quickly, he wrapped his arms around her from behind, loose enough that she could push him away if she wanted. Instead, she turned to face him, fisted her hands in his shirt, and pressed her face to his chest.

They stood like that for a long few moments, neither moving while she struggled for composure. Giving her the time to do whatever she needed to do, he stared over her head trying to take his mind off how good she felt in his arms, because, hell, she was hurting, and even he wasn't a big enough asshole to take advantage of that.

Then her hands were on the move, slowing sliding up his back. Up and down again, then her fingers jaywalked to his front, settling on his abs before she hesitated as if trying to decide if she wanted to go up or down next.

His body knew exactly which way he wanted her to go, but his brain knew better and he caught her hands in his.

Slowly, she lifted her face, her eyes no longer sad. Instead, they seemed lit with a new confidence, as if she knew exactly how much he wanted her. Hard for a man to hide it. A heat joined the confidence in her gaze, one that caused an answering fire low in his belly, quickly spreading outward. "What are you up to?"

She gave him a small, heated smile. "No good. I'm definitely up to no good."

He touched his forehead to hers. "Killing me."

"Tell me you don't want me, Noah."

He could have, but it would be a lie, and he'd never lied to her before. So instead he kissed her, a long, warm, intimate kiss that stole the breath from his lungs and every single thought from his brain, including the one that told him this was still a really bad idea.

"Does Oli have another cramp?"

Olive gasped as they turned to find Joey, cradling sweet little Pepper, faithful Holmes at his side. And behind the menagerie stood Katie, brows up.

"Are you guys married?" Joey asked.

Katie choked on a laugh and tried to cover it with a cough.

Olive shook her head. "Um—"

Katie pointed at her. "You need to be very careful right now, because I just picked up Joey from school, and on the drive over here, he told me all about how he's learning to *not* tell tall tales."

"I think what Olive was going to say," Noah said, "is that it's not what you think—"

"No?" Katie asked, letting a smile escape. "So you didn't just have your fingers threaded lovingly through Olive's hair?" She covered Joey's ears and turned to Olive. "And you. Your hands seemed to be sliding to the south pole."

Noah grimaced.

"It was an accident," Olive said.

Katie outright laughed. "You guys keep telling yourselves that."

Joey, bored with the adults, was nose to the window. "It's raining!"

"So, obviously, it's time to go jumping in puddles," Olive said.

"Yes!" Joey yelled.

Katie gave Olive and Noah a long look. "I'll be outside with Joey while you two figure out why your mouths keep colliding."

When they were gone, Olive turned to Noah, horrified.

Yeah, he got it. Because while he'd been operating under the notion they were a bad idea, kissing her brought him back to the time before their accident, before he'd lost his scholarship, before his dad had died . . . and it gave him a glimmer of an emotion that he hadn't felt since she'd walked away.

Hope.

He had no idea what to do with that.

At his silence, Olive stepped back from him. "Okay, well, I've got some puddles to jump in."

She went outside and he had to force himself not to follow.

A few minutes later, Katie came back in and gave Noah another long look. "What are you doing with my best friend? And let me be clear, you let me have *your* best friend, so I want you to have mine. Tell me you're going to keep her."

"It's complicated."

"Oh my God." She glared at him. "Are you seriously going to screw up the best thing to ever happen to you because . . . what? Because you're an island? A fortress of solitude? That's the dumbest thing I've ever heard. 'It's complicated.' Get over yourself. For once, let yourself be vulnerable and you might actually make yourself happy while you're at it."

"You about done?" he asked dryly.

"Not even close. Remember that time you saved that cat from the well and you stayed up all night with it, keeping her warm and fed? And then, in the morning, she bit you and ran off and vanished, and you decided that was it, no more pets for you?"

"Do you have a point?"

"Just that now you're also turning your back on humans, and I'm worried about you."

"I'm fine."

She sighed. "You're not ready to talk about it. I guess I can understand that since you're not used to allowing your emotions any leg room." She pointed at him. "Just don't be stubborn for too long. Wouldn't want you to finally wake up and look around, and realize you're all alone."

"Like you're ever going to leave me alone in peace."

She snorted, but it didn't sound like she had her heart in it. "Just don't chase away something that could be really good for you," she said softly, and after dropping that emotional bomb, headed out of the room.

He wasn't stupid. He had no doubt that Olive was good for him. In some ways, she had a few of her parents' best qualities. When she felt safe, she was everything he loved in a partner: passionate, fun-loving, and adventurous.

Or at least, she had been.

When she'd first come back into town, she'd clearly buttoned most of that up, burying the old Olive deep. But here and there, little glimmers of the girl she'd been kept appearing in unguarded moments.

And God, he'd loved that girl. He'd needed her too. She'd balanced him out, helped to banish the serious teen he'd been molded into. He'd needed her spontaneity, her playfulness, the unique way she viewed life. Being with her had been the only time he felt free to let go.

Now, once again, he found himself being drawn in, felt his heart engaging. But they weren't teens anymore, they'd grown up and moved on. Their time had passed. He'd found a freedom away from the daily demands of family, and he loved where he was. He couldn't go back, not even for Olive.

Now all he had to do was keep remembering that.

CHAPTER 16

I wanna go see my daddy!"

It was nearing Joey's bedtime, two days after they'd all been at the shop together, and Olive was on Joey duty while Katie spent time with Joe at the hospital.

Currently, Joey lay dramatically on the floor of the living room with Holmes snuggled up to his side and Pepper sitting on top of Holmes, guarding her men.

Olive crouched in front of the gang. "We've got twenty minutes until bedtime," she said to the only human in the mix. "I'm sorry that we can't go see him tonight, but first thing tomorrow, okay? Can you pick something else? A snack? A game?" She gestured to Pepper. "A kitten?"

"Disneyland!"

"I wish," she said on a laugh. "Hey, did you know I'm a fort-building master?"

He perked up a little bit. "You are?"

"Yep. My grandma and I used to have cookies and milk in our forts, and share secrets."

"I've got a secret," Joey said. "Summer Adams kissed me on the playground."

She blinked. *Kids kissed in pre-K?*

"She says I'm her boyfriend. And you kissed Uncle Noah, so that means you're his girlfriend."

"Uh . . . ," Olive said, starting to sweat as she looked around for an adultier adult, but nope, it was just her. "Let's find some blankets for the fort."

"Don't we have to ask Mommy first?"

Hmm. Probably better to ask for forgiveness than permission. "She's busy right now, so let's not bother her." She smiled and he smiled back with Joe's mischievous smile. No wonder he was already dazzling girls.

She found blankets in the linen closet, and they dragged a few of the kitchen chairs into the living room in front of the couch and got started.

Her first two attempts were miserable failures. The blankets were too heavy and kept slipping. They switched to spare sheets, which worked, but let too much light inside for Joey, who wanted to use a battery-operated lantern for a hand-puppet shadow show.

"I've got an idea." Olive went to the laundry area for the step-ladder, which she set up next to the stairs. Her plan: use some of her hair ties around the railing to rig another sheet above the fort, like a canopy, to make it darker inside.

She was on the second rung of the stepladder trying to make it all work when two arms reached around her, taking hold of the sheet and hair tie. She'd know those arms anywhere. They haunted her in her damn sleep. "I've got it," she said.

Proving she didn't, it all began to slip.

Noah caught the sheet. Still on the stepladder, she turned to face him, which put her nose to nose with him. "I had it."

"Building a fort is a team effort."

"Well, then, why don't you and your team go work on the north side," she said. "I'll build the south side." This was sheer bravado on her part, as she had no idea which way was north or south. And there'd been that pesky little white lie about her fort-building skills.

It'd been Gram with all the skills. Whenever Olive had visited her as a kid, Gram would pull out all her sheets and blankets, then drape them over chairs in a strategic way that made Olive feel like she had her own house. She'd tuck Olive inside with a flashlight and then slide in warm homemade cookies and milk.

Noah was admiring the fort so far. "Nice touch with the hair ties. Resourceful."

"Was that a compliment?"

"Yes, and here's another." Leaning in, mouth to her ear, he murmured, "You smell good."

A shiver of arousal went through her, and since that was annoying, she elbowed him to back up.

With a low laugh, he did.

And . . . the sheet held.

"Yes!" Joey said, pumping his fist in the exact same way Noah had done at his T-ball game whenever something good happened on the field.

It made Olive smile. "I'll be back with goodies." Retreating to the kitchen, she stood at the sink, staring out the window as she sucked in a deep breath, trying to regroup.

"What are you doing?" she asked when Noah appeared at her side.

"Breathing?"

She sighed. "I meant with the standing so close thing, the whispering in my ear, the touching . . ." She turned her head and looked at him. "You're confusing me."

"Yeah." He gave her a half smile. "I'm sorry. I'm confusing me as well."

She snorted. "Maybe it's because our mouths seem to think they're magnets?"

He choked out a laugh, then shook his head. "I can't seem to stop myself from getting too close to the fire."

She was the fire, of course, which wasn't exactly a compliment. "Sure you can. Just take a big, giant step back. You know you want to."

His gaze held hers. "Turns out that's not what I want at all." He paused. "The thing is, the way my life is, what I want isn't supposed to matter."

She felt how much he believed those words, but she shook her head. "Well, it *should* matter. What you do isn't who you are, you know that, right? And don't you ever get lonely?"

"Yes." He ran a finger along her jaw. "Are you lonely too, Oli?"

"Sometimes." She hesitated. "More than I'd like to be."

"So why London?"

She opened her mouth, then closed it, stymied on what to say. "I've been there a long time."

"I know. What I don't know is why."

What did he want to hear? That she'd needed to put distance between herself and her biggest mistake—that mistake being how she'd single-handedly messed everything up for the family she'd loved as her own? "London is where I got my first job offer after college."

He nodded. "But then, when you left that job to start your own business, you stayed. Was it really something you wanted, to be so far, or were you running away from something?"

She scoffed and turned back to the window, even as her stomach hit her toes. "That's ridiculous. What would I be running from?"

Although his mouth curved into a smile, his eyes were serious. "You tell me." With terrifying gentleness, he settled his hands on her arms and pulled her around to face him. "Were you running away from me?"

She closed her eyes and found herself mad. "You don't get to ask me that, not when you left Sunrise Cove too."

"I did." He let his hands fall from her. "But I didn't run away and never look back."

"Whatever lets you sleep at night." Suddenly chilled, she hugged herself. "I need to get back to Joey—"

"He's fine. Listen."

She cocked her head then smiled in spite of herself and peeked into the living room to find him on his belly inside the fort, Holmes at his side, Pepper on top of the dog as usual, both listening raptly as Joey read them *Goodnight Moon*, which he'd memorized.

Olive's heart turned over inside her chest, but she ruthlessly ignored it when she met Noah's gaze. "For what it's worth, I'm leaving as soon as Katie feels she doesn't need me anymore. Going back to my life, that is—not running away."

"You think you can walk away from all of us, again?"

"I don't know, Noah. Can you?"

The intensity left his gaze, replaced by a grim amusement. "I guess we'll see."

CHAPTER 17

The next morning, Olive was awoken by an odd, heavy pressure across her legs and was unable to move. Her eyes flew open to find Holmes lying across her, sleeping. On top of the dog sat Pepper, not sleeping. Her sharp eyes were narrowed on Olive. Clearly, the kitten was in bodyguard mode, and it wasn't Olive she was guarding.

"I love him too, you know," Olive said.

Pepper didn't look impressed.

"I'm going to need my legs back."

Pepper licked Holmes's forehead.

Holmes opened his eyes and yawned.

Pepper licked him again and leaped gracefully to the floor, then trotted to the door, where she turned back and gave Holmes an expectant look.

Holmes jumped down with a fraction of the kitten's lithe ability.

"Mew." Pepper looked expectedly at Olive.

Right. She wanted the door open. "I live to serve," Olive said dryly and cracked the door to let the fur babies out, not sure who'd let them in.

She then checked her phone for a message from Buddy or her parents. Still nothing, which meant it was time to take the next step and start looking into yurt rentals. But first, caffeine. She staggered downstairs and found Katie cooking . . . "Blueberry pancakes?"

"Want some?"

"More than my next breath." Olive sat at the island to watch, impressed. "Your cooking skills used to be ordering takeout."

"Things change when you have a kid. Had to learn to eat better."

Olive laughed. "You sound like your brother."

"Bite your tongue." But she smiled. "And who do you think taught me to cook?"

Olive felt her brows raise. "Not your mom?"

"No, we lean more toward murdering each other if we spend too much time in the same ten square feet." Katie expertly flipped the pancakes.

Olive watched, fascinated, even as she realized with new awareness that Katie really wouldn't need her around much longer. It should've thrilled her, knowing she could go home. But . . . well, being needed had been nice.

"What are you thinking about?" Katie asked.

"Once Joe comes home, and I hear from my parents, I guess it'll be time for me to go."

Katie looked up from the pancakes. "Is that what you want?"

"What I want has nothing to do with it. My life's in London."

Katie was quiet as she scooped pancakes out of the pan and poured more batter into it. Then she turned to Olive again.

"Your life's wherever you make it. Are you ever going to tell me why you think you can't make that life here? I know you're holding on to something, but for the life of me, I can't figure out what. If you're over me, over us, just say so."

"*No!* Oh my God, no." Olive's heart twisted that Katie could actually think that. "There are things you don't understand."

"Then help me."

"I would. If I fully understood them myself."

"If it's about something that happened when we were teens, then that's just dumb," Katie said. "It was a long time ago."

"It's not." Well, not exactly. She told herself it was about the simple fact that she'd needed to leave to grow up. And she had grown up. She was incredibly proud of that, of the life she'd built, and more than a small part of her worried that being back here would turn her into that overly anxious, overly stressed, constantly worried if she belonged girl.

Katie studied her. "Does it have something to do with my brother? Because that would also be dumb. Or maybe not, given that you're both two stone walls when you want to be."

"It's about me."

"And your ridiculous need for independence to the point of alienating those who love you?"

Olive had to laugh at how true that statement was. "Well, when you put it like that—" Her phone buzzed. Stephanie. "Work's calling," she said. "We're trying to get the zoo event nailed down."

Katie waved a spatula. "You can run, but you can't hide."

Sure Olive could. She'd been hiding for most of her life, right in plain sight. She was rather good at it, if she did say so herself.

OLIVE GOT A shocking amount done over the next eight hours, migrating from her bedroom to the kitchen to the back patio as needed while everyone came and went throughout the day.

The zoo fundraiser was shaping up to be . . . well, amazing. She had a pet shop donating the cockroaches in exchange for a sign at the entrance of the zoo and placement in all the ads. A Tahoe eatery discounted their catering bill for the same deal. A local bar was providing mocktails named for zoo animals, such as the Bees Knees, Lion's Tail, Flying Goose, and White Dragon. These sponsors, and all the others, would be listed on the swag bags, as well as on the giveaway T-shirts.

When Olive's stomach growled, she shut her laptop and realized from the patio chair that daylight had faded and she sat in the dark. Someone had turned on the lights for her, pretty strings of fairy bulbs that crisscrossed overhead, casting the evening in a beautiful glow.

Gathering her things, she stood up and walked into the kitchen, then stopped short. Seated around the table were Katie, Amy, Gram, and Noah. They all had a laptop open to what looked like lists. But even more confusing, each was also talking quietly on their cell phone.

Noah disconnected his call first.

"What's going on?" she asked.

Gram ended her call as well. "Noah used one of his work programs to cull a list of yurt rentals within a hundred miles of the Mount Eagle area."

Olive stared at Noah.

"What? You asked for help." He shrugged. "So we're all helping."

"Also, the shock in your eyes is insulting," Katie said.

Olive let a laugh escape past the lump in her throat. "I just . . ." It'd been clear that no one else had been all that worried about her parents, but because she was, they'd stepped up. "I'm just so grateful. Thank you."

"Don't be grateful yet," Noah said. "There are still a lot of calls to make." He pointed to the different lists. "These are privately owned yurts. And these are yurts attached to resorts. Then there are yurts on federal property and yurts owned by companies known for metaphysical retreats. We're starting there." He looked up at her. "Unless your gut tells you differently. You know your parents better than any of us."

Olive's gaze slid to Amy, wondering if Amy might pipe up with the information that she too knew Olive's mom. Possibly even knew her better than Olive herself did. But Amy didn't meet her gaze.

Noah used a foot to nudge a chair out for Olive. When she sat, their thighs brushed. Sucking in a breath, she pretended that Noah's screen was the most interesting thing on the planet. Much more interesting than how the soft denim of his jeans felt against her leg, or the fact that he looked sexy as hell with at least two days' worth of stubble on his jaw. Plus, he smelled delicious. It felt like too much goodness, kind of like looking directly into the sun. "They wouldn't be interested in any yurts attached to a resort. They also have a thing against The Man, so I doubt they're on federal land."

"Good point," Gram said.

Noah nodded. "That leaves the yurts on privately owned properties, and the metaphysical retreats."

"The private ones would have to be something woo-woo or ridiculously hippy in the description," Olive said.

"Remember that time they went to live at a llama rescue and

stayed in a yurt?" Gram asked. "I think that was a nudist retreat as well. They do love those."

Olive grimaced. "Maybe we should add nudist colonies to the list."

"Can you think of anything else?" Noah asked. "It'd be great to narrow this down even more."

Olive thought about it. "My mom's becoming known for her natural soap, lotions, and candles. Which means she might be drawn to areas where she could sell at a nearby craft fair. She's also one of the western states' leading photographers on rock stacking, sometimes called cairns. She's taken pictures somewhere known for that. Oh, and we know my dad also sells his weed, along with the products he makes from it, so he might be visiting dispensaries or dealers."

Everyone stared at her.

She ignored that. "Oh, and my mom's been kicked out of state parks for stacking rocks so many times that she's actually on a national database. Stacking rocks is frowned upon on state and federal lands because it can be considered culturally offensive, as well as disrupt wildlife habitats, but that would only be a draw for her."

"Is it possible they've been arrested?" Gram asked. "Maybe they're incarcerated somewhere."

"I mean, it's happened," Olive said. "Twice— No, wait, three times. But they've always called me to bail them out, so I'd probably know that by now."

A stunned silence, during which Katie reached out and squeezed Olive's hand in a rare show of physical affection.

"Aw. Are we going steady?" Olive asked.

"It's just me reminding you that not a single one of us has ever called you for money. We love you, Olive."

"Wow." She smiled instead of crying because she didn't want to be pathetic. "You must really feel sorry for me if you're throwing around the L-word."

"Can you think of anything else?" Noah asked, fingers moving on his keyboard, Mr. Stay Focused on the Task at Hand No Matter What. "I'm checking right now to see if they've been arrested. But is there anything else to narrow down the search beyond soaps and rocks?"

"And the weed," Olive reminded him.

Noah shook his head. "Let's just hope you're right and they're not on federal land doing anything with drugs."

"Doubtful," Gram said. "As Olive said, my daughter-in-law isn't a fan of the government in general. In fact, I think she tried to stop paying taxes, but thankfully even my son knows better than to not pay his taxes."

"Seriously," Katie said to Olive. "How are you so normal?"

"Because of you guys." The words popped out before she ran them past her brain, but it was true.

Amy's eyes filled. "That's so sweet."

Noah handed his mom a napkin and looked at Olive. Something in his expression had warmed, which she decided to ignore. Any more warm fuzzies and she'd need a tissue as well.

Noah used the revised criteria to create new lists, and they began making calls again, this time with Olive helping as well. She made her first call while listening to Noah next to her say into his phone with a deep, authoritative voice, "This is Special Agent Noah Turner from the Investigative Services Branch of the NPS. I'm calling about two missing persons . . ."

Before she could hear more, or figure out why that bossy tone of his was really doing it for her, her call was connected. And so began a very long hour, until she heard something change in Noah's voice as she disconnected with another dead end.

"When?" he asked. At whatever answer he got, he put his phone on speaker and snapped his fingers for everyone to move close.

Which they all did without question. Olive decided she wanted to learn how to do that, command a room with a single snap.

"I've got their daughter here with me right now," Noah said.

"Hello," the woman on his phone said. "As I mentioned, we don't know a lot about them. They paid in cash. Our office is in South Shore. Three hours from the yurt, so I'm not able to check if they're there right now."

"How long did they rent the yurt for?" Noah asked.

"They have another two days."

Olive's mind went blank. She could hear Noah still talking, asking a few more questions, but didn't realize he'd disconnected the call until he said her name quietly.

She glanced up and found everyone looking at her. "You found them," she said, not quite believing it'd been that easy. She got up and took a step back from the table, shaking her head.

Noah stood and reached for her hand, but before he could say anything, she threw herself at him in a hug that was sheer relief. "*You found them.*"

He wrapped her up and hugged her back. "We all found them."

Olive looked at his list, and at the map where he'd circled an area quite a ways north of them.

"It'll take at least three hours to get up there," Noah said. "We can leave in the morning, if the weather is going to hold. I'll check."

"We?" She stared at him. "There is no we. You've got to stay here for Katie and Joe and Joey."

"No," Katie said. "He doesn't. Joe's awake and going to stay that way. And I've got Mom, she can help me."

Amy nodded. "Of course."

"Me too," Gram said.

"No." Olive shook her head. "You've all already done so much for me. I came here to help you, not the other way around. I'm not asking Noah to come with me."

"You don't have to," he said.

"He's going with you," Amy said.

"Most definitely," Katie said.

"One hundred percent," Gram said.

The four of them stared at her. She stared right back.

"Look," Noah said. "The Mini isn't going to make it up there. This is an extremely remote location, with the last leg of it nothing but a dirt fire road."

"I know."

"So you also know it will require four-wheel drive, plus an off-road vehicle for that last leg."

They stared at each other, because the last time they'd been on an off-road vehicle together, she'd destroyed his life.

And hers.

"Why haven't they contacted me?" she asked. "Do you think they ran into trouble on the way up there?"

"Your dad can handle himself," Noah said. "I've been up that way several times for work. There's little to no cell service."

"You think it could be that simple?"

"Yes."

She thought about it. "So either they're totally fine, or . . ." Yeah. It was the "or" she was having trouble with. "Excuse me," she said softly. "I need some air." She stepped out the back door.

The moon was showing off tonight, full and bright, making the few clouds glow. She was staring up at the sky, the iciness of the air making every exhale a little puffy cloud, when she heard the back door open and close.

Katie came to stand at the deck railing with her. "Hey."

"I'm okay," Olive said.

"I know."

They stared at the sky some more, the silence comfortable and filled with all the sweet, sensitive things Katie had trouble saying. Finally, she sighed. "Noah wanted to come out here, but Mom made him play rock paper scissors for who got to go first, and I won. But the thing is . . ."

"You don't have the words?" Olive asked, amused.

Katie sighed again. "Look, if it was my mom out there, I'd go. For what that's worth."

Olive turned to her. "It's worth everything. But I'm here to help you with Joey. Even if we leave at dawn, we'll be gone until late."

"I'll take him with me to the hospital. Mom said she'd come to help out." Katie looked back at the house, and at whatever she saw, she let out a low snort. "Brace yourself. Here comes Mr. Bossy-Nosy-Know-It-All."

Katie walked off and Noah took her spot, leaning on the railing. He didn't look out into the night. He faced Olive, waiting for her to look at him.

With a sigh, she turned to him.

"I'm going with you," he said in that no-nonsense voice.

Because that made her stomach go a little squishy, she ignored it. "I still don't feel right leaving Katie—"

"I'll be fine," Katie said from the doorway.

"And you called *me* nosy," Noah called back to his sister.

"Yeah, because I'm better at adulting than the two of you put together!"

"Hey," Olive said, but also . . . *true*.

Katie pointed at her. "You fled the country rather than deal with conflict." She jabbed that same finger at Noah. "And you. You wouldn't even let me say her name."

Amy, standing next to Katie at the window, laughed until they all looked at her. Then she gestured with her hand that she was locking her mouth and throwing away the key.

Noah, ignoring that and his sister too, said to Olive, "We leave before dawn. Pack light but warm."

"Ha," Katie said. "Have you never met her?"

Noah didn't take his gaze off Olive, clearly waiting for her to object.

She wasn't going to. She wasn't stupid. Even she knew going alone was a really bad idea. She also knew if she had any hopes of finding that yurt and her parents, she'd need someone with tracking and survival skills. And unfortunately, that wasn't her.

It was Noah.

CHAPTER 18

Twelve years ago

Olive, Katie, and Noah were set to graduate in two weeks, and Olive couldn't be less excited. School ending meant that they'd be scattered far and wide from each other: Katie to University of Nevada, Reno; Noah to San Diego State to play baseball, thanks to a scholarship; and Olive would be heading to NYU. She had an offer for an internship for the summer, but she couldn't do it, couldn't give up her last summer in Sunrise Cove.

She actually had no idea what she'd been thinking a year ago when she'd applied. Okay, not true. A year ago, she'd known only that it was time to stop depending on Gram and the Turners, time to learn to be on her own. She'd even been tentatively excited.

But as her departure date got closer and closer, that excitement had been replaced by a growing panic. Leaving everyone she knew and loved had her halfway to a panic attack as she rode Gram's old ATV up to Hidden Falls, to her class's "secret" senior party. Neither she nor Katie felt comfortable at parties, but Joe was going, so Katie wouldn't miss it.

Olive would have preferred to. Noah's kiss had been everything she'd ever wanted, but he was acting like it'd never happened. Fine, they were just pretend, she got it. It'd been her own stupid doing and she had no one to blame but herself, but it didn't mean she had to remain stupid.

She decided that tonight she'd set her sights on someone else, anyone else, and she'd forget all about Noah Turner. Walking through the crowd, she turned at the sound of her name, surprised to see Trev Bates from chem class. She was pretty sure he'd been copying off her tests for months, but he was cute, and one of the few guys who even tried to be nice to her.

"You still with Noah?" he asked.

"Nope."

Trev smiled. "Wanna dance?"

Her heart thundered in her ears because other than that time in middle school when they'd all learned how to dance in PE, she'd never danced with a guy. "Sure."

The song blasting out of the speakers was a slow one, and Trev pulled her close. It was a hot night and he was a little sweaty, but he was smiling down at her and she felt herself smiling back. When the song was over, he took her hand. "Let's go for a walk."

"Um . . ." She looked around for Katie, because, naive though she might have been, even she knew no self-respecting girl should go off into the woods with a guy, no matter how cute, at least not without telling her best friend.

"Don't worry, I'll take real good care of you," Trev promised, pulling her along.

"Olive."

Noah stood in front of them, arms crossed, face blank, eyes cold. "What are you doing?" he asked.

"Going for a walk."

Noah looked at Trev, one of his teammates, and his eyes went from cold to ice. "No."

Oh, he had some nerve, not wanting her for himself but still holding her back. "Let's go," she said to Trev.

"He thinks because you've never done this before that you're an easy target," Noah said.

Olive had a very slow fuse, it took a lot to rile her, but she went straight to seeing red. "Just because you don't want me, doesn't mean no one else does."

Ignoring this, Noah looked at Trev. "Trust me, she's more trouble than she's worth."

Trev let go of Olive's hand and walked away without a second glance.

They now had an audience of at least fifteen other kids, and horror and humiliation crawled up her throat. Her flight instinct had her whirling and running, heading as fast as she could toward where she'd left the ATV. It took her a moment to start the thing because it was ancient, and another to swipe away the angry tears she refused to acknowledge. Before she could hit the gas, someone slid onto the ATV behind her.

Noah.

"Get off," she snapped.

"No."

She elbowed him in the gut, but he refused to budge. Fine. She hit the gas. It was slow going on the temperamental ATV, which was meant for only one rider, but it was better than walking. Halfway home, a surprise storm hit hard and heavy, deluging them in seconds.

"Stop," he said in her ear. "Let's switch. I'll drive—"

She didn't stop, she drove through the crazy rain on the narrow, curvy dirt road. Freezing, shaking, drenched, she gasped in shock as a massive branch fell across the road right in front of them, forcing her to stomp on the brakes. But it was like trying to dock the Queen Elizabeth II, *and she went into a slide, finally coming to a messy stop only a few feet from the fallen branch.*

"I'll drag it aside," Noah said. "Keep one foot on the brake and the other revving the engine so you don't stall."

When she nodded, he hopped off and began dragging the huge branch off to the side.

A strong gust of wind hit, nearly knocking her off the ATV, but she managed to hold on, even as her wet boot slipped from the brake. She screamed as the ATV leaped forward, right at Noah.

Then right into Noah . . .

Present day

The soft whir of the heater clicking on was the only sound in the room when Noah opened his eyes. He didn't have to glance at his phone to know that it was 4:58 in the morning. His body always woke him just before his alarm.

He drew a deep breath and let it out slowly, trying to wake up because the next two minutes were all his. No family to appease. No work. No Joey padding in on bare feet and taking a flying leap, landing on his belly, bouncing as he yelled "it's morning!" No stressing over Joe's recovery.

These two minutes were sheer luxury.

Definitely not a substitute for a day off, which he probably needed. Or an actual vacation for that matter, which seemed even more unlikely. But still, he treasured these 120 seconds because—

Beep-beep. Beep-beep. Beep-beep.

Aaaand time. He rolled out of bed, brushed his teeth, and reached for the shower valve, wanting the water hot, hot, hot— only to go still at the sight of a bunch of silky, lacy underthings hanging from one end of the shower to the other.

They were dry, so he took them down, his callused fingers gliding over silk, lace, and cotton. By the time he set them in a neat stack next to the sink, he needed a cold shower, which didn't improve his mood any. Knowing he was going to spend the entire day in close proximity to the woman who left him torn between running for the hills and kissing—among other things—he dressed, mentally preparing himself for the hours ahead.

A few minutes later, he was outside in the icy dawn to load his truck, including his Razor, a modern version of Gram's old ATV. For one thing, the Razor was a UTV—utility terrain vehicle—which was far more powerful and actually meant for two people to ride, side by side.

When he heard footsteps, he was shocked. Mostly because Olive had never met a morning she liked, and he'd expected to have to wait. Leaning back against the truck, he took in her weak smile and raised a brow. "Having second thoughts?"

"About going to look for my parents?" she asked. "No. About going with you?" Her smile turned a bit more genuine. "Definitely."

His own smile was knowing. "Smart woman."

She offered him coffee in a to-go cup, which he gratefully took. "Thanks."

She sipped from her own cup, her gaze drifting to the Razor. To her credit, there was zero hesitation. She wore jeans, hiking boots, a knit cap, and a cute white puffer jacket that was more fashion than function. She'd dropped a dainty little backpack at her feet. He'd have been impressed at how little she'd packed, but there was also a huge duffel bag that made him laugh. "I could pack the entire T-ball team in that bag."

"Hey, your bag isn't so small itself."

"It's a go-bag."

She eyed it. "The only thing I know about go-bags is from TV. Why would we need a bag filled with survival stuff?"

"So we have everything we might need in an emergency survival situation."

She paused. "Do you anticipate an emergency?"

"Always." He took a look at her face and bit back a sigh. "Ninety percent of my job is mundane, boring investigative work. But that other ten percent can turn deadly in a hot second if I'm not prepared." He hoisted the bag. "So I'm prepared. Always."

"How prepared? Like, do you have cookies in there?"

"No, but I'm betting you do."

She looked away. "Maybe."

Yeah. She totally had cookies in there.

"So what's in the go-bag that makes you prepared for anything?" she wanted to know. "Condoms?" The minute the word came out, she slapped a hand over her mouth, like she hadn't meant for the word to escape. "Never mind," she quickly said. "Don't answer that."

He smiled. "Let me know if you change your mind and want to know." He nudged her duffel with his boot. "Those are some heavy cookies."

"It's stuff to eat, for the both of us. Keep it up and I won't share." She tossed him a protein bar. His brand. Favorite flavor. "Breakfast of champions."

He stared down at it, then back at her. "Okay, who are you and what have you done with Olive Porter, the woman who hates mornings, hates healthy food, and disagrees with hiking boots on principal because they aren't flattering?"

She didn't smile, and his faded. Because now he could see past her bravado to the exhaustion in her eyes. "Did you sleep at all?"

Ignoring that, she picked up her small backpack. "We doing this or what?"

"Yes—" He stopped at the notification that hit his phone. Tapping the link, he blew out a breath.

"What?"

"I've been watching the weather since last night. It was fine then, and also when I checked after my shower a few minutes ago. But now there's an alert for a possible surprise storm." He looked up. "It could blow in late this afternoon, fast and hard. The good news is that if it does, it should be over by midnight. We could wait until tomorrow—"

"What are the chances of precip?" she asked.

"Twenty percent, but—"

"That's nothing." She tossed her backpack in the truck and started to reach for the big duffel bag, but he beat her to it, slipping the strap over his shoulder. "Olive."

"*Noah*," she said, mimicking his deep tone.

Smart-ass.

She tipped her head back to look him in the eye. "Are you forgetting I spent the first fourteen years of my life living off the grid in a virtual tin can?"

He'd never forgotten a single thing about her. "We're going to be on a UTV—"

"It has a roof."

"Yes," he said. "But it's open on the sides, no windows, no protection from the elements." His gaze met hers. "In a potentially big storm. Ringing any bells?"

She held up a hand, like she was making a solemn vow. "I promise not to run over you."

"I'm not worried about your driving," he said. "Well, okay, I'm worried about your driving. But I'm more worried about mental trauma."

"Yours?" she asked sweetly. "Or mine?"

He sighed.

Her amusement faded. "I'm sorry. It's just . . ." She shook her head. "I'm worried if we wait, they'll be gone. I need to see them, Noah. Need to make sure they're okay."

What she didn't say, but what they both knew, was that she needed to see them . . . before she left again.

Stepping close, she put her hand on his chest. "I get the logical thing is to wait, but being back here is like stepping into a time machine. I'm feeling less and less like the capable, successful woman I turned myself into, and more like that lost, insecure, uncertain teenager who doesn't know who she is or where she fits in the world."

The words, softly and earnestly spoken, broke something inside him. He knew how she'd felt back then. Just as she, and only she, knew *he'd* felt the same. "Let's get on the road, then," he said gruffly. "We're wasting daylight."

He didn't have to tell her twice. She hopped into the truck, no hesitation, no fear, no worries, apparently one hundred percent confident in his abilities to take care of them.

He had the skills. He'd absolutely keep them safe. Physically. But mentally or emotionally? That was most *definitely* outside his skill set, as she should know all too well.

NEARLY TWO HOURS later, beneath a turbulent, churning, gunmetal gray sky, they left the highway, turning onto a narrow, curvy two-lane road to climb up.

And up.

His passenger hadn't said much, and neither had he, though their silence felt oddly . . . comfortable.

Soon enough they left the asphalt behind. It wouldn't be long before they'd leave his truck behind too, going the rest of the way on the UTV. His passenger squirmed and pressed her hands over her belly. He glanced over at her. "Hungry?"

"Starving."

"Me too." He stopped right in the middle of the fire road. It was single lane, and there were no other vehicles stupid enough to be out here at this time of year with a storm brewing. And it was brewing. The wind had kicked up, rustling the pines towering all around them.

The minute he turned off the truck, Olive was out of her seat belt and up on her knees, turning in the seat, reaching into the back for her bag. He resisted looking at her sweet ass for at least a fifth of a second.

Progress.

When she plopped back into her seat, her hands full of food, he had to laugh. "You bring the kitchen sink too?"

Her eyes narrowed. "Do you want me to share or not?"

"Yes, please."

She had cheese, crackers, apples, peanut butter, chips, and a variety bag of mini chocolate bars.

If he hadn't already, he'd have fallen for her right then and there. "You're amazing."

"True story."

With a laugh, he pulled out his pocketknife and sliced up two apples and a stack of cheese while she opened the crackers and pulled out the peanut butter.

A few minutes later, she was licking crumbs off her thumb with a little suction sound that nearly killed him.

"This is all a woman really wants," she said. "Food."

He slid her a glance. "Right."

"No, really."

He gave a slow shake of his head. "In my experience, pleasing a woman is a lot more complicated than cheese and crackers."

"Maybe you've been with the wrong women."

"True story."

She snorted, but he was way too curious to let it go. "You're saying food is enough to satisfy you?"

She shrugged. "I'm saying I wouldn't mind someone feeding me once in a while. Nothing fancy, my choice would be . . . tacos. And maybe it'd be nice to hear I'm beautiful once in a while."

His heart ached that she didn't have that, because she absolutely deserved it. "Tell me you want more than tacos and pretty words."

She stuffed an apple slice ladened with peanut butter into her mouth.

Subject closed, apparently. They cleaned up, and Noah said, "At the next place where there's room, we're going to leave the truck behind."

She nodded, knowing that from there to the yurt, they'd wind up the mountain with switchbacks that the UTV could handle much better than his truck.

Two minutes later, he found a good spot to stop and looked at Olive. "We'll be okay."

A rough laugh escaped her. "Who are you trying to convince, you or me?"

"Both."

Her gaze dropped to his mouth and everything inside him reacted. Leaning in, he kissed her without thinking. When he realized what he was doing, he started to pull back, but with a sexy-as-hell little murmur of complaint, she gripped his shirt with two fists and held on tight. When they broke apart for air, he saw a matching raw hunger in Olive's eyes and he had to close his own. "Oli—"

"I know. Bad idea."

Yes. Because if kissing her had been a mistake, touching her was an invitation to mutual destruction. He slid on his jacket and got out of the truck. The wind had kicked up and the temperature had dropped. He still had his doubts on this being a smart thing, but Olive wasn't going to give up now. Or ever. It wasn't in her nature, and, honestly, it wasn't in his either.

So he backed the UTV down the ramp. When he started loading up their bags, Olive was there, helping. He handed her a helmet, put on his, and then started the engine, meeting her gaze. "Last chance to turn back."

She stared straight ahead, her eyes and mouth, no longer softened by their kiss, had turned grim. "No."

Okay, then. But he'd been driving off-road vehicles his entire life, and also for work. He knew he could get them there. In what condition would be another matter. The temperature had dropped and she shivered. "Cold?"

A negative shake of her head was his only answer. He gave her a long look.

"I'm fine."

"Uh-huh. Now the truth."

She sighed. "I'm just remembering the last time we were out in the wilderness in a storm, okay? The memory's messing with me more than a little."

"It's not going to happen again," he said firmly.

"Because we're on a different fire road?"

He flashed a smile. "Because I'm driving."

"Wow."

He let out a low laugh. "I'm kidding."

Her eyes narrowed. "So you won't mind if I drive, then."

"You'd have to pry the steering wheel out of my cold, dead hands."

She tossed up her own hands. "So you *do* mind."

"Let's just say this isn't the place I'd be interested in letting you drive."

"Where, then?"

He hit the gas.

"*Where, then?*" she repeated, having to yell over the engine and the fierce wind.

He slid his gaze to hers and waggled his brow.

"Seriously!" Her eyes went wide in disbelief. "Your bed? *That's* where you'd let me drive? Oh my God, you're *such* a guy."

Guilty as charged. But the brief smile that flashed across her face, telling him he'd coaxed her out of her own head at least, had been worth it.

Five minutes later, it started raining. Fifteen minutes, and the windshield wipers were having a seizure. Seeing the road had become a luxury, and when his tires slipped in the mud, the rear end fishtailing, Olive gasped. "Hang on," he said, steering them out of the spin before stopping. "You okay?"

Her breath came in little pants and she had a grip on the Oh Shit bar. "Why wouldn't I be?"

He did love her sass. "We're closer to the yurt than my truck now, so it's probably safer to keep going than turn around at this point."

"Agreed."

Still, the going was slow, and twenty-five minutes later, he stopped.

Olive squinted through the downpour to the vague outline of a yurt. "This is it? I don't see any other vehicles. And is that a second, smaller yurt off to the side?"

"That's the outhouse."

She looked at him in horror.

"No running water," he said. "Don't worry, I have several gallons of drinking water in the back."

She studied the yurt. "Maybe something happened to their van, and they walked in."

He had his doubts on this. The place had a feel of vacancy to it. But this being her show, he waited for her to make a move to get out. When she didn't, he nodded. "I'll go take a look around back. Maybe they parked there for some reason."

He exited the Razor straight into hell—if hell had rain coming down in thick, heavy sheets, that is. Gusts of wind slanted the rain in a sharp angle, making it difficult to see much.

Olive appeared at his side. "They could be on a hike," she shouted.

"In this weather?"

"They don't always think things through."

No shit. They never had, at least when it came to Olive.

The yurt was the size of a VW bus. They walked around it to the back but didn't find a van. Or anything. Completely drenched to their skin by then, they returned to the front door, which Olive knocked on while Noah peered into the sole window.

No signs of life.

Olive tried the handle. "It's locked."

"Not a problem."

"You're going to B and E?" she asked.

"No B." He flashed a smile. "Just E."

CHAPTER 19

O live watched as Noah pulled something from his cargo
pants pocket and lowered himself the best he could, his
weight on his good leg. There was the sound of a click and he
rose—with more than a slight grimace—and opened the door.

She didn't ask if he was okay, because he was male, and
therefore would either ignore her or say he was fine. "So we
are breaking and entering," she said instead. "You just bumped
that lock."

"Nope." He met her gaze, his own revealing nothing. "When
we got here, the door was unlocked."

She rolled her eyes, and he almost smiled. "There's clearly no
one using this place," he said, and shrugged out of his jacket to
wrap it around her. Drenched on the outside, on the inside it
was warm and smelled deliciously like him, and was big enough
to completely encompass her and her useless jacket that hadn't
lived up to its waterproof promise. "But—"

"You're cold," he said.

"As are you!"

He shrugged. "I'm better at going with the flow."

She started to get snippy about that, but . . . well, truth was truth.

"Get inside," he said. "I'm going to get our bags. Don't want to leave them in the Razor since you brought enough food to feed the entire bear population."

She froze and stared at him.

He shook his head with a barely there smile. "You've been in the big city too long if you've forgotten what it's like out here."

Another truth. In the Tahoe National Forest, bears were very cute, very scary menaces. They broke into unlocked cars and ate everything they found, including center consoles and steering wheels. They broke into unlocked garages and tore into refrigerators and cabinets. Basically, if something smelled good, the bears found it and ate it. "Be careful."

"My middle name."

"Yeah, right," she muttered, watching him walk off, hearing his low laugh. "Wait! Your jacket!"

But he was already gone. Shaking her head, she went inside, turning in a circle, taking in the yurt in its entirety. It was small but seemed strongly constructed, which was good given the intensity of the rain hitting the roof overhead. She was surprised to find it at least sparsely furnished with a loveseat, a small table with two mismatched chairs, and a bed, all in bright oranges, reds, and greens.

Her parents would be right at home in the sixties setting, but there was no sign of them, no sign of anyone having been here for some time, if the layer of dust meant anything. So either they'd decided not to come, or . . . they'd never made it for whatever reason. Pulling out her phone to call the rental company to ask if they'd heard from her parents at all, Olive stared down at the screen.

No service.

Not a surprise. People who didn't live in the Tahoe region never believed it, but there were still huge pockets where internet and phone service didn't exist. Maybe Noah would have an idea of what to do. Realizing he hadn't come in, she went to the door.

The rain made it nearly impossible to see a foot past her own nose. Rainwater poured off the small alcove, probably put in place to protect the opening of the yurt from the elements, but all it really did was completely hinder visibility.

"Noah?" she yelled, her voice immediately swallowed up by the noise of the storm.

He didn't call back to her.

A gust of frigid air sent a few strands of her hair fluttering across her face and she impatiently shoved them back. Suddenly unbearably anxious, she cupped her hands around her mouth. "This isn't funny!"

Silence.

Dear God, if he'd gotten himself eaten by a bear, she'd never forgive him. Never. Ever. *Dammit.* Sucking in a breath, she ran out into the rain. At the UTV, the rain was coming down so hard that she nearly missed the tall, leanly muscled shadow at the back of the vehicle.

Noah stood there, palms on the Razor, head bowed, a stillness to his body that made her rush toward him. She was nearly there when her boots lost their traction in the mud. For a single heartbeat, she waved her arms, trying desperately to find her balance, and then she went down hard, landing on her butt.

Noah stepped toward her, his limp far more pronounced than it'd been that morning.

"Are you hurt?" he asked, offering her a hand.

"Just my pride. Unlike you!"

When she didn't take his hand, he simply reached down and pulled her upright on his own, jaw tight. "I'm fine," he said in a low voice.

"Noah—"

He turned his back on her. "Let it go."

"I can't!"

That had him stopped and slowly spinning back.

"Look," she said, trying to lower her voice. "This is what friends do. Worry. Watch each other's backs. Stand by each other. So deal with it!"

"*Deal with it?*"

"Yes! And what happened? You didn't answer me when I called out for you."

"Nothing happened, I didn't hear you."

When she just stared at him, he sighed like she was some huge trial. "The leg locks up sometimes if I stay in one position too long, or when it's cold. It's no big deal." And with that, he limped toward the yurt, all three bags hanging off his shoulders.

God save her from idiot alphas. "I can carry my own stuff!"

He didn't slow down, leaving her running after him. Inside, he dropped the bags and turned to take in the place, water sluicing off him. His shirt was so wet it clung to him like a second skin, emphasizing just how fit he was, and she felt her mouth go dry—which really ticked her off. "I thought you'd been eaten by a bear!"

He gave a snort of laughter. "Would you have missed me?"

"Yes," her mouth said, once again without permission from her brain. That did it. She was never going to speak again.

After a stunned pause at her admission, Noah smirked. "You were just afraid the bear would also eat all your snacks."

He didn't believe that she'd have missed him, and she wasn't sure if she was relieved or not. While she was thinking too hard, he moved stiffly to the woodstove.

"I can start the fire," she said.

"I've got it."

"Your leg—"

"Stop treating me like a feeble-minded invalid."

She stared at him, then lowered her voice with effort. "Maybe it's because you're *acting* feeble-minded."

"I'm *acting feeble-minded*," he repeated with more than a hint of disbelief.

"Hey, if the shoe fits."

The sound that came from deep in his throat spoke of irritation and bad temper. Well, good then, mission accomplished, and she looked around for something to throw at him that wouldn't maim or kill him. Nothing. But hold on . . . she had a little packet of M&M's in her pocket. She wished they were peanut M&M's, because they'd hurt more, but with her having a sensitivity to peanuts and all . . .

"Hey!" he yelped when she beaned him in the back of the head with a blue M&M. Craning his neck, he glared at her.

"Be glad I can't find a weapon," she said and kept throwing M&M's because she couldn't stop herself. Clearly, she'd lost her mind.

Thunk. Plink. Rattle—the noises the candy made as she threw them depended on what they hit. Well, except the one that beaned him square in the forehead now that he was facing her. That one didn't make any noise at all.

Neither did the one he caught in his mouth.

"*Show off.*"

Chewing, he raised a brow. "You about done?"

With a huff, she shoved the empty wrapper in her jeans pocket and turned to rifle through the cabinets. Empty, except . . . She grabbed the lone item—a bottle of whiskey. "Found dinner." And with that, she chased away her to-the-bone chill with a sip that burned all the way down. "How long until you're okay to head back?"

He stared at her like she'd lost her mind. "We're not driving back in this crazy-ass storm."

Panic swirled in her gut. "But—"

"We're not leaving, Olive. It's not safe."

She looked around the yurt and swallowed hard. "How are we going to stay here without killing each other?"

He turned back to the woodstove. "I'll stay on my side and you stay on yours."

She eyed the single, bare, full-size mattress that suddenly looked very, very small.

"You can have it," he said without even looking at her.

"Not making you sleep on the floor," she muttered. "We're adults. We can share."

Another shrug, like he didn't care one way or the other, which felt like an insult. She looked at him and realized his pants were covered in mud like hers. "You clearly fell too," she said. "Did you hurt yourself?"

"Did you?"

"Wow." She put her hands on her hips. "So now we're three?"

Instead of responding, he crouched before the woodstove, his movements so carefully precise, she knew he was in far more pain than he was letting on.

"Seriously?" she asked his back, the one that looked strong and capable. What was it about a guy's back that did it for her?

Or maybe it was the broad shoulders suitable for taking on un-bearable weight.

Actually, it was most likely his very fine ass . . .

Ignoring her, he began to methodically build a fire.

"You're doing it wrong," she said.

When he didn't take the bait, she tossed up her hands and turned to their bags. Maybe he wanted to be a stubborn ass, but she did not. She wanted clean, dry clothes and she wanted them yesterday.

Except there was a problem.

Nowhere to go to change. What the hell, she decided. He had his back to her anyway. She kicked off her wet boots, pulled off his jacket and then hers, and then her sweatshirt and T-shirt. Finally, she unzipped her jeans. The problem with wet denim wasn't that it was wet, but that it'd cemented itself to her skin. It took a lot of struggling and shimmying to get the jeans down, but finally she was free. Which was when she real-ized the silence in the yurt was deafening. She looked up and locked eyes with Noah, his own dark and filled with things that made her swallow hard. "What?" she asked with all the bad temper she could muster.

"It's Wednesday," he said.

"Yeah? So?"

He nudged his chin toward her lower half, so she looked down, belatedly remembering that today's undies said *Fri-Yay* across the front. "What, you've never seen a girl wear the wrong day undies before?"

That won her another almost smile, she could tell. But she was still mad at him, so she dug through her bag and pulled on her backup clothes. She then turned to the small—make that postage-stamp-tiny—kitchenette. She needed tea. She always carried a few emergency tea bags with her because in her opinion, caffeine was an entire food group. Only . . . no running water, no electricity, no gas.

And to think, people rented places like this for fun. Still, she'd eat the dry tea bag before complaining to Noah, who she wasn't ready to forgive for his multiple transgressions, the biggest being that he didn't want to be with her. Not that she intended to tell him why she was mad, not even upon threat of death or dismemberment. But she was for sure no longer speaking to him, although given that he hadn't attempted to talk to her, she wasn't certain he appreciated that fact.

A muffled oath had her turning around. Mr. Handy in Any Situation stood hands on hips staring down at a very small little line of smoke. No fire. Not even a spark.

"I don't think glaring at it is going to help," she said.

He ignored her.

Fine. So the not speaking to each other was mutual. Whatever. She nearly turned away, but she caught it.

He was shivering.

"Noah," she said, and when he didn't answer, she moved closer and tried to turn him to face her, which wasn't easy because he resisted. Damn stubborn brick wall. In the end, she simply walked around him to his front. Reaching up, she cupped his jaw. His cold jaw. He'd hidden it well, but he was just as frozen as she was, and, in fact, was still very wet. "You need to change. I'll get the fire going."

"It's going. It'll catch any second now."

"Uh-huh."

Mr. Perfect didn't believe her so she dropped to her knees and knocked his stack of wood over.

"Hey."

Doing the opposite of what he had, she started with the largest pieces of wood on the bottom and then placed the kindling on top to assist in oxygen flow so the fire could burn down to all the underneath layers. When she saw the first lick of flames, she nodded, stood, and turned to Noah.

He was seated on one of the two kitchen chairs, jaw tight. He'd removed his shirt but was still in his cargos and boots.

When she realized the way he sat with his bad leg stretched in front of him probably meant he couldn't easily bend it to get his boots off, never mind his pants, her bad temper faded and she crouched low to unlace his boots.

"What are you doing?"

"What does it look like?" she asked, giving her voice a heavy dose of smart-ass rather than sympathy, knowing his stupid pride would hate even a hint of the kinder emotion.

Men were dumb.

"I can take off my own damn boots," he snapped.

"Sure." She sat back on her heels and gestured for him to have at it.

When he just glared at her, she shook her head and leaned forward again and finished removing his boots and wet socks. She eyed his pants next.

"No," he said wearily. "Just give me some room."

She did him one better and left his stubborn ass to go tend to her fire. Which turned out to be totally unnecessary because the flames were flickering to life. She glanced over her shoulder and found Noah on the bed under a blanket. "Where did the blanket come from?"

"My duffel bag."

Right. The emergency and survival gear. Not that she could

think straight beyond one single thought: *What was he wearing beneath the blanket?*

The wood crackled and warmth began to spread through the entire yurt.

"It's a good fire," Noah said with absolutely zero sarcasm—which, dammit, made him a better person than her.

"It's always fascinating to see you work under pressure," he said quietly. Genuinely.

"Why would you want to see me work under pressure?"

His smile was wry. "Under pressure is where you see what people are really made of. No time to clean up who you are or what you do. Pressure shows you what a person fears most."

"Yeah? What do you fear?"

His smile was tight. "More than I used to. You?"

"I fear we'll run out of snacks."

He snorted.

"Okay, hotshot," she said. "What do *you* think I fear?"

He didn't laugh off her question, instead spoke seriously. "You fear being labeled by the way you grew up, so you hide the real you from the world you built around yourself. All without realizing the real you is amazing—as is."

She realized her mouth had dropped open. How could he possibly know her fear, and worse, understand it better than she could herself?

He gave her a crook of his finger. "Come here."

Said the big bad wolf . . .

At her hesitation, he smiled. "Nervous?"

"No." More like turned on, which really ticked her off. But apparently her feet didn't get the message because they took her to the side of the bed. "Do you need something?"

"Yes, for you to get in. You look like you're still cold." He patted the space beside him.

Back to his badass alpha-in-charge self, she could see. But he was right. She was still cold. Really cold, especially her fingers and toes. And her nose too. What was with that?

When he reached out and took her hand in his, she sighed. His had warmed and melted her resistance because she wanted to be warm too. "Fine." She climbed into the bed. "But *only* because I'm worried about you."

"I know," he said with some amusement as he hauled her into him and wrapped his body around her.

He wasn't naked, but nearly. All he wore were knit boxers and she almost moaned—until she realized he was shaking with silent laughter. Fine. She *had* moaned. "You're a jerk."

He pressed his face into her hair and held her tight. "And *you're* one of the strongest, most amazing women I've ever met."

The unexpected compliment made her squirm.

"Olive." His voice was low, husky. "Killing me."

When she realized how she'd been moving against him, and that he'd had a very male reaction, she froze. *Eep.* "Sorry."

"Don't be. Most action I've seen in months."

She snorted, but then their gazes locked and held as the rain battered the yurt around them, reminding her they were stuck out here in the middle of nowhere until the storm abated.

With one bed.

CHAPTER 20

Olive knew she should move away from Noah, but his leanly muscled, tall frame was solid and warm, and her own body refused to give him up. It wasn't often that she could let a silence go by without filling it, but in that moment, with the fire crackling, the drum of the rain pounding on the roof of the yurt, and the delicious heat of him seeping into her, she felt oddly at peace. It made little sense. Actually, it made no sense.

The unplanned intimacy should've made her uneasy, but it didn't. Instead, she felt an ease she couldn't explain, like they were out of time and place.

Maybe . . . maybe whatever happened here could stay here. "Like Vegas."

Noah raised a brow.

"Nothing," she said quickly. "I didn't mean to say that out loud."

A slow smile crossed his face. "Like Vegas," he repeated. "As in whatever happens in Vegas stays in Vegas?"

"No, of course not!" But also . . . totally.

His smile widened. "You just squeaked. Means that's a lie."

Great. "How's your leg?"

"What leg?"

Closing her eyes on a rough laugh, she dropped her head to his chest. "I shouldn't have asked you to do this."

"Because you're not a fan of visiting Vegas?"

She rolled her eyes, but then lifted her face to his, her smile fading. "Because I know it's drudging up old memories."

He was quiet a moment, but his eyes were locked on hers as he lifted a hand and gently stroked a finger along her temple, tucking a stray strand of hair back from her face. "I'm not sorry I came," he said. "I couldn't stomach the idea of you making this trek alone."

"Not to mention there was no way I *could've* done it alone," she muttered.

"Was that a thank-you?"

That made her laugh. "Yes. A big thank-you." She hesitated. "I owe you."

"And I owe you for coming back to Sunrise Cove to help out, so let's consider us even."

"I'm not sure I was all that big of a help," she said.

"Just your presence is a help. I know I've been . . ." He shook his head, clearly looking for the right words. "Distant. And you were right on the mark about old memories surfacing."

"About us?"

"That," he said. "And other stuff that happened between then and now."

She cocked her head and studied him. "Your dad?"

He nodded.

"I'm sorry," she said softly. "He died so fast after his diagnosis."

"Yeah, and it didn't help that just before that, he was barely speaking to me, and vice versa."

She looked down at their joined hands, at the way his thumb lightly ran over her knuckles. "He was hard on you, but he loved you."

Noah laughed roughly.

The truth was, in her opinion, his dad hadn't really understood Noah. He'd wanted a puppet. But Noah was no one's puppet. All he'd ever wanted was to be accepted just as he was, imperfections and all.

"I could never please him," he said. "It got worse after our ATV accident. He knew what the doctors said, that a career in baseball would be improbable, but he still pushed me. And when I pushed back, he wanted me to find a way to stay in baseball, or get a business degree and take over the shop."

"Neither of which you wanted."

Noah shook his head. "As soon as I rehabbed my leg and was mobile again, I left to work in the forestry department. I got the experience I needed in law enforcement and special investigations, and was invited to become an ISB special agent."

"And that made you happy."

"Oh, hell yeah. The freedom to be who I am . . ." He hesitated. "I came home when I could, especially when my dad got sick. He didn't soften through that, by the way. Nothing got better between us. I guess I thought we'd have time to figure our shit out, but we didn't."

"Noah." Her heart ached for him. "I'm so sorry."

He shook his head. "When I look back objectively, I can see that it wasn't all bad. My growing up years. He taught me discipline, and how to harness my impulses. I was a wild card, and in that regard, he was good for me. I mean, I didn't think so at the time," he added with a wry smile that stirred something in her chest. "But he taught me to be proud of what I do. It was a turning point for me. I def wouldn't have the life I have now if it hadn't been for his influence." He squeezed her hand. "And we're going to find your parents. You guys still have time to find middle ground."

She looked into his eyes, saw his own regrets, and felt her heart squeeze. "*That's* why you're helping me."

"I'm helping because I care about *you.* I'm just saying that when we do find them, maybe you can take the time to open up and express how you feel about your relationship."

"No regrets," she said quietly.

Eyes on hers, he nodded. "No regrets."

She cleared her throat. "So, um, speaking of regrets . . . we didn't get a chance to talk at your dad's celebration of life. I'm sorry about what happened to him. How you lost him. Tell me you know what happened wasn't your fault."

"I do, but I still feel like shit for not fixing things sooner. Luckily my mom and sister don't seem to hold it against me." He cocked his head. "And . . . you knew that already."

"Yes, because I didn't ban Katie from saying your name." She laughed at his wince. "I've always asked about you, kept up with what you were up to." She paused. "Truth?"

"Always."

"I soaked up any info about you that I could get."

Their eyes locked and held for a beat before he said, "I know it was a long time ago, but I'm sorry I hurt you that night at the party."

She managed a genuine laugh. "You mean when I wanted to sleep with you, but you refused so I acted like an idiot by throwing myself at Trev What's-His-Face, only to have you tell the whole world I was a virgin, and that if he slept with me, you'd kill him? Oh, and then when I tried to take off—mortified, by the way—you jumped on my grandma's ATV with me, and . . . well, you remember the rest."

He grimaced. "I like my version better."

She laughed again. "Do tell."

"I thought Trev wasn't good enough for you, and I *definitely* knew I wasn't good enough for you. And I never said I wouldn't sleep with you, just that I wouldn't do it that night, not with emotions running so high. I offered you a raincheck." A faint smile curved his mouth. "You told me where to stick that raincheck."

She had. "I might've been hasty."

He shook his head, not willing to be sidetracked. "There was no way in hell I was going to let you drive home by yourself because I knew you weren't experienced enough to even be on that ATV in the first place, but it wasn't like your grandma knew you'd"—he used air quotes—"'borrowed' it."

She narrowed her eyes. "Rewind back to the you weren't 'good enough' thing."

His eyes softened. "I wasn't, Oli. I was a fuckup, an adrenaline-fueled fuckup who craved nothing more than getting away from anything that resembled connections and roots. You were so sweet and naive, and I—"

"*Sweet and naive?*" she asked, her voice going up a few octaves. "*Sweet and naive* implies the personality of . . . a golden retriever!"

He shook his head, thankfully not smiling or she'd have to hit him. "Not sweet and naive like a golden retriever," he said. "Sweet and naive like a kitten—with sharp teeth."

When she laughed, he smiled. "You were also sarcastic, and maybe a little wary, but never jaded." He looked marveled by that. "You found joy in simple things and were quick with a smile."

"*Were?*"

"*Are*," he said. "Also smart as hell, sharp as the pocketknife you always carried, and resourceful. You didn't take shit from anyone. Still don't. You were—and are—incredible."

"So then why—"

"Because you wanted everything I was trying to escape from . . ." He ticked off the reasons on his fingers. "Emotional ties, roots, family . . ."

Right. He'd spent his growing up years having to be something, someone, he wasn't. And now that he was free to be his own person, he didn't understand—or care—that love, true love, wouldn't require him to change. It took her a moment to brave her next question, but she had to know. "You see anything changing for you anytime soon?"

He paused, regret in his gaze now. Cupping her face, he rested his forehead against hers. "I've always been so sure the answer to that question would forever be no, but looking into your eyes makes me hesitate."

Her heart skipped a beat, but if she'd once been naive, she was no longer. "Don't give me false hope, Noah."

"I'm trying not to. I'm just saying, if I could change for anyone, it'd be for you."

"That's the thing," she said. "I'd never ask you to change a single thing about you." She started to climb out of the bed and heard him take a deep breath before catching her, then tugging her back to kiss the bejeezus out of her.

"What was that?" she asked breathlessly.

He flopped to his back and stared up at the ceiling. "Hell if I know. You drive me crazy."

"Flattering," she said with a good amount of sarcasm. Hard to pull off when she was still panting.

His smile was wry as he rolled to his side, propping his head up with a hand to look at her. "If it helps, you're the only one who can make me crazy."

They stared at each other, the air going supercharged. Not with bad temper like it had been only a few moments ago, but with . . . awareness. Anticipation and hunger pulsed around them in tune to the rain coming down. The fire crackled, and Noah's intoxicating scent surrounded her. How was it after such a long day that he still smelled so good? Or the way he looked at her, like he thought she was beautiful and remarkable, his pupils darkening with heat and desire.

Even knowing this wouldn't, couldn't, be a thing, she still wanted him. And given that at the moment she happened to have him all to herself, she scooted close enough to feel every inch of him against her, some of the inches making her heart pound in a matching rhythm of the rain pounding the roof. With a sound of need, she fused her mouth to his.

Something she already knew about Noah—he loved to kiss, and he was unbelievably good at it. He started off slow and deep and delicious, but eventually moved his focus from her mouth to nibble down her neck. The sensation drew a throaty moan from her, one that had him pulling back just far enough to look into her eyes. "The raincheck's over a decade old," he murmured, his voice husky low and sexy as hell. "Any chance it's still good?"

Here was her problem. Noah was like fire. Hot and consuming. She wanted what he was offering, but she wasn't stupid. She knew it was all he had to offer. Or at least, all he *would* offer.

And yet, there was something behind his smile, a haunted cast that made her suspect he needed the connection with her every bit as much as she needed it with him. He'd shared a side of himself that she'd never seen before, and now she wanted to do the same. "You're just in time," she said. "It was about to expire." Needing him even closer, she threw a leg over his.

He winced, but tried to hide it.

"Ohmigod," she gasped. "Did I hurt you?"

"No."

"I totally did."

"Maybe just a little."

"I'm so sorry!"

"I'm fine."

"Are you sure—" But she never finished that sentence because his big, warm hands slid under her shirt and cupped her bare breasts. His heartfelt groan was nearly as thrilling as his touch.

"Pain is a small price to pay for where this is going," he said roughly.

"Yeah?" She leaned into his big hands because they were the best thing she'd ever felt. "And where is this going?"

He nipped her earlobe. "Wherever you want it to."

She wanted *him*, more than she could remember wanting anything, even if he had stupid rules about it. Even if it was only for the moment. The moment would at least be all consuming and blazing, and would eradicate the cold she felt, inside and out. "I want a home run."

At her use of the baseball term, he laughed that rare, deep, full-throated laugh of his, and then slowly, holding her gaze, giving her plenty of time to change her mind—*as if*—he slid her shirt up and over her head, tossing it behind him before kissing her again, a questioning kiss that she answered with a resounding demand of *more*.

He answered by removing any and all remaining clothing between them, which at this point was only her sweat bottoms and his knit boxers. Taking him in, that hard warrior's body, had desire and hunger skittering through her. Seeing it echoed in his gaze, along with something more than just a need for sex, something deeper, something from his soul, something that existed for only her, had her heart thundering in her chest.

His hands danced over her entire body from top to bottom and back again, always in motion, always in tandem with his knowing mouth, until she had to bite her bottom lip to keep from begging for more. Closing her eyes, she arched into him in silent surrender, all rational thought gone. The only thing she could focus on was his touch, teasing one minute, serious the next, until, fingers fisted in his hair, she begged after all.

He gave her everything she wanted, and when he lifted his head and whispered, "About that condom you asked me about . . ."

Slipping out of the bed, she went to his survival bag and pulled out the condom in an inner zipped pocket, laughing as she turned back to the bed. "I take back everything I said about your go-bag."

He was laughing too—until she rolled the condom on him. Because as she touched him, taking her time about it, he switched to a combo of a rough groan and heartful swearing. When she'd finished torturing him, he reversed their positions with an easy strength, pressing her into the mattress, spreading her out beneath him, kissing and touching every inch of her. She was trembling from aftershocks when he finally slid inside her, the exquisite fullness having her moaning already, clutching at him.

He lifted his head, eyes dark with hunger, forearms on either side of her head, his big hands fisted loosely in her hair. "Hello, Oli." He smiled. "It's been too long."

A sobbing laugh escaped her as she clutched at him, viscerally brought back to five years prior when they'd run into each other at his mom's fiftieth birthday party. They'd had an argument about . . . God, she couldn't even remember. She'd gotten so mad, she'd put her hands on his chest to shove him away, but her brain had become confused and she'd yanked him to her instead. And . . . they'd accidentally slept together.

She, of course, had very maturely slipped out of his bed before dawn and caught a plane rather than face any fallout. Chickenshit, that's what she'd been. Because there'd been fallout anyway. Her heart, for one, and maybe even his.

She'd seen him a few times since then, of course, but they'd never talked about it, or even acknowledged that it'd happened, not once.

He said her name again, in a voice that had her looking into his eyes, driving that night from her mind.

She was talking raw, scorch-the-earth, sheet-clawing sex, with the silk of his voice sliding over her body like a caress, the intensity in his eyes burning into her.

The man had a single-minded focus that could make her forget everything, including her resolve to not fall in love. She simply couldn't get enough of him, and she sure as hell couldn't hold back. Around them, the room was dark, save for the luminescent glow coming from the woodstove. Silent, except for the crackling of the fire and their twin moans of pleasure, and of course the ever-present rain falling, a dissonant symphony of water cascading off the rusting and weathered metal of the yurt's frame.

She honestly had no idea what she'd expected. It certainly hadn't been that she'd completely lose herself in him. But she did. She lost herself, even as she was found.

After, they lay there entwined under the blanket, the fire bathing them in flickering light. The romance of it all struck her and she wanted to lift her head, look into his eyes, and know what they'd just shared meant something to him.

But she didn't, afraid she'd see something she didn't want to.

They dozed, but she was too keyed up to stay asleep. At her side, Noah's breathing was deep, slow, and even. He looked utterly relaxed and completely peaceful.

And totally doable.

Gah, she needed to get a grip. And *not* on one of his body parts. As always, he stirred up a maelstrom of powerful, complex emotions inside her, some of which didn't even have a name.

As if he could feel her thinking too hard, he shifted slightly, and their arms brushed. Then she felt his fingers reaching, touching hers, entwining their hands together, which he settled on his chest, right over his heart.

Turning her head, she found him watching her. There was a barely there smile curving his mouth, but his eyes were serious. "You okay?"

She smiled. "I think you know exactly how okay I am."

He gave a gentle tug on her hand, but it was the pull of his personal force field that had her crawling into his arms. She knew him well enough to know exactly what that force field was made of too—the intensity of his personality, the power of his will, and the sheer focus of his attraction to her, which in turn bound her to him as well. She knew she should pull back and walk away, or she'd drown in him.

But she didn't move.

He pushed some hair off her face, then wrapped a strand around his finger.

"I suppose it's gone wild from all the rain," she murmured, knowing she had to look like a hot mess.

"I love it. I love the no-makeup look too. You look like the girl I remember."

She groaned and he flashed a smile, but he wasn't making fun of her. She knew he meant what he'd said, and her chest went warm. Because she liked the boy he'd been too. So much. And it no longer surprised her to realize that she liked the man he'd grown into as well. Maybe even more than the boy, and now something fluttered inside her chest. Her heart, probably rolling over and exposing its underbelly. She supposed this was what fully loving someone felt like. It kinda sucked, especially when you were in love by yourself. "You said you came with me because you care about me."

"Yes." His smile was half amusement, but also half something else as he echoed her earlier words back to him. "This is what friends do, Oli. Worry. Watch each other's backs. Stand by each other."

Right. *Friends.* Welp, she had no one to blame but herself. She tried to come up with something to say, but Noah's breathing evened out again before she could. Apparently, his brain was kinder to him than hers was to her. Knowing sleep wouldn't happen, she started to slip out of the bed.

Noah's warm hand caught hers. "What's wrong?"

"Nothing."

"Lying again," he said quietly.

She sighed. "I don't want to keep you up."

"Here's an idea," he said in a sleep-gruff voice that was sexy as hell. "You can worry about your parents, you can watch me sleep, or you can come closer and let me take your mind off the things you can't do anything about, and then maybe sleep a little as well. The choice, as always, Oli, is yours."

Turned out, sleeping was overrated, though they did eventually catch some Z's. A few hours later at dawn, the icy rain had moved on, and as the sun slowly rose, so did steam off the ground. There was nothing as magical as Tahoe after a storm—the colors seemed deeper somehow and the trees swayed lightly as if in happiness.

They weren't the only ones. Olive and Noah spent some time having a breakfast of each other, and then breakfast with each other.

The second wasn't nearly as nice, seeing as it consisted of cold food from Olive's duffel, when what she wanted was crispy bacon, eggs, and pancakes. Big, fluffy pancakes.

Noah smiled at her from across their picnic on the bed. "When we get out of here, I'll buy you the biggest, most decadent breakfast you can imagine."

She grinned and he kissed her. He had his moments.

Then, from somewhere in his pants on the floor, his phone buzzed with an unfamiliar tone.

"What's that?" she asked, watching him slip off the bed. She couldn't help herself, the man looked amazing without a stitch of clothing on.

"It's my work phone," he said, searching his clothes for the phone.

"You had it with you? It works out here?"

"Yes, and yes—it's a satellite phone."

At his flat voice, she sat up. "Something up?"

"If they're calling me while I'm on leave after I begged to be put back on duty and my request was turned down flat, then yeah. Something's up." He answered the phone with a short "Special Agent Turner." He was quiet, listening, moving across the yurt like a cat, pulling on his now dried jeans in his usual economical yet unconsciously graceful movements.

"Yes," he finally said, his expression distant. "I understand. But I can't come in. I'm stuck in Tahoe."

He said a few more things as well, which Olive didn't catch because . . . *he was stuck here?*

When disconnected, he tossed the phone aside.

Unable to hold her tongue, she said, "Excuse me. *Stuck here?*"

He ran a hand down his face but still didn't say a word.

Hating how her emotions blew hot and cold with anger when it came to him, she drew a deep breath. Apparently, she needed a weather forecaster to tell her what to feel. "How can you be *stuck* with family?"

"There's a lead on the guy we were chasing when Joe got hurt." He picked up his shirt and turned it right side out before meeting her gaze. "I owe it to him to solve this case so it's not all for nothing."

"Okay." She nodded. "I understand that. But you're not cleared for work yet. And Joe just woke up. He still needs you looking after his wife and son."

Noah just looked at her, and she got it like a jackhammer to the chest. "You don't want to be here. With your family." *With me* . . . "You want to be back out there."

"I do," he said quietly. Unapologetically.

The sound in her head, the one of a vinyl record coming to a screeching halt, was the sound of her own secret fantasy of the two of them making a go at this thing dying, and dying hard.

CHAPTER 21

To say the ride back to Sunrise Cove felt awkward was probably the understatement of Noah's life. Which was why he didn't do this.

Whatever the hell *this* even was.

They didn't speak on the Razor. Completely normal for him. Not normal for Olive.

He'd been so sure she'd light into him once they were in his truck and could hear each other better, but she didn't. She sat in the passenger seat the very picture of calm—something she'd clearly learned since they'd been teens, because back then she hadn't been able to hide a single thing from him.

She was definitely hiding now.

He was inclined to let her, because why hash this out and hurt her more? Except . . . he hated to leave things unresolved between them.

Again.

And now they'd been intimate. He'd known sleeping with her would complicate everything, but what they'd shared last night had been so much more than sex. He could still see her in that yurt, the faint glow from the fire gently lighting the bed where she lay, skin glowing, a soft, sated smile on her face. They'd spent long hours taking each other apart and putting each other back together again.

Although if he were honest, he still didn't feel back together. Olive had destroyed him, in the very best of ways. It wasn't often he spent a night in a woman's bed, and even less often that it'd meant something to him.

But last night . . . He didn't even have words.

And then this morning, with her hair all Girls Gone Wild, those deep green eyes heavy lidded and sleepy . . . she'd been irresistible. He knew she'd have said she looked a hot mess, but to him she was the most beautiful thing he'd ever seen. "Are you hungry?" he asked when they got off the highway in town. "I can stop—"

"No, thank you."

He nodded. Okay, then, leaving things unresolved between them it was.

"Hello?"

He glanced over, thinking he'd missed something she said, but she was on her phone.

"Yes," she said with the first genuine smile he'd seen since they'd slept-*not*-slept together. "Thank you." She disconnected and leaned back, looking relieved. "That was Buddy."

"The guy you found on your parents' farm."

"Yes. He said my mom just called him. They decided the yurt was too remote and difficult to get to in their van, so they went camping instead."

"What campgrounds?"

Olive snorted. "Oh, they think actual campgrounds are for wusses. They were headed to some open land somewhere, off the grid. They borrowed a phone to call Buddy. Apparently, they lost theirs and didn't want to spend the money for a new one right now."

He slid her a look. "And the reason they called him and not their daughter?"

She hesitated, her eyes filling with shadows, and he was struck by an urge to erase them and then track down every single person responsible for putting them there in the first place.

Except, he was one of them. In fact, he was probably at the head of the line.

"The call wasn't about me," she finally said. "They wanted to check and make sure Buddy had been able to get some things harvested before yesterday's storm hit. He did ask them to call me."

"So . . . they're calling you next?"

She looked at her phone. The phone that was most definitely not ringing.

Noah chewed on that for a moment, his chest tight. It'd always been like this for him when it came to her. He wanted to solve all her problems. Which was dumb, because she had a core of inner strength like no one else he knew. She didn't want him to solve anything for her. No, what she wanted was something he didn't know how to give.

His love.

But her parents sure as hell should've given that to her. He and his parents had most definitely had their issues. His dad had been controlling, wanting him to live the life he himself hadn't been able to. His mom had been, and still was, nosy and pushy, wanting him to settle down. But even though he couldn't remember not knowing his role in the family—having to be perfect and having no needs of his own—he'd never doubted they loved him, in their own way.

Olive crossed her arms and looked out her window. "Don't you dare feel sorry for me. They love me." She paused. "In their own way. And anyway, it was never love I lacked. I lacked for . . . stability. Security." She said all this to her side window. "Also, they did say they'd catch up with me soon."

He glanced over at the back of her head and wondered if Buddy had made that last part up, or if Olive had. Or hell, maybe he was just too cynical and it was true. He really hoped it was.

When they pulled into the driveway back at Katie's, Olive opened the passenger door before Noah had even shut off the engine. He barely managed to grab her hand to stop her from sliding out.

Her face was unreadable as she gave him a brows-up, the "what?" silent.

What could he possibly say to make her look at him like she had when he'd been deep inside her, her pleasure-filled eyes locked on his? He started to open his mouth to say *Let's talk about how to keep this thing going between us . . .*

But that was his heart speaking, and he took orders only from his brain, which was currently yelling at him to keep his mouth shut because otherwise he'd be leading her on.

"Look," she said, beating him to the punch. "I'm good with everything that happened on the mountain, okay? I've got no regrets. Truly. But I'm not built like you. If we continue"—she bit her lower lip—"well, I'll get emotionally attached. And we both know that won't work for you. So I need a little space." Tugging her hand free, she grabbed her bags and walked into Katie's house without looking back.

She was *going* to get emotionally attached? As in she wasn't *currently* emotionally attached? Because he was most definitely there. Hell, he'd always been there. That wasn't his problem. Nope, that honor went to the fact he'd been doing his damnedest to not get *more* emotionally attached.

Shaking his head at himself, he remained in the truck and called his boss. He knew from Neil's earlier call there was going to be a meeting with all the people involved in the case, but he hadn't been able to get the details. "Sorry," he said when Neil picked up. "Got back to you soon as I could."

"Still stuck with family?"

Noah winced. Olive had been right. It sounded bad, and he was an asshole. Okay, so she hadn't said that part, but it'd been heavily implied in her tone. "Not at the moment. When's the meeting?"

"Tomorrow. Zoom in."

"I'm fine to drive down—" But he was talking to air. He thunked his head to the steering wheel a few times because he'd gotten into a fight with Olive for absolutely no reason. With a sigh, he got out of the truck, then froze at the sight he'd missed because his head wasn't in the game.

A dusty, ancient VW bus from a decade long gone sat at the top of the driveway on Olive's grandma's side. The back window was almost completely covered in stickers from a myriad of places across the country, so he couldn't see if anyone was inside, but voices from the side patio drew him in.

Olive clearly hadn't noticed the van either, since she'd gone straight into Katie's house. He turned to Gram's and could hear a few people talking: Olive's parents, Ace and Violet, and . . . his *mom?*

He picked up speed and found the group on Gram's patio. His mom looked absolutely furious, but even more shocking, she had a finger in Violet's face. "And a good mom doesn't let her children worry about her—*ever!*"

"Hey, I *am* a good mom!" Violet said, gesturing with a glass of what could've been water, but was more likely moonshine, since making it was one of Ace's talents.

"Yeah?" Noah's mom asked. "*When*, Vi? Name one time!"

Vi's grip on the glass tightened and Ace smoothly grabbed it from her, probably because he didn't like to see his efforts go to waste.

Not that Violet seemed to notice. "I gave Olive freedom and the room to make her own mistakes. Unlike you and Chuck, who never gave your poor son a single inch of rope. You're lucky he turned out so well—unlike you. You were the meanest kid on the planet, and that hasn't changed, I see."

Noah looked at his mom, stunned to find tears shimmering in her eyes.

"Okay," she said. "Maybe I was a rotten teen, but—"

"Try biggest bully in our school on for size," Violet said.

Gram stepped out her back door. "Just got home from the senior center to hear shouting." She took in the tense faces, then landed on Violet. "I know your mama raised you better than this."

"No offense," Violet said wearily. "But this is none of your business."

"It's her house," Amy said.

Violet narrowed her eyes and opened her mouth, but Ace lifted his hands in a calming gesture. "Ladies—"

"Zip it, Ace." Violet stepped up to Amy so they were nose to nose. "This isn't your fight."

Noah's mom never took her gaze off Violet. "Fine. I was awful, okay? But I was just a kid. Do you know what's worse than being an awful kid? Being a bad grown-up and an even worse *mom*. And that's what you are. A horrible, no good, rotten mom. Do you even know what your girl can do? No, you don't, because you don't keep up with her like you should! Olive is *amazing*, and you're missing out on her life."

"You mean because I don't micromanage her?"

Noah heard fast footsteps coming across the driveway and turned just as Olive appeared, looking stunned. "Mom? Dad?"

"Hey, kid." Ace moved to her and slung an arm around her shoulders. "Long time no see."

Olive hugged him. "I've been searching all over for you guys. You're both all right?"

"Of course," he said and gave her a squeeze.

Olive smiled but was clearly distracted by her mom and Noah's mom still standing nose to nose and glaring at each other. "*Mom?*"

"Hold on, baby, I'm in the middle of something."

"See?" Amy said, tossing up her hands. "Even now, you can't put her first."

Katie came up behind Olive, looking horrified. "Mom, you can't talk to Violet like that. I had to turn on a show for Joey super loud so he wouldn't hear. What the heck is going on?"

"Honey, I love you, but stay out of my business."

Violet pointed at Amy. "And you stay out of my business! Olive's an adult, and she handles her life accordingly. We support her. Well, not *support* support, because that's not our job, but she's free to do whatever she wants."

"She was a child and you let her move away from you!"

"She was a teenager! Old enough to know she didn't want to live on the mountain any longer. Living there was my choice, not hers, so of course we let her come here. But if I'd known you were going to insert yourself into her life, I'd have done things very differently."

"Oh my God," Amy said, tossing up her hands. "Your delusions know no boundaries."

"Look at her." Violent gestured to Olive. "She turned out perfect. Well, maybe a little uptight." She smiled at her still stunned daughter. "Don't you worry, baby, I've got some gummies that'll help that. We should give Amy some as well. She's so uptight, she probably squeaks when she walks."

"Do you mean *weed*?" Amy asked, sounding horrified. "You want to give your daughter *drugs*?"

"Wow." Violet looked at Ace. "Someone's forgetting how much she used to love her cute little roach clip—"

"Hey, we were in high school! Everyone smokes in high school, you jackass!" Amy yelled.

"That's it. Ace, where's my drink?"

"Right here." Amy took it from Ace and tossed it right in Violet's face.

"Oh my God, *Mom*!" Katie rushed to Violet. "Are you all right?"

"Of course, but thank you, honey, for asking." Violet licked her lips, then slid a look at Ace. "You're right, that's your best batch yet." And then she picked up the entire pitcher, still about three-quarters full, and dumped it over Amy's head.

"Enough." Noah waded in and grabbed his mom at the same time that Ace took hold of Violet, both women spitting mad.

"I can take her!" Violet yelled, trying to air swim to Amy, who was currently fighting Noah to get loose. "Mom, what the actual hell. *Stop.*"

Amy shoved free of him and yanked down her very wet sweater. "Don't mind us. That was a very long time coming."

And then, polite as one can be with hooch dripping off the end of her nose, she nodded to Ace, jabbed a finger at Violet, and strode off across the driveway with her shoes going *squish squish squish* with every step.

Katie looked at Olive and her whole family. "I'm so sorry."

"Not your fault," Ace said, and led a soggy Violet into Gram's house.

"What the hell just happened?" Olive asked, sounding boggled.

Noah shook his head. "I don't know—" But before he could finish his sentence, Olive, ignoring him completely, followed after her parents into Gram's house.

He turned to Katie, but she was gone too. So he crossed the driveway, bypassed the big house, and jogged up the steps to his mom's place above the garage.

She didn't answer the door, but he could hear the shower going, so he let himself in and waited. Clearly he was missing a whole big backstory here since he hadn't even realized his mom and Olive's had been in school together. He supposed that made sense, given that Gram was Olive's dad's mom, not Violet's mom. Violet hadn't grown up on this street, and by the time he, Katie, and Olive had become friends, Olive was already estranged from her parents. It hadn't even occurred to them that their moms knew each other previously.

But his mom should have told them. Or at least told Olive.

His mom appeared a few minutes later in a robe, a towel wrapped around her hair. She went straight to her little galley kitchen, opened her freezer, and took a long pull from the bottle of vodka she had in there.

"Day drinking now?" he asked.

"There's a first for everything." She turned to him. "And don't start."

"Oh, I'm going to start. What the hell was that?"

She shrugged.

"*Mom.*"

"You know what? Fine." She jabbed a finger at him. "But you go first. What's really going on between you and Olive?"

He crossed his arms over his chest.

She matched his stance.

He rolled his eyes.

"Yeah, that's what I thought," she said. "I knew there had to be a good reason you weren't trying to date any of the perfectly amazing women I threw at you. Look, work your life away, don't fall in love or give me grandchildren, whatever. But if you'll excuse me, I've got a family-sized bag of cheese puffs calling my name and I like my privacy after I've made a complete ass of myself."

He gaped at her. "No apology for never telling me about your and Violet's past? And what about Olive? You didn't think back when she first showed up in Sunrise Cove all those years ago that she might want to know the history between you and her mom before you took her under your wing?"

"I was afraid she wouldn't let me get close to her if she knew."

He was boggled. "That was her choice to make, and you took it from her by lying."

"Omitting," she said. "Big difference. And quite frankly, I'm shocked no one ever outed me before this. It might be the only secret Sunrise Cove never let loose of."

He shook his head. "Olive's not going to understand. And how could she?"

Her mouth tightened. "I'm not going to apologize to you for the hard mom choices I've had to make. In fact, the only person I owe an apology to is Olive."

"You're right," he said, and left, needing to get eyes on Olive and make sure she was all right.

When he crossed the driveway again, he found Gram alone, sitting outside sipping hot tea. She smiled sweetly at him. "Sorry, hon, but if you're here for Olive, she went out for a bit."

Sounded about right. "Do you know where I can find her?"

"I'm pretty sure she doesn't want to be found."

That tracked.

She eyed him with sympathy. "You look tired."

"Story of my life lately."

She nodded. "It's been a rough go. It must feel like a lot." She smiled warmly. "I guess it's a good thing that you need rain along with sunshine to grow." She got up. "Oh, and one more thing. You were always my favorite choice for a boyfriend for Olive, pretend or not." And with that, she went inside her house.

"Did everyone know?" he asked no one. Shaking his head, he unloaded the Razor, and then took off in his truck. Twenty minutes later, he was sitting next to Joe's hospital bed, each of them eating a Jell-O. His red, Joe's green. Proving his motor skills were coming back, Joe flicked Jell-O at Noah and got him right in the face, so all things considered, it was looking pretty good for the guy recovering from a TBI.

"What's going on with you?" Joe asked. "What don't I know?"

Noah concentrated on scraping out the last of his Jell-O. "You don't speak for two weeks and suddenly you're all curious about my life?"

Joe made a weird face and Noah realized he was trying to give an eye roll. "Don't hurt yourself."

"Dammit," Joe muttered. "They still won't roll. Come on, out with it. Talk to me. Why are you moping?"

"And now you want to talk about my *feelings*? You better check and make sure you still have your man card."

Joe pointed at him. "Toxic masculinity alert."

"Okay, that's it." Noah swiped the stack of women's magazines on Joe's side table into the trash.

"Hey, the nurse brought me those, and I wasn't finished reading about being seen." Joe pointed his spoon at Noah. "The moping. Explain."

"I *never* mope."

"B.S. You mope like a girl."

"I mope like a girl?" Noah asked with disbelief. "Now who's exhibiting their toxic masculinity?"

"You're right. I'll restate. You mope like a toddler. A *boy* toddler."

Noah rolled his eyes. "I'm trying to remember why I sat by your bed while you were taking a two-week nap, wishing you'd wake up and talk to me."

"Aw." Joe grinned. "You missed me."

"I did, but hell if I can remember why."

"Stop stalling." Joe gave him a get-on-with-it roll of his hand.

"Shit. Fine." Noah scrubbed a hand down his face. "I hate what happened to you." And just like that, his throat got tight. "I'm so sorry. I know those are just words, but—"

"Wait." Joe looked confused. "What the hell are you sorry for?"

"The accident. The whole you-almost-dying thing. What do you mean what am I sorry for?"

Joe blinked. "You realize it's called an accident because it's just that, an *accident*. No one ever sets out to purposely crash."

"I was driving. I'm responsible."

"Look," Joe said. "We both know how much you like to take the blame for everything. I don't know if it's because you always had to do that growing up, or—"

"That has nothing to do with—"

"Keep interrupting the recovering coma patient," Joe warned, "and I'll be happy to show you just how strong and recovered I am by kicking your ass."

Noah snorted.

"You know I can."

"I know no such thing," Noah said. "Especially if you're referring to our last time in the gym—"

"Where I knocked you on your ass."

"Only because you told me our boss had just walked into the gym, and when I turned to look, you sucker punched me. Now can we get back to discussing my feelings on your current situation?"

"You mean you want to whine some more about how bad you feel?" Joe shook his head. "Bite me."

Noah closed his eyes and shook his head. "Can we get serious?"

"Do we have to?"

"You didn't deserve this, Joe. No one deserves what happened to you—"

"Noah, from the bottom of my heart, I need you to do one thing for me."

"Anything."

"Good answer," Joe said. "What I need is for you to shut the fuck up. Because shit happens, all right? Shit happens all the damn time. You know this better than anyone. Let it go, man. Let it go before it eats you alive."

Noah swiped a hand down his face. "I'm trying."

"Try harder," Joe suggested.

"Oh, you're right. Up until now I've only been trying medium hard." Noah shook his head, disgusted with the both of them. "Listen, you have no idea what it was like. Katie was . . ." He shook his head. "Devastated. *Beyond* devastated. She managed to find a way to blame herself as well. Said you two had been in a big fight the night before and she couldn't handle knowing that you might not understand how much she loves you and needs you in her life."

Joe looked startled. "I know how much she loves me. How can she doubt it?"

Noah shrugged. "I've got no idea how the female brain works because I haven't been reading *Cosmo*."

"No shit you don't know how the female brain works."

"Hey."

"Tell me I'm wrong, I dare you," Joe said. "I mean, I get you not wanting to be tied down, but *everyone* deserves love and affection. Even your stubborn ass."

Katie and Joey appeared in the doorway. Katie eyed their faces curiously, clearly sensing something was off. "Bad timing?" she asked.

"Bad timing is your specialty," Noah muttered.

His sister put one hand over Joey's eyes and used her other to flip him off. "And your specialty is being clueless about women," she said.

"Is this about Olive?"

"Well, give the man an A. Maybe not all hope is lost for you after all." She turned to her husband and smiled sweetly. "Brought you lunch. Just don't tell your nurses because it's a burger and fries. And don't you dare share with this moron."

"I love you to the moon and back," Joe said fervently. "But . . . would you mind giving me and Noah thirty more seconds?"

"Of course, especially if you're going to give him shit."

"That's a bad word," Joey said.

"You're right, baby. I'm sorry. Let's go raid the vending machine."

"Yes!" Joey yelled.

When they were gone, Joe looked at Noah, his smile fading. "I've got one more thing to say to you, and I want you to turn on your ears this time, man. It's going to piss you off, which should help with that guilt problem you're having, but it's no less true for it."

Noah slid him a wary glance. "What?"

"Do you remember when you and Olive got in that ATV accident and the shit hit the fan in every single corner of your life?"

"Gee, not ringing a bell at all," Noah said dryly.

"Ha-ha. So you remember, then, that Olive was driving. Did you ever blame her for what happened?"

He'd walked right into that trap, hadn't he. "No." True story. He'd never blamed Olive for that night. He'd blamed himself, for all of it, for not making sure she had a better handle on the ATV, especially in that crazy storm, and for letting the incident blow up his entire life.

Joe lifted his hands in the universal sign for a touchdown.

Noah shook his head. "But—"

Joe pointed at him. "No. No *buts*. I have spoken. This is the way. I rest my case." His smile faded at the look on Noah's face. "What? What did I just say?" He blinked. "The Olive thing?"

Noah opened his mouth and then shut it.

"It is! It's about Olive." Joe gave him the gimme hands. "Tell me. No, wait, let me guess. You slept with her."

Noah dropped his head back against the chair and stared up at the ceiling.

"Holy shit, I was just kidding." Joe smiled. "I thought she'd rip your throat out if you even looked at her crooked. You slept with her? Are you two together now?"

Noah pressed the heels of his hands against his eyes. "Yes. No."

"Because . . . you're an idiot?"

Noah dropped his hands and stared at him. "Because I can't give her what she deserves."

"Right, Mr. Island of One."

"She's my sister's best friend," Noah said in his defense.

"And I, *your* best friend, wanted *your* sister. You didn't mind."

"Because you waited a few years to make your move. You waited until Katie was ready for the likes of you."

"You never gave Olive that chance."

Noah shook his head. "It's not about that. We grew up, we changed. Our lives are too different. There's nothing between her and me, and there won't ever be." With that, even knowing he was being a complete dick, Noah turned to the door to go and . . . froze.

Because there in the doorway stood Katie, Joey, and . . . Olive. Well, more accurately, Olive's back as she made tracks.

And this time he deserved it.

"Well," Joe said quietly into the silence. "You were clearly looking for a way to make her mad enough to walk away from you and you found it. Admit it, loving her is scarier to you than being first through the door, unarmed and without a vest, at a crack den."

"He won't admit a damn thing," Katie said. "Refer to my earlier comment about him being stupid and clueless."

Ignoring them both, Noah dropped his head for being cruel enough to hurt the best woman he'd ever known. He deserved what he'd get out of life—nothing. He cut his eyes to Joe, who actually managed to roll his eyes this time.

Right. No mercy for a fool.

CHAPTER 22

O live left the hospital, escaping to the lake. She took a walk along the water and just let herself be in the moment. Not thinking about the past or any regrets. Not thinking about the future, however murky it might be.

But eventually, she got tired of her own company and headed to Gram's house. Her parents were there. Her mom refused to discuss her and Amy's fight, saying only that it didn't involve Olive and she didn't want anything to affect her relationship with the Turner family.

Sweet, but misguided, though Olive agreed to shelve the discussion for the night. As for what her parents *would* discuss, they felt horrible for worrying her and had apologized profusely, and Olive was going to take that at face value and let it go.

She had bigger problems. Gram said Noah had come looking for her, but talking to him was the last thing she wanted to do. And since the first thing she did want to do—more of what they'd done in that bed in the yurt—was also the worst thing she could possibly do for herself, she decided to take her exhausted butt across the driveway to Katie's and upstairs to bed.

She'd just peeled out of her clothes and into pj's when she heard a soft knock. She opened right away, assuming it'd be Katie.

It wasn't.

Noah stood there, hands above his head braced on the jamb, face pensive. At the sight of her, his eyes warmed, heating in that way he had of melting her bones. She returned the look, putting every single feeling she had for him into it, and then . . .

Shut the door on his face, engaging the lock.

She'd thought for sure that getting the last word, even though she'd not uttered a single syllable, would've helped her sleep.

But it didn't, and during the long hours of the night she told herself it didn't matter. He'd done her a favor by being honest.

And maybe one day she'd even believe it.

THE NEXT MORNING, Olive's alarm went off, this time at oh dark thirty. Holmes didn't budge, but Pepper lifted her tiny, rumpled head and gave Olive a slit-eyed glare for daring to disturb her beauty sleep.

"Good thing you're cute," Olive muttered, and sighed. The sun wasn't even up yet. Somehow, she'd seen more sunrises since being here than she had in her entire life. Was she a morning person now? Was she suddenly going to start singing in the shower and be that crazy person who smiled at perfect strangers while in line at the coffee shop?

She'd probably have ignored the alarm, but she'd promised Amy a week ago that she'd make herself available today to help at the family shop's annual blow-out sale. It'd be all hands on deck, including a certain pair of hands that could make her body do just about anything they wanted.

"It's not going to be a problem," she said to her audience of two. Holmes and Pepper just looked at her.

She sighed. "You're right. It's going to be a problem."

Katie poked her head into the room. "You okay?"

"Of course," she lied, thankful that Katie could rarely pick out a lie. "My parents showed up, so everything's okay."

"And I'm glad about that," Katie said. "But actually, I was talking about whatever happened between you and my idiotic brother."

"Whatever did or didn't happen isn't going to happen again, so there's no need to discuss."

"Okay, then." Katie nodded, then paused. "But really, are you okay?"

"I will be." *Soon as today was over.* "Are you planning on staying late at the hospital tonight? I could get Joey bathed and in bed if you need. I'm also available to vacuum."

"That would be great, even if the first offer is only so you'll have a five-year-old buffer between you and Noah, and the second because vacuuming means you won't have to talk."

Olive winced. "Am I that transparent?"

"Yes, but I don't care. I've fired myself from cleaning the house. I didn't like my attitude and I got caught drinking on the job. It was Joey's leftover chocolate milk, but still. Plus, I'm still tired from yesterday's tired, and I've already used up tomorrow's tired. So yes, I'll take you up on your offer. Just don't you dare let my brother chase you out of here." She hesitated. "I realize that sounded bossy and demanding, and I'm supposed to be working on that, so I'll rephrase. Can you please make sure you don't let my brother chase you out of here?"

"I never let a man chase me anywhere."

Katie nodded. "Good." She looked at the time. "Gotta run."

And so did Olive if she wanted to avoid bumping into Noah before she had to see him at the shop. To that end, she took the shortest shower in the history of ever, quickly pulled on some clothes, and tiptoed downstairs.

Only, she forgot that Noah had ears like a bat.

She'd just reached for the front door handle when he said her name from behind her. Closing her eyes briefly, she turned to face him.

His mouth curved slightly. "Sneaking out?"

"No." She took in his wry expression and sighed. "Fine, yes, I'm sneaking out."

He drew a deep breath. "Two things. One, I'm sorry about my mom. For what it's worth, I didn't know any of our moms' history."

"Not your fault."

"Maybe not, but the hospital was. What I said . . . I'm sorry about that too. I'm not dealing with any of this well."

"Me either." She blew out a breath. "You're bad for my mental health."

He looked stricken at that and she shook her head. "No, sorry, that wasn't fair. You've never been anything but honest."

"I just don't want you to feel like you have to avoid me."

She got that, but being with him had been more than a physical act for her. Far more. It'd been . . . an emotional journey. All night she'd replayed the images of what they'd shared, the things they'd done to each other, her utter lack of inhibitions with him, the total abandon he'd drawn from her, and it'd all been so exquisite and erotic, she wanted to cry just thinking about never having it again.

But she *couldn't* have it again, or she'd lose herself in him. She wanted what she couldn't have, and trying to pretend otherwise was just lying to herself. "I won't need to avoid you forever," she said. "Just until you get old, grow a beer belly, and lose some of your teeth."

He looked pained.

"Get over it," she said on a mirthless laugh. "You know what you do to women. In high school, you used to run them into walls."

"I can think of a much more enjoyable reaction to elicit from a woman than running her into a wall."

"Yes, and it's forever etched in my memory what you are capable of doing to me without even trying."

"Right back at you." He stared at her for a beat. "And I don't care how old we get, I'm still going to want you."

Oh, damn, that was sweet, and she'd never been able to resist the rare Sweet Noah. She poked her head past him and peered up and down the hallway. No one. Good. Fisting her hands in his shirt, she backed herself to the front door and tugged Noah's head down to hers.

"Olive—"

"One last kiss," she murmured. "Just one. We clear?"

He looked into her eyes for a long beat, surprisingly solemn, before he nodded. "Crystal." Sliding one hand to her hip, the other flat on the door next to her head, he rubbed his jaw to hers like he was a big cat. A big, wild, feral cat. "One last kiss," he murmured roughly. "As long as you're okay with it."

If she was any more okay with it, her clothes would melt right off her body. In fact, her purse and keys had already fallen out of her hands, clattering to the floor.

Noah lowered his mouth to hers in a sweet, tender, loving kiss that short-circuited her central nervous system, and by the time he lifted his head, she was breathless. She knew she had working knees, but where had they gone? Plus, why had she said one last kiss? Why hadn't she said two? Or a hundred?

He bent and scooped up her things, handing them back to her. She stared at him. "Why do I let you do this to me?"

On an exhale, he drew her into his body, hugging her. "I could ask you the same question."

She took in the genuine emotion playing across his face and shook her head. "The way you look at me, how you touch me . . ." She stopped there because she wasn't sure what to say that hadn't already been said.

He looked away for a beat. "Sometimes I just need to look at you, touch you."

This caused a sharp internal lurch that twisted her stomach into a pretzel. She had to force herself to disengage from him. "I need coffee." She started to walk away, but his hands settled on her shoulders and caught her from walking the wrong way, turning her in the direction of the kitchen. Kissing the top of her head, he gave her a nudge.

Katie was at the table working on her laptop. Olive sighed. "I thought you'd left."

"And miss you and Noah trying to convince yourselves neither of you needs the other—with your tongues?" She got up, poured a cup of coffee, and handed it over.

Olive took it gratefully. "It's complicated." She studied Katie's screen. "Did you know you have fourteen thousand tabs open?"

"Don't touch them, they're my emotional support tabs. Just don't ask me which one the music's coming from." She paused. "So that was some kiss."

Olive choked on her coffee.

"Want me to hit him for you? It's the perfect scenario because he won't hit me back."

"I definitely don't want you to hit him, jeez."

Katie shrugged. "Let me know if you change your mind. I'll be at the shop in twenty."

"Me too. Gotta make a quick stop next door."

Outside, Olive sucked in some of the icy morning air, which would hopefully clear her head. When she headed across the driveway and knocked on the van, her mom slid open the van door wearing nothing but a smile. "Honey!"

"Mom!" She slapped her hands over her eyes. "*What are you doing?*"

"Went for a sky clad walk. I didn't used to have to get up so early to do it, but apparently this generation is a bunch of prudes. I didn't want to get arrested."

"You mean again. You don't want to get arrested *again*," her dad said mildly from behind her mom, thankfully *not* sky clad himself.

"That too." She smiled at Olive. "Since you don't want to relax with an edible, you should go walking with me tomorrow morning. It's freeing."

"Hard pass. Can you please put on some clothes?"

Her mom laughed, but tugged on a robe and belted it. "Tea?"

Olive looked at her warily.

"Just plain ol' tea, honey."

"No thanks, I've got this coffee. I only have a moment. I'm working at the shop's big sale today." Olive sat at the small but cozy table. "Did you know that no one's ever offered me drugs except you? I guess I've never looked cool enough."

Her mom looked surprised. "Are you sure? Because I think

you're the coolest person we've ever met." She looked to her husband, who nodded his agreement.

Olive snorted. "You're just trying to soften me up before we talk about the fight you had with Amy. Which, by the way, we're going to discuss, even though you refused last night."

"I'd much rather discuss the intensity I sensed between you and Noah," her mom said.

"Nice try. He's off the table."

"Well, so is my and Amy's past."

"Mom, you tossed a drink in her face."

"Trust me, she deserved it. End of story. Moving on."

Olive couldn't say she was surprised. Her mom could be a stone when she wanted to be. An unmovable stone. Olive sighed. It was possible she hadn't fallen far from the tree. "I told you this last night, but want to say it again. It's really good to see you."

Her mom covered her hand with her own. "I'm sorry we concerned you, but you should never be worried about us."

"You didn't pick up any of my calls. Of course I was worried."

"I got distracted," her mom said. "I've, um, sorta got a secret. I wasn't going to tell you until I got further in the process, but I can't keep it inside." She beamed. "This trip we took, it was for work. I was taking pictures for my book!"

Olive blinked. "Your book?"

"A coffee table book on cairns."

"I thought rock stacking was frowned upon now."

"Hence the book, in case the practice goes away entirely," her mom said. "I've got a publisher offer and everything, and only two months to put it all together, so I've been scrambling." She reached for Olive's hand and squeezed gently. "Honestly, we didn't try very hard to keep the phone operational. It was a beautiful detox situation, just immersing ourselves in nature.

You work too hard. You could really benefit from a nature immersion yourself."

Olive turned her hand over so she could entwine their fingers. "Going out into the remote wilderness and being completely disconnected is relaxing for *you*. For me, being in civilization and able to plug in and connect . . . *that's* how I relax."

Her mom gave a soft smile. "It's okay. We're different, I get that. It's so good to see you, Olive. Thanks for always being you."

"One of the true gifts I got from you," Olive said. "You always understood that I needed a different life. That you let me go live with Grandma all those years ago means everything."

Her mom looked surprised. "Well, of course. It wasn't easy to see you leave, but what *was* easy was wanting you to be happy."

"It wasn't easy to let me go?"

Her mom blinked, then set her tea down. "It was the hardest thing I've ever had to do. You didn't know that?"

Olive paused. "We don't often tell each other how much we care." *Or at all . . .*

"Oh, honey." She looked regretful. "People don't always say 'I love you.' More often, they *do* things that show it. Showing's always better than telling."

"Like letting your teenage daughter move away," Olive said softly, getting it.

Her mom nodded, and emotion clogged Olive's heart. "Thanks, Mom." She looked at the time and winced. "And I'm sorry, but I've got to go. It's going to be a madhouse at the semiannual sale."

Her mom pulled her in for a hard hug. "Love you."

Olive choked out a soggy laugh. "Love you too."

Her mom watched her move to the door. "Amy doesn't deserve you."

"She's always been good to me." Olive met her gaze, and at her mom's pensive look, stopped. "Maybe you should tell me why you two hate each other."

Her mom scoffed. "Like she hasn't already told you."

Olive shook her head. "She hasn't."

"Then you should ask her why I hate her."

Knowing it was a waste of breath to push, Olive started to go out, then stopped again. "Are you going to be gone when I get back?"

Her parents looked at each other. "We thought we'd stick around until you go back to London. That will probably be any minute now that Joe's awake, right?"

Right. She kept forgetting that she was free to go home. It was an unwelcome surprise to find she wasn't ready. "I don't know. Joe's still in the hospital and all . . ."

"Probably not for much longer," her mom said. "But if you're going to play it by ear, we can too."

CHAPTER 23

Twelve years ago

"You need to stop dwelling," Katie said, and plopped into the chair at Noah's hospital bedside.

Noah sent an incredulous look to his sister. "I've never dwelled a day in my life."

"Not true." Katie paused. "And I miss Olive too, you know. She came to see you before she left. You were out cold, she didn't want to wake you."

Her Dear John letter had been propped up next to a water bottle at his bedside, saying nothing more than she was sorry, she'd decided to take an internship and leave for New York early, and she hoped he could understand.

Basically, she'd left town like the last four years hadn't happened.

Katie offered him some water, but he shook his head and closed his eyes, not willing to admit he missed Olive too. "Dad's furious with me, any possible baseball career is over, and you want me to stop dwelling," he muttered. "It's not like I ran

myself over with that ATV, you know." This wasn't fair and he
knew it, but exhaustion and pain had worn him down.

"Well, who stands in front of an ATV?" Katie asked.

"The guy trying to clear the road for the ATV!"

"You're fast, you should've run. Remember that time you got
that home run in like five seconds? You couldn't do that when
your life was actually on the line?"

With a sigh, Noah reached for the pain meds pump and hit
the button like he was playing Whac-A-Mole . . .

Present day

When Olive got to the Turner Rents & Supply's semiannual
sale, it was organized mayhem. Amy and Noah were running
the front while Katie and Olive handled the customers.

They had ducklings, baby rabbits, supplies for everything
outdoors, equipment on deep discount, and also Holmes and
Pepper, because Joey had a meltdown about leaving his "brother
and sister" home alone.

On top of all that, they also had a crowd.

Olive honestly had expected to hate every second of it, but
being outside in the early-spring sun, helping kids hold the
ducklings and rabbits, while not a single person mentioned how
she'd once run over the town hero, did her a world of good.

"Hard to hold on to negative emotions while holding a fuzzy
little baby, isn't it?" Katie asked, having come up to her side.

"I'm not holding on to negative emotions."

Katie snorted, and as she walked off, tossed back, "I might
not be great at reading people, but your shoulders are at your
ears."

"I don't know what you're talking about," Olive said to no one, but she consciously lowered her shoulders.

"Olive?" This from a woman around her age with two little girls, clearly twins, in her arms, each with a candy bar in their hands, the chocolate mostly melted and all over them. "Olive Porter, is that you?"

She smiled politely. "Can I help you?"

"It's Holly McNeers," the woman said. "From school? I'm Holly Freestead now."

Right. Holly had been . . . well, obnoxiously perfect. One of the most popular girls in her grade, she'd also been class president and homecoming queen, among other things—such as someone who'd been rumored to have gone out with Noah a few times. "Gone out with" being a euphemism, of course, for what Olive had hoped to do with him that long ago night at the party.

Holly hoisted her little girls further up on her hips. "I heard you and Noah are a thing now."

In Olive's mind, she was cool, calm, and collected. In reality, all systems were down. "You heard wrong."

Holly arched a single brow. Damn, Olive really wished she could do that. "Is there something I can help you with?"

"Yes, actually," Holly said. "Or so I hope. I've got a candle shop. It's very popular." Then she lowered her voice and leaned in. "That's a lie. I hear you're the best PR person on the planet. What you're doing for the zoo is just . . . incredible. I need to hire you."

"You . . . want to hire me?"

"Here, hold this." Holly thrust her two chocolate mongers—er, children—into Olive's arms and then proceeded to search her purse while the twins stared at Olive.

Olive stared back.

"I like your hair," one of them said, and then touched it with her chocolate fingers.

"I like your clothes," the other said, and touched Olive's top.

It didn't matter since she already had dirt streaked across her front and a questionable stain on her jeans from where she'd been loving up on a sweet black Lab puppy earlier. "And I like the chocolate perfume you're wearing."

The girls giggled.

Holly finally found her phone and asked for Olive's contact info. "So we can get together soon and discuss?"

Olive nodded. "Sure."

Holly took back her girls, who waved, and then they were gone.

"Fraternizing with the enemy?" Katie asked, coming back to Olive's side.

"You vanished on purpose."

"Of course I did." Looking entirely unrepentant, Katie moved on. "What did she want?"

"I should refuse to tell you."

"But you won't."

Olive rolled her eyes, even if she was right. "She wanted to talk about my handling some PR for her candle shop. Weird, right?"

"Maybe not. I actually think she grew up." Katie looked at Holly's retreating back. "A few years ago, she apologized to me for being so awful in high school."

"Wow. Did you do that thing you do, where you pretended to be deaf so you didn't have to talk to her?"

"Nope. I let her take me out to lunch."

Olive raised both brows. "So who's fraternizing with the enemy now?"

Katie shrugged. "You're the only friend I've ever needed, but you haven't been around."

That sucked up Olive's good humor in a blink and she opened her mouth to apologize, but Katie shook her head. "It's okay. I understood why you left and stayed gone."

"Do you think you can explain it to me?"

Katie's lips curved.

"I'm actually being serious."

"You know why," Katie said. "Because of your erratic up-bringing and a few assholes you gave your heart to, you don't trust love."

Olive stilled. Was that it? Four simple words to explain why she felt so messed up all the time? It couldn't be that simple, could it?

"And you still don't," Katie said. "Because if you did, you and Noah would be doing more than having a secret thing that you're both pretending you're not having."

"Noah and I are not having a thing, secret or otherwise. I mean . . . I thought we were, but it turns out we're not, so . . ."

"I didn't mean to upset you."

"You didn't. Really," she said at Katie's doubt. "I just never . . ."

"Knew that you avoided love?" Her best friend and sister of her heart nodded. "We know."

Oh dear God. "*We?*"

Katie grimaced and started to walk off. "I think my mom's calling me."

"Coward."

Katie waved without looking back. "Sticks and stones!"

Olive sighed and looked around to see where she was needed.

"Excuse me," a male voice said, catching her attention. He was midthirties, good-looking, with a smile that turned him from pleasant to handsome.

"You're Olive Porter," he said. "You and Noah—"

"We're not a thing, secret or otherwise!"

The man looked startled. "Okay . . . but that's not what I was going to say."

"Fine. Yes, I ran him over. *One time!*"

The man blinked. "Maybe I should start over. I'm Scott El-lison. I own a local café, the one on Lake Drive? We're looking for a PR person and Noah highly recommended you."

"Oh. Sorry," she said, feeling ridiculous. But also . . . Noah had recommended her? "You're the place that makes the crack fries, right?"

"Crack fries?"

Batting a thousand . . . "As in they're addicting."

He laughed. "Yeah, that's us. Maybe I should put that in the advertising—come for the crack fries, stay for the burgers." He grinned. "Do you think we could set a meeting?"

"Of course."

They exchanged contact information, and when he walked off, she found herself smiling. Feeling pretty good about herself for a change, she turned and plowed into a brick wall named Noah.

His hands came up to absorb the impact, keeping her upright when she would've bounced off him and hit the ground. "Sorry," she gasped.

"No problem." He flashed a wry smile. "Other than the ear-lier kiss, this was the best two seconds of my day so far."

She'd seen him working on some equipment, wielding tools with an expertise that had really done it for her. What was it about a guy who could work with his hands? And why couldn't he be bad at something? "That rough?"

"Just busy." He looked around. "I think the entire town is here."

"It's the ducklings. They're a big draw."

"That's not what's drawing me," he murmured.

Nope, don't buy into it, her brain tried to remind her body, but her body wasn't having it. She made the mistake of looking up into his warm golden-brown eyes and lost her breath. Then there was the fact that she was still plastered up against him. "Noah—"

"Not here." He took her hand and started walking with her in tow.

She didn't ask him where they were going. At the moment she didn't care. All she could think about was how his warm, slightly roughened hand felt in hers, how his ass looked in those jeans, how his back seemed so strong and sinewy beneath his T-shirt, and how fast could she get his mouth on hers. Clearly, she'd lost her mind.

He pulled her into the empty office and turned to her. She'd been about to say something to him out there, she was sure of it, but hell if she could remember what.

"Olive?"

"Yes?"

"You're . . . staring at my mouth."

She scowled. "Ignore me."

"I've never once been able to do that, and believe me, I've tried." Stepping into her space bubble, he lowered his head. "Maybe we should try again to have that one last kiss."

Excellent idea, because with his mouth on hers, she couldn't say anything stupid, right? "Yes."

She hadn't even gotten the single-syllable word out before his lips were warm on hers, causing her brain to cease working and the floor to fall out from beneath her feet. Someone moaned. She was pretty sure it was her as she pressed even closer to his big and very hard body—

"Mommy, look! They're kissing again!"

At the sound of Joey's voice, Olive nearly jumped out of her skin.

Noah didn't jump. In fact, he took his damn time pulling back, slow to let his hands drop from where he'd been holding her close, one at the small of her back, the other threaded in her hair.

Joey stood very close at their side, head tipped back to see them, wearing a chocolate mustache and beard. His "siblings" were sitting like sentinels, dog and kitten on either side of him. "Hi!"

"Hi." Noah ruffled his hair. "Did anyone ever tell you that the chocolate is supposed to go in your mouth?"

Joey grinned. "Want some?" He held out his fisted hand, opening it to reveal a semisquished, mostly melted small candy bar.

"Sweet offer," Noah said. "But pass."

Joey looked at Olive.

"No, thank you," she said, her eyes meeting those of Katie, who stood in the doorway, brows arched.

"Can I play Candy Crush on your phone?" Joey asked Olive.

She'd taught him how to play one day in the hospital when he'd been bored. She swiped her phone screen, opened the app, and then handed her phone over. "Good luck, little man. I kicked some serious booty on my last round, so you've got a lot to live up to."

He grinned and sat on the floor to concentrate on the phone. Holmes sat with him. Pepper was very busy attacking Noah's bootlaces.

Noah scooped the kitten up by the scruff of her neck, just like her mama would've done. But since she appeared to think that Holmes and Noah were her mommies, she merely starting purring, switching her tactics from beating up his bootlaces to batting at his nose.

Noah chuckled, then carried her over to Holmes. "Keep your baby in line."

Holmes licked Pepper from chin to forehead, and Pepper snuggled in, her eyes closing in bliss.

Katie was tapping her foot on the floor impatiently as she stared down her brother and Olive. "Tell me you two still aren't a thing. Go ahead, I dare you."

"We're not," Olive said.

Katie arched a brow and said, "No? Because from where I was standing . . ." She crouched and covered Joey's ears. "You were attempting to climb into each other's bodies. If you'd stop trying to keep this a secret, you two could kiss wherever the heck you wanted, you know that, right?"

Olive rolled her eyes and went over to a tall filing cabinet. "I don't know about Noah, but I came in here looking for something."

"Like what?" Katie said.

Olive opened a drawer and had to wave her hand at the dust bunnies that arose in the air. She coughed, and then stilled, because in the drawer was a framed collage of old pictures. Pulling it out, she stared at the pics of Amy and Violet as teenagers, arms around each other, grinning.

"What's wrong?" Katie asked, and came closer, peering over Olive's shoulder. "Huh."

Noah pushed off the wall to take a look just as Amy came into the room. She took in their faces. "What?"

Katie handed her the frame. "After your fight with Violet the other night, I assumed you two had always hated each other."

Amy took in the pictures, then quietly set the frame back in the drawer and slid it closed. She turned to Olive. "I'm sorry. I owed you the whole story the other night, but I wasn't ready to face it." She paused, looking worried, regretful, and . . . guilty? "Once upon a time, Vi and I . . . well, we were best friends."

"I don't get it," Olive said. "All that time I lived next door to you, when you treated me like one of your own, when you knew I was having a hard time with my parents, you never said anything, not about you two hating each other, and certainly not about being best friends before that. You never even let on that you really even knew her."

"I know." Amy drew a deep breath, shuddered it out. "I always thought she'd rat me out, but she never did. I was so relieved that I just kept telling myself no one needed to know. But I was wrong." She paused. "We met in middle school and became instant best friends. It lasted until our freshman year, when we had a falling out and never made up, and . . ." She hesitated. "I'm ashamed of this, I really am. But your mom, she was . . . different. She marched to her own beat, didn't care what anyone thought."

"Like me and Olive," Katie said softly.

Amy's eyes had gone suspiciously shiny, but she nodded. "Yes. And all I wanted was to be normal. So when the popular kids started talking to me and inviting me to hang out with them, I was thrilled. But then they made it clear I couldn't bring Vi with me into the fold." Her mouth tightened. "So I started being mean to her. I was . . . awful," she whispered. "It took her a while, because she was that kind of a person, she didn't want to give up on me."

"But she did?" Katie asked, sounding angry, *very* angry.

"She didn't want to, and it took her a long time, but yes, she did finally give up. We stopped communicating. We graduated and life went on, and then, all those years later, when Olive came to live with her grandma . . ." She looked at Olive again. "I loved you right from the start. I thought maybe I could make amends by taking care of you."

"Mom"—Noah shook his head—"you know that's not how it works."

"Not to mention," Katie said, "all those times you told me that being normal was overrated, that I was special and people would realize they were wrong for how they treated me—when all along, *you* were those people! You were the mean girl!"

"Yes." Amy looked tortured. "And I'm sorry. All I can say is that I was a different person back then, and one I'm not proud of. For what it's worth, I told your mom this too. Just this morning, right before I came in here, in fact."

Noah turned to Olive and asked softly, "You okay?"

"It was a long time ago." She looked at Amy. "Whatever went on between you and my mom is in the past, I consider it none of my business. I know you only as a warm, compassionate, loving mother. You took me in and treated me like one of your own. You didn't have to do that, but you did."

Amy's eyes filled as she hugged Olive to her. "Thank you," she whispered.

Katie was shifting on her feet, something she did when anxious or faced with too many emotions.

"Katie needs a subject change," Olive said.

"No, that's not it." She closed her eyes and scrunched up her face, then opened them and looked at Olive. "I need to say something too."

Olive's heart knocked around in her chest. "Do I want to hear it?"

"I think so." Katie bit her lower lip, then finally said, "I'm sorry I never say the words, but I feel it. I do. I love you."

"Aw," Olive teased around a throat thick with sudden tears. "Did that hurt?"

Katie dropped her head and laughed before meeting Olive's gaze again. "Only minimally. I'm sorry I never say it when you need to hear it."

"Don't be. You're just better at show than tell. And also, I love you too."

Katie smiled. "To the moon and back, right?"

"To the moon and back."

Amy was watching, swiping at her tears. "Are we all okay?" she asked quietly. "Did we get out everything that we need to in order to move on?"

The last thing Olive wanted to do was cause a rift over something that belonged in the past. "We're okay, even if I'm sure we all still have our own secrets."

Amy swallowed hard, since obviously she still had a secret from her kids, a big one—that her husband had extracted a promise from Olive to leave and not look back.

Not that Olive would judge. She had a secret too. Hers being, of course, that despite her efforts to the contrary, she was still in love with Noah—something she had no intention of sharing with anyone. Ever. "We should probably get back out there—"

"Wait." Amy swallowed hard. "I'm . . . not done confessing."

Olive turned back, already shaking her head. "Amy, don't. It's not worth it."

Both Katie and Noah looked confused.

"What's not worth it?" Noah asked, moving closer to Olive.

Amy never took her gaze off Olive. "You love my son, right?"

Everyone's head swiveled to Olive, whose heart had just stopped.

"Mom," Katie said, sounding horrified. "You can't put her on the spot like that. If you're going to do it to anyone, do it to Noah."

"It's okay," Olive said, because she didn't see a reason to hide anymore. She let out a breath and met Noah's gaze. "Yes," she said quietly. "Yes, I love your son."

Noah didn't often broadcast his feelings, preferring to show the world a strong, impenetrable front. But it was gone now.

"She always has," Amy told Noah. "It's the reason she never explained why she left all those years ago. Because when you love someone, you protect them. And she most definitely was protecting you."

Noah shook his head, not taking his gaze off Olive. "Protecting me from what?"

It was Amy who spoke. "The night of the ATV accident, your dad asked Olive to leave. Said you would need time and space to heal, and it would be best for you if you did that without distractions. Otherwise, Olive never would've left Sunrise Cove and all the people she felt so safe with."

Noah's eyes narrowed on his mom. "Are you kidding me?"

Amy's eyes went shiny with more tears. "I'm sorry I didn't tell you sooner. I didn't know either, at first. But shortly before he passed, he told me. And then he was gone, and I didn't want one more thing to taint your memories of him."

He stared at her. "You should've told me anyway."

Olive was caught by surprise when she felt Noah's hand slide to the small of her back, gently nudging her around to face him.

"This is why you left? Why you stayed gone?"

Not seeing any reason to hide it anymore, she nodded.

"Olive," he said softly, his voice filled with aching emotion.

Only five minutes ago, she'd have welcomed that tone from him, but something inside her couldn't take it. She didn't want him this way, not because of a secret from the past when they'd been young and stupid, a secret that no longer mattered.

Okay, she'd been the only stupid one, but still. "Don't be mad."

He looked horrified. "I'm not. At least not at you."

"Why?" she asked, throat raw. "If not when I was eighteen, then certainly in the years after I should've realized that my staying gone hurt you. So if you're not mad at me, don't be mad at your parents either." Unable to keep the tears from her voice, she went on anyway. "Your dad did what he thought he had to do to protect what he saw as your future, and right or wrong, he saw that future as baseball, not me."

"My parents were authority figures to you," he said, shooting his mom a long look that, to her credit, she winced at, but she didn't try to defend herself. "My dad never should've put you in the position that he did, or at the very least in the following years, he should've taken it back. My mom should've done the same, if not when he told her, then certainly after he died."

"They did me a favor," Olive insisted. "I didn't realize it until after I'd left, but it forced me to go out and find a life for myself. And I did, a good one." She gave a smile that hopefully signaled she was fine despite the quiver in her voice. She definitely needed a moment in private, maybe two . . . So when Noah reached for her, she took a step back. If she let him touch her right now, she'd fall apart. And she was barely loosely put together to begin with. "I'll be back, okay?" Then, before he, or anyone, could stop her, she left.

CHAPTER 24

In Olive's wake, Noah turned to his mom and sister.

"Go," they said in unison.

He strode to the door, stopping at a tug on the hem of his shirt.

Joey looked worried. "Does Olive have an owie?"

Noah crouched down. "Yeah, little man, she does."

"Is it your fault?"

"Yes." No, he hadn't known what his dad had done, but he'd let ego and pride keep him from making contact after she'd left, hell, even after he'd left. He'd just . . . let her go. And now she was out there trying to process everything on her own because he hadn't made himself emotionally available to her.

"You haz to say you're sorry," Joey said solemnly. "Daddy says you can't hurt people, especially the ones you love. And you love Auntie Olive, right?"

"I do," Noah said softly.

"Then she'll forgive you," Joey said earnestly. "She's nice like that."

Noah hugged the kid, who was smarter than he was.

"You need help?" Joey asked.

"I think this is something I have to do myself, but I appreciate the offer."

Joey nodded sagely.

Noah ran through the shop. Or tried. He was stopped no fewer than five times. By the time he got to the parking lot, there was no sign of Olive or the Mini. He was already calling her as he got into his truck.

Joey answered. "Hi!"

Shit. Olive hadn't gotten her phone back from Joey when he'd taken it to play a game. "Hi, bud. Take good care of this phone, all right?"

"I will! Bye!"

Noah didn't find Olive at Katie's house. But her mom was standing on Gram's porch watching him. "Problem?" she called out.

"Have you seen Olive?"

"No." She raised a brow. "You look panicked. Is something wrong?"

Noah was known for having a resting hard face, for being able to hide all emotions and personal feelings. He wasn't known for looking panicked. He opened his mouth to calmly assure Olive's mom that everything was fine, so it shocked the hell out of him when instead he said, "I screwed up."

Violet nodded. "Well, admitting it is half the battle." Her smile was wry. "I should know. I've done it often enough."

"Do you have any idea where Olive would've gone?"

"No, but what I do know is that you won't find her, not until she's good and ready. I'm sorry, I know that's not much help, but while you're waiting her out, maybe you should decide if you're in or out."

"In or out of what?"

She gave him an eye roll. "Her life. Look, she's had a lot of people be drive-bys, myself included. If you're in, be smarter than me and let her know." And with that, she turned and walked inside the house.

Noah was still standing there when Katie pulled up with his mom and Joey in tow.

"We shut down for the day," his mom said. "I couldn't concentrate."

Katie looked at Joey. "Why don't you go play in the sandbox for a few?"

Joey whooped and ran across the grass to his sandbox.

Noah's mom turned to Noah. "I should've told you everything a long time ago."

"I wish you had."

She squeezed his arm. "I know, me too. I was so afraid if you knew, you'd leave Sunrise Cove soon as you could, but that's no excuse." Her face crumpled. "But then you left anyway. And you so rarely came home, I was afraid to chase you away for good. And then when Olive showed up to help Katie and I saw how much she still cares about you . . ." Her eyes filled. "And how much you still care about her . . . I knew just how bad it would be if it all came out."

Noah drew a deep breath, not willing to be moved by her tears. "Why did Dad do it?"

She sniffed and blew her nose. "He thought he was protecting you. It was the night of the accident, and he was scared and worried. We all were."

Noah shook his head. "But he had no right to blame what happened on Olive before he even knew the story."

"I know," she said. "But you have to understand what it was like that night for the people who loved you. Your dad . . . he was so very proud of you, of the scholarship you'd gotten, of your bright future in baseball, and all he could see was how it'd been taken away—"

"No," Noah said. "I'm having a hard time believing he was acting in my best interests, especially knowing what I know now."

"Was he a hard man? Yes. And also not great at talking about his feelings—"

Noah snorted.

"But son . . ." She moved closer, waiting until he looked at her. "It's not too late for you."

"What does that mean?"

"She means you're shit at talking about your feelings as well," Katie said. "And yeah, I know. Pot, kettle. Only *I* managed to break the emotionally bankrupt mold and not only fall in love, but also admit it out loud." She softened her voice. "It's never too late, Noah."

Wasn't it? He'd sent mixed signals to Olive, and that was the result of his own deep-seated and misguided fears. In spite of the confidence and strength he projected to the world, on the inside, he was still that kid who'd pretended to be perfect to keep his family whole. To this day he wasn't sure he'd ever been loved for who he really was, on the inside—a deeply flawed human being just doing the best he could.

No, that was a lie. Olive loved him. She hadn't said the words until today, but she'd never needed to. He'd known, he'd always known. It was his very own miracle. And what had he done?

Push it away.

Push her away.

"What can I do?" his mom asked quietly.

He closed his eyes, reliving the past, and all the things he'd ever said and done to show Olive she could no longer reach his heart because of how she'd left—when leaving hadn't even been her choice.

Not to mention, he'd left too.

He'd been trained for many years not to overreact, not to judge. Taught to look past what the surface story told him. And yet he'd done the opposite of all that where Olive was concerned. "This isn't all on you, Mom. I hold plenty of the blame. I'm going to go look for her."

Which he did. After a few hours, he had to admit that her mom had been right—until she wanted to be found, he'd have to do what he hadn't done before.

Trust her to come back.

He ended up at the hospital to see Joe. He found him in PT. He'd been moved to the rehab wing of the hospital, with the plan to come home within a week if all continued to go well. It was stunning how much he improved every day.

Noah had never been so grateful for anything in his entire life.

He kept Joe company through a brutal PT session, working on his own PT for his leg while he did. When he saw Joe faltering through a set of leg presses, he casually said, "Joey could do better."

Joe gave him the bird, but indeed pushed harder.

Joe's physical therapist, Kenny, an ex–football pro, laughed. "I should get every patient to bring in their best friend."

Joe gave Kenny the bird too. Probably because he was too winded to talk. Noah, doing leg presses, could understand. Pain and muscle fatigue had his bad leg shaking like a leaf.

"Push harder," his smart-ass BFF said.

Noah returned Joe's earlier gesture and flipped him off. Joe gave a breathless laugh, and damn, Noah nearly cried like a baby at the sound.

Joe waited until Noah had started another leg exercise before casually saying, "I know we've already talked about this, but I've got an update. A little birdie told me you and Olive are going to keep doing the deed. Or whatever the kids are calling it these days."

Noah's legs slipped right off the machine, which both Joe and Kenny thought was hilarious. "You heard wrong," he said grimly.

"So . . . you didn't come home from the overnight at the yurt glowing like a virgin after his first time?"

Noah was great at lying. It was a skill he'd acquired at work talking to asshole criminals.

We'll make sure you get bailed out right away if you come quietly.

Yes, I totally believe you're innocent even though the shit you stole is right there in your truck for all of us to see. Absolutely, I believe it landed there magically.

Only, he'd never developed the ability to lie right to the face of someone he cared about. But evading and misdirecting? Yeah, he had that down. "Amazing what being off work can do for a guy's complexion."

"Yeah," Joe said dryly. "My three-week stay at the spa has done wonders." He looked at Kenny. "This guy had a shot at the second most amazing girl on the planet when we were in high school—I married the first most amazing girl—and he blew it big time."

Kenny shook his head. "Man, every guy's stupid in high school. I let The One walk away *twice*. Took me five years to get my head out of my ass and beg her forgiveness."

"And did she? Forgive you?" Joe asked.

Kenny waved his left hand, the one with the wedding band. "Best decision I ever made."

"Me too," Joe said smugly.

They both looked at Noah with pity.

"Hey," he said. "I'm glad for you guys, I really am. And I like the idea of the institution of marriage. It's just never been for me."

Joe looked at Kenny. "He's got daddy issues. Thinks he needs freedom from family and ties and roots. Including the woman he loves."

"But family and ties and roots are the very things that make life worth living," Kenny said.

They both nodded self-righteously.

"Look," Noah said. "I care for Olive. Deeply." So fucking much he ached with it. "But we're different, okay? We want different things. I'm happy both working and living in the wilderness, and she's a big-city girl now, by choice. I can't ask her to give that up."

"He's a little bit country, I'm a little rock 'n' roll," Kenny sang, deeply off-key.

Noah rolled his eyes, put on his headphones, and got on the treadmill to run. Okay, so it was more a fast walk since running still hurt like a bitch. But it was a lot easier than figuring out what he wanted to say to Olive. When they'd been fake dating, deep down he'd known there'd been nothing fake about his feelings for her. Even though he hadn't had the words back then for what he'd felt, he knew it'd been the first time he'd ever loved someone.

Since then, he'd thought he'd been in love several times, but when those relationships had run their course, he knew he'd been mistaken. No one in his life had ever gotten him the way Olive did, which scared the shit out of him.

But maybe on top of that fear sat something else. The knowledge that he wanted to be done turning his back on something that felt so right. Looking up, he realized he'd gone four miles. Kenny was on to his next client. Joe was sitting on a bench watching Noah with a worried look on his face.

"Shit, I'm sorry. Why didn't you wave or yell at me that you were done?"

"I did both," Joe said. "You were somewhere far, far away."

Noah got off the treadmill and mopped up his face with a towel before sucking down the rest of his water.

"Deep thoughts?" Joe asked.

Noah shrugged.

"So . . . yes."

"Fine, yes." Noah tossed his towel aside. "And you're right. I don't want to lose Olive, even though I know she deserves someone far better than me."

"What are you talking about? You're the best man I know."

"I can't give her what she needs."

"And what is it you think she needs that you can't give?" Joe asked in a tone that made it clear he thought he was talking to an idiot.

"Oh, I don't know . . . stability, security, a guy who comes home at a decent hour every night, not to mention one who can open his heart?"

"Has she asked you for any of those things?"

When Noah scowled, Joe shook his head. "You ever think that what she deserves is you, as is?" He smiled. "That's good, right? I got it from one of those morning talk shows."

"Shit. We gotta get you out of this place."

"That's all I'm saying." Joe's smile slowly faded. "Look, no one's saying you have to jump right into marriage or anything. Just take it slow, go at the pace that's right for you. It's not like you have to label your relationship right now." Joe winced. "Sorry, I shouldn't have said the R-word."

"I'm not that afraid of the word."

Joe tried to raise a brow and failed, making Noah find a laugh. He stood up and headed out.

"You going to go see her, right?" Joe asked his back. "Tell her hi for me! Tell her she's welcome for all the good advice I gave you!"

CHAPTER 25

Olive spent a few hours thinking too hard as she took a drive down memory lane, going to all her favorite places around the lake. At the first place, she and Katie had hiked up to a bluff and jumped off into the lake, screaming in terror because it was so much higher than they'd anticipated. The thrift shop where she, Katie, Joe, and Noah had made each other buy crazy clothing and then strode into their favorite burger joint like they were dressed for prom. The beach where she'd sat and watched Noah and Joe and a whole bunch of other guys in one of their dads' boats, taking turns wakeboarding. Her favorite pizza parlor, where she and Katie had put quarters into a vending machine, winning each other fake rings they pretended had been given to them by their boyfriends . . .

Eventually, when it got dark, she got tired. Gone were the days when she could stay up all night reading or hanging out with Katie. Which meant it was official, she was old.

Finally, she ended up back in Sunrise Cove. Not ready to face anyone at Katie's house, she went to Gram's. Her parents were out somewhere taking pics. Gram had bunko night going in the kitchen, so Olive made herself scarce by going up to the attic to see if any of her old stuff was still around.

When she climbed the ladder and crawled through the trap door, she froze, stunned. Apparently, she wasn't done taking that trip down memory lane. Not a single thing had changed in all the years she'd been gone. Well, except for a fairly thick layer of dust. She'd lived in a small bedroom downstairs, but the attic had been her haven. When things had been tough for her at school, Gram had helped her turn the attic into a secret getaway, including a full-size, four-poster bed complete with mosquito netting that Olive had thought made it look like a princess's bed. There was a chest at the foot of the bed, still filled with her stuff: books, teen magazines, a few photo albums, and some bedding for the nights her teenage self had slept up here pretending the rest of the world didn't exist.

Daylight was long gone, and there was no electricity in the attic, so she hiked down two flights of stairs and gathered some cleaning supplies, along with a battery lantern.

And then she got to work.

It took several hours, but the attic no longer had an inch of dust or cobwebs anywhere. She really hoped any spiders watching her had gotten the message and taken off for greener pastures.

Tired, but her mind clearer than it had been, she sat in the window alcove. Staring out at a glorious moon playing peekaboo in and out of the streaky clouds floating across the dark sky, she tried to access where her mind was at.

She wasn't mad at anyone. She knew that much. Well, maybe at herself for holding on to the past. She was still watching the night go by when she saw Noah pull into the driveway. She closed her eyes, but when she heard the knock at the front door two flights down, she didn't have to guess who it was.

Then she heard the front door open and shut. Dammit, Gram. She eyeballed the megaglass of wine she'd poured herself after finishing cleaning, tempted to down the whole thing. But chances were good she'd need all her facilities operating at one hundred percent.

Voices drifted up the stairs, and she knew Gram had pointed Noah in her direction.

And sure enough, thirty seconds later, his head appeared in the trap door. Noah glanced around the room, then climbed through before crossing the room to the window seat.

When she looked up at him, he handed over the phone she'd left with Joey, then came to her side, his gaze searching hers. Since she was pretty sure he could see all the way to her soul when he looked at her like that, she closed her eyes.

"I'm proud of you," he said quietly. "Of how you always stay true to yourself. I don't think I've ever told you that, but I should have."

The words a surprising balm on her heart, she opened her eyes.

His were full of more emotion than she'd ever seen from him, with concern and worry and affection leading the pack. "I'm sorry about my parents—"

She put her fingers over his lips. "Not your fault." She handed him her glass. He took a sip and handed it back to her, watching her closely.

"I don't want to talk about it," she said. "It's in the past, where we're leaving all our other crap."

"You asked me for space," he said quietly. "Would you like for me to leave?"

What she wanted was to feel something, anything that would remind her that she wasn't alone, that her life mattered, that *she* mattered. "I'd rather you stay." Setting the wine down, she stood, gesturing with a head tilt for him to come with. She stopped in front of the girlish bed that was barely big enough for one person and looked up at Noah. "Do you want me?"

"Always."

She melted a little bit at that and stepped to him, fisting one hand in his shirt, sliding her other into his hair, pulling him down for a kiss. He let her have her way with him, then lifted his head. "There are people in the house."

She bit her lower lip. "You mean because I might make noise?"

"*Might?*"

"I can't help it!"

His smile was soft, affectionate. "I know. I love it." He kissed her this time, and when they finally came up for air, she took a step back. She relieved herself of her top, then started working on her jeans, which, damn, were a little snug. She blamed the pizza. Catching a foot, she nearly went down. That she blamed on the wine.

Luckily, Noah caught her, and she gave a breathless laugh. "I should definitely cross erotic dancing off my list of future job possibilities."

He didn't smile. Instead his eyes blazed with heat and hunger as he took her in standing there in just a bra and undies. Backing away from her, he closed the trap door, then dragged the chest in front of it.

Then he came close again and she gestured to his fully clothed body. "You're behind."

His smile was pure bad boy.

Her knees wobbled, but she held her ground, crossing her arms, waiting for him to strip. She wasn't the only one who had armor, and she wanted him to reveal himself to her.

He reached over his shoulder, fisted his hand in the material, and pulled his shirt off. If she did that her hair would look like a squirrel's tail—and dear God, why did he always smell so good?

Without another word, they took turns. Her bra, his boots and socks, her bikini panties . . . Then he met her gaze as he reached for the button and zipper on his jeans, undoing both torturously slow, making her practically pant with anticipation.

When he was finally free of his clothes, he stalked to her, sliding a hand into her hair, tugging her head back so he could drag hot kisses down her exposed neck while the fingers of his other hand splayed wide against her rib cage. Her eyes closed as he brushed his lips almost questioningly over the pulse racing at the base of her throat before lifting his head. "Yes?" he murmured.

That he would still ask for permission would've melted her into a puddle of desire if she hadn't already been there. He had a hand tangled in her hair, his lips inches from hers, unmoving. Waiting patiently. His eyes were sheer erotic hunger, and she knew what came next would be all-consuming, blazing hot, and, best yet, would drive all the negative thoughts and worries from her brain. "Yes," she breathed.

And then they both sort of lunged into each other at the same time. They'd shared a lot of kisses, but none had been anything like this. Somehow he put everything he had, every part of him, into that kiss, showing her more of himself than in all the years they'd known each other. The real him, the one that so far had always been safely kept guarded by his inner brick walls. She'd knocked some of them down, but she'd been so sure she would never get through all of them.

Until now.

She had no idea what had changed for him, and it didn't matter. Reciprocating his surprising openness, she in turn let him see into the darkest corners of her soul, let him feel the deepest emotion in her heart.

Lifting his head, he looked at her, *really* looked at her, and then smiled. "You know you've got all the power here."

She smiled, and he laughed, which always did something to her, healing something deep inside of her that she hadn't even realized she was holding on to.

Picking her up, he tossed her onto the bed, and then followed her down.

"Hurry, Noah."

"No," he said very gently.

And not another word was spoken for the rest of the night. Well, because her softly and desperately whispered "more," "don't stop," and "harder" didn't count, right?

CHAPTER 26

Olive lay flat on her back breathing hard, hair in her face obscuring her view of the attic beams high above. Her body was still humming, her mind perfectly emptied of thoughts—other than to wonder if any of the spiders residing up there in the beams had watched what she and Noah had done to each other. She turned her head to look at him.

He too lay on his back, eyes closed but clearly not asleep. At least if his curved lips meant anything. At her slight movement, he rolled toward her, propping his head up with his hand as he smiled—the full, rich smile that was so rare, the one that seemed to be for her alone. Secretly, she loved the fact that there was a side of him that was for her only, not shared with any of the outside world. It chased away her loneliness. *He* chased away her loneliness with his easy affection and the obvious way he cared about her. "That was . . ." She paused, unable to find a word for what they'd just shared.

He tugged her to him with a sexy, sure smile. "Mind-blowing? Earth-shattering?"

"Hmm." She shrugged. "I was going to say it was . . . *okay*."

With a laugh, he nipped her shoulder. "Maybe you should give me another shot so I can improve my rating."

If he did any better, she'd die, death by orgasms. And he knew it too. Noah had zero inhibitions. He never held back, letting everything he felt show, making her feel incredibly powerful and sexy.

It was addicting.

He was addicting. But . . . "How did we get here?"

Reaching out, he toyed with a strand of her hair, wrapping it around his finger. "Lots of luck on my part. And some questionable decisions on your part."

She laughed. Damn, the man really knew how to make her feel good. A problem, because in her head, there were pretty much three levels of existence: bad, neutral, and okay—with *good* being a pipe dream. *Bad* was learning her boyfriend and a good friend had been going at it behind her back. Or when she'd had to sell her car to eat. *Neutral* was having an all right but unexciting job with a steady income and an apartment, and being able to go shopping once in a while. *Okay* was nearly the same as neutral, but she could afford to subscribe to a few streamers.

None of the above scenarios required a man, but, like frosting on a cake, it'd be nice and might even elevate her to the elusive good level of existence. Still, the worry that she might mess it up with Noah was high.

But . . . wait a minute. She and Noah didn't have a commitment, so how could she mess it up? Well, okay, by getting emotionally attached. Except like it or not, that had already happened. It was her own secret, but it didn't make it any less true.

So she had two choices. Walk away now, or take what she could get until she left. *Ding, ding, ding*, she chose door number two, and she'd deal with the consequences of that when she was back in the UK, licking her wounds.

And there would be wounds.

But that was Future Olive's problem. For now, Present Olive would just enjoy every minute of every day she had left here, especially the minutes with Noah. So until things fell apart, she would add a fourth category to her list of emotional states— blissfully, stupidly, tentatively *happy*. "Speaking of questionable decisions," she said. "You might be onto something with your no ties, no strings thing."

He shook his head. "I'm definitely not."

"I don't know, I'm thinking it might be good for me because if the past is best left in the past, then worrying about the future is best left for, well, the future."

"You're talking about us," he said carefully.

"I think you mean the non-us. Since we're not an us."

"Feels like there's at least a little bit of an us." His voice was light, almost teasing, but his eyes were dark and serious. Intense even. "I don't want to hurt you, Olive. Not ever again."

"You can't." Bold words, possibly true, but possibly not. She was just going to have to hold on to the fact that she had left once before and had learned to live a life of her own choosing on her own terms. She could survive it again. Probably.

He held her gaze for a long moment. "Are you leaving?" he asked softly.

"Well, not today."

Eyes filled with something she couldn't name, he pulled her in closer. "You're not going to vanish, are you?"

"No."

"Promise me. I want a goodbye this time, Olive. I don't want to go another decade without being in touch."

She met his gaze, which was deadly serious. He meant it. He wanted to stay in contact, and . . . she wanted that too. Why had she ever thought leaving and staying gone was a good thing to do? Maybe because she'd been a stupid eighteen-year-old. Maybe because it took two to keep in touch . . . Don't go there, not while everything felt good. The past was in the past. "Promise."

His phone vibrated, but he made no move to reach for it. Suited her just fine. She was done watching everyone else live their lives while she sat on the sidelines of hers. Her plan was to climb into the driver's seat of her world and figure her shit out. Beyond that, the plan needed work. But at least she knew where to start. "You said something about improving your rating . . . or was that all talk?"

She was rolled beneath him before she'd taken her next breath. "I'll show you all talk," he murmured. "Until you're begging for mercy."

She didn't need mercy, but there was plenty of begging.

WHEN THE MORNING light woke Noah, he automatically reached for Olive . . . and encountered nothing but sheets. Cold sheets. He eyed the time. Nine? He'd overslept twice in a row. The reason for that put a stupid smile on his face.

He checked his phone. Neil had left a text that he'd gotten permission for Noah to come into the Yosemite office. There was something going down with the case he'd been working on for nearly a year, a murder investigation. A woman in her mid-thirties had vanished on a remote trail and was reported missing by her husband. The guy had told the authorities his wife had been anxious and depressed, and he'd hoped the trip would do her good. It hadn't. She'd fallen off a cliff three hundred feet to her death.

Noah and his team had gathered evidence that the husband had pushed her off that cliff, but he'd vanished, seemingly off the face of the earth.

And then yesterday new evidence had surfaced—a distant relative owned a cabin in the Yosemite area, and it was believed the husband was holed up there.

The takedown was happening tonight.

Noah couldn't lead it, but his consolation prize was an offer to run command, and he was going to take it. He'd have to leave within the hour, but he'd do anything to get his foot back in the door at work.

He dressed and made his way downstairs. At the kitchen table sat Gram and her three boarders eating breakfast. All gawking at him.

He nodded at them. With a snort, Gram got up and poured him a coffee. "The walk of shame looks good on you," she said.

Not wanting to put Olive in the position of having to explain anything, he said, "It's not what you think."

"Sure." Gram handed him the mug, waiting for him to take a sip before she casually said, "Oh, and your shirt's on inside out."

He choked on the coffee, then looked down at himself. His shirt was on correctly.

Gram grinned. "Gotcha."

Shaking his head at her, he left via the back door and crossed the driveway, stopping in surprise.

Olive and Joey were tossing a softball back and forth. To be fair, Olive was tossing and Joey was mostly missing the catch and running after the ball as it bounced away, but it did something inside his chest.

Warmed it.

"Don't forget to keep your eyes open," Olive was telling the kid. "Try catching the ball by wrapping your arms around it and cradling it to your chest."

Joey nodded sagely and at the next throw kept his eyes open as he wrapped his arms around the ball, and . . . caught it. Whooping with delight, he jumped around, celebrating himself, making Noah smile as he came closer.

Joey, catching sight of him, beamed. "Uncle Noah! Uncle Noah! I caught it! Did you see? Did you see?"

"I did. Great catch."

With a laugh, Joey flung himself at Noah, one hundred percent confident that he'd be caught, having no idea what failure tasted like. Noah hugged the kid close. He knew it was unrealistic to hope he never knew failure, but he hoped like hell Joey would hold on to his innocence as long as possible.

The front door opened. "I've got pancakes!" Katie called out.

Joey wriggled to get free and ran toward her, yelling, "I caught the ball, Mommy, I caught the ball!"

"Aw, so proud of you." Katie looked over Joey's head and smiled at Olive and Noah. "There's plenty of food. Come join."

Noah picked up Joey's forgotten ball and looked at Olive. "Do you think he knows that my sister's pancakes are like bricks?"

She laughed. "Maybe she's better at them now."

"I can assure you she's not."

That won him another laugh. "I remember the time we took them outside and used them for batting practice," she said.

"That was fun." He tossed her the ball. "Until my mom made us clean up the mess."

She threw the ball back at him. "Us? There was no us. You took off and left me and Katie to do it."

"I was a jerk."

"Only once in a while," she teased. They continued to play catch, reminiscing over the things they did as teens. Eventually, she held on to the ball and met his gaze. "There's something I can't figure out. Why didn't you ever just tell your dad you didn't want to keep playing?"

"I should have."

Nodding, she threw the ball.

"It's just that baseball was the only thing we had in common," he said, and tossed it back.

She caught the ball, looking at it for a long beat before meeting his eyes. "I know I've said this before, but I think it bears repeating. I'm sorry I couldn't keep control of the ATV and that you got hurt. Whether you wanted to play or not, what happened that night took away your choices and your link to your dad."

Not missing the sudden waver in her voice, he moved to her. "Olive." He tipped her face up to his. "Nothing that happened to me, not the ATV, not losing the scholarship, or my dad, none of it was on you."

She started to speak but he gently set a finger on her lips. "None of it," he repeated. "I put your hands on the steering wheel, knowing you had zero experience, knowing you were so cold you were shaking, knowing I should've turned the ATV off and set the brake. What happened wasn't on you, please tell me you believe me."

She let out a shaky breath. "Some part of me does. I think the problem is that I've never quite figured out how to move on."

"You just do. Best that you can."

She stared at him for a moment. "Is that what you do in your life when things get rough? Move on? From . . . letting people in? Opening your heart? Love?"

"Best that I can," he repeated gently.

"Right. And that works for you." She looked around. "But no matter how much I want it to, and I *really* want it to, I don't think I can make it work for me."

"I know."

Something happened then, an emotion came and went in her eyes. Sorrow? Regret? It was already gone, but he couldn't pretend he didn't see it. "Oli, you know how much I care about you, feel for you—"

"I do." She took a step back. "I also know there are limits to those feelings."

Were there? He was losing perspective on that the more time he spent in Sunrise Cove, and with Olive, knowing that a part of him wanted with her what Katie and Joe had.

"I misled you," she said softly. "When I told you time heals all wounds." She shook her head. "I should have said time heals *most* wounds. Most, but not all. Not this one. Not you."

"Oli—"

"It's okay. I don't think talking about it again is going to help. I know where you stand, and I get it." She backed away. "I'm going to go eat some bricks—er, blueberry pancakes." She flashed a smile short of her usual wattage and walked into the house.

And he let her.

FOUR HOURS LATER, Noah was in the Yosemite office, sitting in front of a bank of computers, headset in place, providing backup as needed to the four agents in the field. He'd had to shove the stuff with Olive down deep in order to give everything he had to the job and keep the men out there in the field safe, but he was aware of the weight of it in the back of his mind.

When the takedown happened, it went so fast, it felt almost anticlimactic. After, Neil appeared at his side. "Great work, Turner." He paused. "I know how much work you put into this investigation. I also know you're disappointed you couldn't be out there." A small smile crossed his face as he looked Noah over. "Did you think by your being dressed, I might change my mind and let you go without being cleared for field work?" he asked, referring to the fact that Noah was in full uniform, including multiple weapons.

"Habit."

Neil nodded, studied him thoughtfully, then kicked a chair out and made himself comfortable. "We've never had an op go down so smooth."

"Lots of man-hours into this one," Noah said.

"Yes, most of them yours."

"And Joe's."

"And Joe's," Neil agreed. "But Joe isn't coming back."

Noah froze. "What?"

"He didn't tell you?"

Noah drew a deep breath. "No."

"He called me yesterday, said the job no longer suited him. He wants to be around more for his wife and kid. Said something about helping his wife's family run their equipment shop. That's your family's shop, right?"

Noah nodded, thoughts racing. *Why hadn't Joe told him?*

Neil was quiet for a long moment, and Noah, never one to give himself away, waited. His boss was fair. Strict, taciturn, irritable, but fair. And he never sat around without a very good reason. Noah was just starting to wonder if the guy had fallen asleep with his eyes open, when he finally spoke.

"I'm retiring too." He eyed Noah for his reaction. "At the end of the quarter."

Noah was stunned. Neil had always said he'd leave only when his cold body was dragged out of here. "What changed?"

"Me. I've got grandkids now, in San Diego, and the wife's making noises about moving closer to them." He looked at Noah speculatively. Shrewdly. "You'd make a great supervisor of the western offices. You've got a knack for investigating."

"I enjoy it," he said. "Which is why I've always been in the field."

Neil nodded. "Yes. But you have a way with keeping all the balls in the air, for multiple cases, for *all* the cases we've got open. You also have a way with people—"

Noah snorted.

Neil smiled. "Meaning you know when they're full of crap. Most of the time we operate up to our knees in shit, and yet somehow you always manage to figure a clean way out. This job, it eats most people up and spits them out, but you . . . you thrive on it."

Noah didn't know what to say. Neil had never been one to dish out compliments. "Where are you going with this?"

"We need you back. We need you back yesterday, but in a bigger capacity. In an overseeing capacity."

Noah had never been interested in overseeing other people. Not in his business life, and not in his personal life. Maybe down the road he'd enjoy a desk job. But this particular desk job would take him away from home much more than he already was, and for far longer periods. "I wasn't looking for this."

"That's what makes you the best for the job. You'd travel more, spend a bunch more time in D.C., but you'd have your fingers in all the pies. Oh, and the salary goes way up. You're at the top of a very short list of candidates, and the powers that be are excited about you. I don't have to tell you what that means."

No, he didn't. "I'll think about it."

Neil nodded. "That's all we can ask."

It was nice to be asked. Very nice. And as he drove back to Sunrise Cove instead of staying in Yosemite for the night, he did exactly what he'd promised. He thought about it. But those thoughts actually went to Joe, who'd never loved the work the way Noah had. It'd been a paycheck, a means to an end, a way to support his family. Nothing more. Not like for Noah, who'd considered the job a way of life, and thrived on it.

The thing was, Noah had thought he knew what he wanted out of life. Freedom. Adventure. Space. And he'd had those things. He'd loved those things.

But there was an odd and growing restlessness inside him that said maybe he had something better to say yes to.

CHAPTER 27

S o you made a mistake thinking you could remain emotionally unattached," Olive said. "Whatever. It happens."

No one responded.

This was because it was nearly midnight and once again she
was alone in Gram's attic. She loved her London flat, she did.
But she'd never felt as completely at home there as she did here,
in the house she'd run to as a teenager, the house where she'd
grown into her own person, the house where she always felt the
most herself.

"And there's something else," she told the quiet attic. "In spite
of that mistake, I don't want to leave."

She hadn't expected this. She'd been so sure that by now she'd
be chomping at the bit to get back to the life she'd so carefully
built for herself six thousand miles away.

Being here wasn't supposed to feel so right. It wasn't her life
anymore. But sitting on the bed, no makeup, hair piled on top
of her head in a messy bun, she felt more like herself than she
had in a long time. She was in her oldest, comfiest clothes: her
zip-up hoodie with *Not slim, kinda shady* written across her chest

and sweat bottoms she'd stolen from Noah all those years ago—
yes, she still had them. She'd rolled the sweats at her waist but
she still tripped over the long, frayed legs whenever she walked.

So she didn't walk. She sat on the bed hugging a pillow while
watching *The Shining* on her laptop. She'd seen the movie a
hundred times, and it still scared the crap out of her.

A knock sounded on the access door and she nearly jumped
out of her skin. Before she could leap up and hide under the bed,
the door slowly creaked open. Grabbing her phone, she hoisted
it like she was a pro baseball pitcher, prepared to chuck it at
whoever's head dared to show itself.

When she saw a tall shadow, she froze, arm still raised in
indecision.

"Go ahead, I probably deserve it."

She nearly collapsed in relief as Noah stepped out of the
complete dark and into the meager light cast by her laptop. He
stood bedside in cargoes and a forest green windbreaker with
Federal Agent printed in bright yellow on a pec and down one
arm, clearly armed to the teeth and looking deadly sexy and
deadly dangerous to her heart and soul. She put a hand to her
chest. "You scared me."

"Why aren't you sleeping at Katie's? Because of me?"

She grimaced inwardly. "No. It's because of me. What are you
doing here?"

"I wanted to talk to you."

"It's the middle of the night."

"I know, I'm sorry. I just got back. I could see the glow of
your laptop from the driveway, so I knew you were awake. Can
we talk?"

"About?" she asked warily.

"About earlier. When I was a dick."

"Which time?"

He gave a rough laugh, stared at his boots for a moment, then lifted his head. "You're right. Let's start at the beginning. That night of our high school graduation party, when you were going to sleep with the biggest asshole on the planet—for your first time."

Oh boy. So they were going to go there. Okay, then. She scooted over and gestured for him to sit.

He paused to unload his weapons—gun, knife, another gun—setting them on the chest at the foot of the bed before sitting at her side, stretching his long legs out and leaning back with a sigh that sounded exhausted.

"We both know you were the one I wanted that night," she said. "But you'd turned me down. So what did it matter to you who I slept with?"

"What did it matter—" He broke off and twisted to face her. "It mattered, because of this." He kissed her, a sensuous, erotic kiss that shut down her brain.

By the time he pulled back, she'd forgotten why she'd wanted to chuck her phone at his head.

"It mattered," he said quietly, rubbing his jaw to hers like he was a cat. A big, dangerous wildcat. "Because *I* wanted to be the one kissing you. Touching you . . ."

She put a hand on his chest and nudged him back a little so she could think. "At the risk of repeating myself, you'd turned me down."

He shook his head. "I didn't. I said it wasn't the right time. I wanted it to be because you wanted me, not because you wanted to lose your virginity."

She blinked. "I didn't get that memo."

"Because you were hell-bent on not listening to me that night.

And then when I saw you being tugged by Trev to his dad's truck so you could be a conquest of the party, I lost my shit."

No. Nope. "You told him I was more trouble than I was worth!"

A very small smile curved his lips. "Which was true."

The opposite of amused, she narrowed her eyes. "You embarrassed me in front of our whole class!"

"Not my finest hour," he admitted. "But I was panicked and worried."

"You never panic or worry."

He lifted a shoulder. "Panic's rare for me, I'll give you that. But I'm a pro at worrying, especially about those I care about, and Olive, I cared deeply about you. I did what I did so he would walk away without hurting you."

She was still reeling about the caring deeply thing. "You thought he'd hurt me?"

"Yes." He paused as if weighing his words, then shut his mouth.

"Oh, don't hold back now."

"It was a bet," he said flatly.

She stared at him. "What?"

"If he'd slept with you, he'd have won a bet between him and some of his idiot friends."

Okay, that was a blow she hadn't seen coming. She stared into his eyes and saw nothing but honesty, so she decided to give him some honesty right back. "Trev never had the power to hurt me. You, however, did. And it was you who hurt me that night."

"Which I'll regret to my dying day."

Everything, from the tense line of his body to his soulful eyes, told her that was true, and went a long way toward healing a part of her she hadn't even realized needed healing. "And the other times you were a dick?"

He looked at her for a long beat. "I've got something I'd like to show you first."

She let a small smile curve her lips. "I've already seen it in all its spectacular glory."

He choked out a laugh. "Not what I meant, but good to know. Can I . . . would you come with me somewhere? Please, Oli?"

He seemed so serious, too serious, and her sassy mouth couldn't let it be. "Will there be food?"

"Whatever you want," he said.

"Popcorn?"

That got her a smile. "Yeah," he said. "There will be popcorn."

"Chocolate?"

"And chocolate."

She laughed. "You're just saying that to lure me in."

And even though they both knew she'd been lured in by him a long time ago, he stood and held out his hand. "You willing to take a chance and find out?"

CHAPTER 28

Olive followed Noah over to Katie's, waiting while he left his sister a note. Holmes was asleep, not in his bed, but sprawled out on his back on the couch, legs straight up in the air, snoring like a buzzsaw.

Sitting near his head was Pepper, wearing an adorable pink collar, to which was attached a small sign that read: *It's been zero days since I attacked shoelaces for no reason.*

Olive gave them both some love, and then Noah was back, taking her by the hand. A minute later, they were on the road, the interior of the truck lit only by the ambient light from the dash, the air warmed by the heater, making it feel cozy and . . . intimate.

Noah drove them around the lake via the west side, heading south. After a while, he turned away from the water and up. At first, there were other houses, but the higher they went, the fewer structures she saw. Just over an hour from when they'd left Sunrise Cove, they turned into a driveway at the end of a wooded lane.

The moon lit things up enough for her to see a cabin in front of them. Noah sent her a smile, and they got out of the truck. They walked around the side of the cabin to the back, where there was a large patio and a view of the lake far below, which took her breath away. "Wow," she whispered. "Beautiful."

"This place belonged to my grandma," he said. "My dad's mom. She thought her son was, and I'm quoting her here, a 'horse's patoot,' so she left the cabin to me and Katie. My dad didn't mind, he hated how far out of the way it is. And since Katie wanted to buy Mom's place, and Mom wanted that too, I bought out Katie's half of the cabin so she'd have the money."

Olive turned and took in the structure, which had all the charm of an old mountain cabin but somehow looked new at the same time. "Looks like there's been work done."

He shrugged. "She's old and needed some TLC. Over the past few years, whenever I wasn't in Yosemite at work, I was here, restoring things. It's a beautiful old place, and private."

"It suits you," she said softly.

He unlocked the back door and led her inside. The wood floors were new and beautiful, and she loved the exposed beams high above. Furnishings were sparse to say the least. The large living room held a massive TV and oversized couch. Nothing else, unless you counted the beat-up running shoes against one wall.

"Until Joe and I got into that accident, I was working pretty much nonstop," he said. "I've got a small efficiency apartment in Yosemite, but it's personality-less and filled with whatever the management company had in there. I'm looking forward to doing more here when I've got the time."

He meant if he ever slowed down, which she didn't see happening. Since that thought was depressing, she moved away from him. She'd kicked off her shoes when they'd first come in and the wood floors were clean and cool beneath her feet as she walked through the beautiful old rooms. Ending up back in the kitchen again, she stared out the window over the sink at the patio and wooded yard.

"Drink?" Noah asked quietly at her back.

When she nodded, he pulled a bottle from a small wine rack and opened it, pouring them both a glass.

"Back to the next time I was a dick," he said as if they'd never stopped their earlier conversation. "It was five years ago when we slept together before we talked things out."

She looked away. "Because I left before we talked."

He set his glass down, and then hers, before tipping her face up to his. "I knew better, knew we needed to talk first, but I . . ." He gave a wry smile. "I wanted you so very badly." His smile faded. "But after, when you'd gone, I felt like I took advantage. I'm so sorry, Olive."

She shook her head. "I wanted you just as badly."

"Then why did you go?"

She hesitated, wondering how much she should say, then decided she needed to say all of it. For her own sake, if nothing else. "Because when I left, the first time," she clarified. "After our accident, you . . ." She looked him in the eyes. "You didn't try to contact me. We saw each other here and there at family events, but you didn't go out of your way to check in with me. If you'd really wanted me in your life, you'd have started a conversation about why I'd left. Instead, you just let me go and never looked back."

He closed his eyes for a beat and nodded. "Exhibit number three of me being a dick. You're right and I've always known it. I'm sorrier than I can possibly say. I had way too much pride and ego back then. If I could change it, I would—"

"It's okay."

"It's not. Not even close." He ran his fingers along her temple, warm and gentle, stroking a wayward strand of hair off her face as he looked into her eyes, his solemn. "You deserved more—"

She put a finger over his mouth. "The past is in the past, remember?"

"I've changed my mind on that."

"Oh." She felt the hit of that like a one-two punch to the throat. "Okay. Um, I understand—"

"I doubt you do." He held her gaze. "Olive—"

"No." She tried to pull back, but he caught her. "I don't need the spiel again," she managed to say in a calm voice when she felt anything but. "I get it. I really do. But you have to let me go."

He let go of her arms only to gently cup her face in his big hands, his thumbs wiping away a few tears that had escaped without her permission. "I need to make clear what I haven't until now," he said. He looked away for a beat, blew out a breath, then slowly brought his eyes back to hers. "It scares the hell out of me how much I need you, and I'm not talking about the insane chemistry we have in bed."

Her heart skipped a whole bunch of beats. "What does that even mean, then? You don't do relationships. You don't want a girlfriend."

He smiled. "Do you *want* to be my girlfriend, Oli?"

"I want to be less confused." She shoved him back a step. "Everything feels upside down, and now Mr. I Don't Do Relationships is throwing words around."

"Yeah, I'm surprised too," he said. "But I finally figured some things out today." His smile turned wry. "Better late than never, right?"

She crossed her arms. "What things?"

"For one, I've been a fool when it comes to you. More times than I even knew, as it turns out."

"Do you think you can narrow some of them down for me?"

Very gently, very slowly, probably giving her time and room to kick him if she wanted, he reeled her back in. "I learned early on to be what everyone wanted of me. That's no secret. I thought that was the only way to receive love. And as a result, I've been . . . shy . . . about sharing myself."

That tumbled a disbelieving laugh out of her. "Like you have a shy bone in your body."

"Maybe not in my body. But definitely in my heart. I've been . . . unwilling . . . to share it with anyone. Except you."

Since that nearly melted her into a puddle at his feet, she locked her knees and narrowed her eyes. "Keep talking."

"My heart's been in the palm of your hand since we were fourteen."

Her heart squeezed, but she shook her head. "You expect me to believe you hid that fact all this time?"

"No." He didn't smile, his eyes were deadly serious. "I honestly don't expect you to believe any of this. But it's the truth. It's my truth. Grew up having to be perfect, remember? I'm a pro at hiding my feelings. Or I was."

She kept looking into his eyes, the ones that now were suddenly open, revealing his emotions. It stole her breath and, she was afraid, let in a little bubble of hope. "Okay, well, I've got a secret too."

He waited with a patience she couldn't have summoned on her best day. "I've been moderately successful at business," she said. "But as for my personal life . . ." She gave a slow head shake. "My life, the part of it that matters anyway, is here. Katie, Joey, my grandma, my parents, your mom . . . you." The relief she felt at the admission nearly brought her to her knees. Or maybe that came from the way Noah was looking at her, his golden-brown eyes reflecting everything she felt right back at her. "I care about you," she managed to admit. "Well, as much as you let me." She paused. "Okay, maybe a little bit more. That's the scary part."

He touched his forehead to hers. "Please don't throw me away, not yet, Oli. I already can't stand thinking about what it's going to be like when you're gone."

Her emotions felt raw as her heart cracked in two as she took in the want, the longing on full display in his expression. His emotions were as raw as hers. "I'm not throwing you away. I won't. I'm moving back," she said, shocking herself with the revelation. "I can work from anywhere, and there's no longer a reason to stay on the other side of the planet. At least I hope not—"

With a rough, male sound deep in his throat, eyes lit with something she was afraid to name, he hauled her into him, wrapping her up in those warm arms. "Olive—"

"If you've just realized this is a mistake, that you don't really want me like that, tell me right now," she said, preempting him in order to manage her expectations.

His laugh was rough. "I want you *exactly* like that. I want you so much more than you can possibly imagine. From the moment I saw you again, it all came back to me. Or hell, if we're being honest, I don't think it ever went away."

She shook her head, confused to her core. "Then why—"

"You know why. Nothing about my lifestyle allows for a relationship."

"Plenty of people in dangerous jobs are also in relationships. Joe, for one."

"He's retiring."

Shock hit her. "What?"

Noah squeezed his eyes shut, then opened them again. "I shouldn't have said that. My boss just told me today. Joe hasn't said anything. Which means he hasn't told Katie yet, so you have to keep it to yourself."

Olive's thoughts raced. And a myriad of emotions hit her. "Katie's going to be happy to hear it."

He nodded. "Because she's always been freaked out that something bad would happen to him. And then it did."

"What happened to you guys could've happened anywhere, on the job *or* off."

"I'm coming to accept that." The pad of his thumb rubbed gently over her cheek. "I'm sorry I've held you at arm's length."

"And now?" She held her breath for his answer.

"I don't know that I'd be any good at a relationship," he admitted. "History says no. But . . ."

"Oh, don't you dare stop there."

His lips curved wryly. "But . . . I'm willing to try if you are."

"Why the change?"

"My boss is also retiring from running national command. He wants me to consider the position. It'd be a huge promotion and a lot more money."

"Congratulations," she said with what she thought was admirable calm.

"But," he went on, "base of operations is in D.C., and even then, he's always on the road and works crazy hours." He paused. "I'm turning it down."

She drew in a shaky breath. "Why would you do that?"

"It's not what I want. It's not what I see for myself going forward."

She couldn't help the new little leap of hope her heart gave. "You always said you didn't see yourself giving up the lifestyle."

The corners of his mouth slightly curved. "Fear's a bitch."

"Come on. Nothing scares you."

"Plenty scares me." He kissed her softly. "You, for example."

She gave him a *get-real* look.

"It's true," he said on a low laugh. "You make me want things I didn't want to want."

Nerves had her taking a lap of the kitchen, running her fingers along the countertop, looking out the window into the night aglow with the moon and a trillion stars as the ball of worry she'd been carrying deep inside clenched painfully. "I'm not asking you for anything."

"I know. You never ask for anything for yourself. Ask me what I want, Oli."

She swallowed hard. "What do you want?"

"You. I want to be yours. I want you to be mine."

That ball of worry melted away as if it'd never existed. "That sounds . . . serious."

"It's frighteningly serious." From the other side of the kitchen island, he gave her a smile with a whole bunch of charm and a touching amount of vulnerability to go with it. "You should know, I brought you here to beg you for a shot at making a long-distance thing work until we could figure something else out. But then you said you were moving back. Did you mean it?"

A small picture frame leaned against the granite backsplash. It had three pictures in it: one of his family, one of him and Joey, and . . . one of the two of them in a kayak on the lake. She couldn't remember when it'd been taken. "Yes," she said. "I meant it."

"I took this place on because I felt like there was a hole in my life," he said to her back. "But I learned an empty house can't fill a hole. Recently I've been dreaming of filling it with someone, not something." He paused. "You."

Spinning around, she stared at him.

He was resting his back against the counter, his arms folded loosely, his feet crossed at the ankles. Deceptively casual.

She drew a breath. "You want to go from seeing each other once in a blue moon to . . . me living here?"

He nodded.

"With you," she clarified.

He nodded again.

She chewed on her bottom lip, shocked by how good that sounded. "You don't think we should take our time figuring this out without the pressure of having nowhere to get away from me?"

"I don't plan on needing an escape hatch from you, Oli."

She looked away.

"You need an escape hatch?" His voice was still quiet, his body the picture of calm.

While she on the other hand was starting to sweat in places she didn't know could sweat. "Is it hot in here? It feels hot in here suddenly."

His mouth quirked, but now there was tension in his shoulders and his eyes hadn't left hers. "You need an escape hatch."

"No." She shook her head. "No. I just . . . I'm going to irritate the shit out of you. I eat ice cream right out of the container. I load the dishwasher like a two-year-old. Ask Katie, she grounded me from loading the dishwasher *ever*. Plus, sometimes I live out of the clean laundry basket rather than putting the clothes away, and—"

"You think I care about any of that?"

"You're a neat freak," she reminded him.

"I am not a neat freak."

"You are."

He blew out a breath. "Okay, maybe. But that doesn't mean I expect you to be."

"What *do* you expect?"

"Nothing more than what you want to give me freely."

Oh. Oh, that was a great answer, and most of her tension vanished. "You promise?" she whispered, because he never broke his promises.

"I promise." Reaching out, he tugged her back into him. He was still leaning back on the counter, now with her standing between his legs, hands on his shoulders, looking up at him.

He brushed her hair from her face. "You've become a part of me," he said. "As important and basic as breathing." He kissed her softly. "I feel things for you that I can't even name." His face became serious again. Very serious, very intent, his eyes focused on hers. "I love you, Oli. So much."

She slid her hand up his chest to feel the comforting rhythm of his heart, going a little faster than his usual. He wasn't quite as calm as he seemed. "I love you too, Noah. I think I always have."

For a beat they stood there in mutual surprise. After all the time they'd spent avoiding it, their emotions and feelings for each other were finally out in the open. She felt freer and lighter than she had in a long time, and smiled up into his still serious expression, seeing his answering smile slowly spread across his face. "You really love me?" she asked.

"I mean, how could I not love the woman who isn't willing to let me make the worst mistake of my life?"

"What mistake is that?"

"Trying to keep you out of my heart. Oli, I honestly can't remember *not* loving you."

The second he'd said he loved her—*he loved her!*—she'd taken her first deep breath of the night, and she let herself relax into something very new for her. *Anticipation, happiness, faith.*

"You never said what it is *you* want," he said.

What did she want? He'd just given her everything she'd ever dreamed of. "How about the promised popcorn and chocolate?"

He gave a rough laugh. "Please tell me you want more from me than that."

"Yes, but you've already given it to me."

"You deserve so much better than me," he said. "I'm sorry it took me so long to get my head out of my ass."

She smiled demurely. "The important thing is that eventually you did get it out of there."

He laughed again, rocking her gently back and forth. "Say it again."

She met his gaze as she slid her fingers into his hair and met his mouth with hers. He tasted like everything she'd ever wanted. "I love you. I can't remember not loving you."

The last of his tension left him. "I didn't know how much I needed to hear that." His voice was filled with more emotion than she'd ever heard from him before. "I used to think my internal GPS was broken because it never led me anywhere I wanted to go."

"And now?" she asked.

"Now it's finally led me home."

CHAPTER 29

When Noah woke, he was on his back, covered by the most amazing woman on the planet. He kept his eyes closed a moment, soaking it all in: the night before, the words he and Olive had said to each other, then hours of not speaking at all, communicating solely with their bodies. He didn't have to open his eyes to search hers and try to guess what she might be thinking; neither of them were hiding anymore.

He looked down. Snugged up against his side, Olive was burrowed into the meat of his shoulder, an arm and leg thrown over the top of him. He could tell by her breathing she was still out. They hadn't gotten to sleep much more than an hour or two ago. He could use a bunch more hours, but the sun was high and slanting in through his bedroom window and across the bed. The air was frosty, but beneath the down comforter, their bodies generated a heat that warmed every last dark corner of his heart.

Then he realized Olive had woken and was quietly studying him. "Regrets?" she asked softly.

"Only that I can't make you breakfast in bed. I haven't been here in weeks and I don't have any fresh food."

"It's okay. I have the feeling we don't have time for that anyway. I can hear both of our phones going off." She sat up. "The real world is calling."

He sat up too and pulled her onto his lap so that she was straddling him. "This is the real world, Oli."

"Is it?" she asked quietly.

He let his voice fill with promise. "Yes. I'm yours, and I want to be yours."

She stared at him, then smiled. "Okay."

"Okay." He really didn't want to do this, but . . . "We should get back for Katie and Joey."

"Agreed." She slid out of bed without a stitch of clothing on and turned coyly back to him. "Coming?"

He groaned. "You're a cruel, cruel woman."

"What?" she asked innocently. "You're the one in a hurry. I'm going to take a really fast shower."

He was out of bed in a flash. "We'll shower together to save time."

Note that they did not, in fact, save time at all . . .

SEVERAL HOURS LATER, Noah led Olive into his sister's house by the hand. The living room was quiet, so he took the opportunity to press her back against the closed front door and kiss her. "The first time I met you, I had no damn idea I'd come to love you with everything I've got."

"'Damn' is still a bad word," Joey said.

They both turned around to find they had an audience crowded in the open doorway to the kitchen. Joey, Katie, Noah's mom . . . and—

Joe, leaning on Katie, one arm slung around her shoulders, the other holding Joey's hand.

"You're home!" Noah strode over and hugged him hard, too choked up at the sight of him to say anything else.

Katie smiled at Olive. "What, I don't get a hug?"

Olive's jaw dropped. "Really? I can hug you?"

"No, I was just kidding."

Olive hugged her anyway. As usual, Katie endured it, hands down at her sides, but she was smiling.

Joe was still holding tightly onto Noah. "If you think the hug's gone on too long, it's because my legs have decided to take a nap."

Noah gently pushed him into a chair. Joe swiped an arm over his wet eyes, and Noah wasn't too proud to do the same. "Man, you're a sight for sore eyes."

"Seems fair," Joe said. "Because *everything* I own is sore. And you know I don't like to be the only one suffering."

Katie made a funny sound deep in her throat and everyone turned to look at her. She had tears streaming down her face.

Olive gasped at her. "Are you . . . crying?"

"No, *you're* crying." She went to swipe her tears away.

"Stop!" Olive yelled. "Sorry. It's just that I've been prepping for this moment since we were fourteen, so don't move!" She pulled tissues from her pocket, which were slightly wadded. "I've had these for a long time."

"Ew," Katie said.

"But good 'ew,' right?" Olive asked.

"No, you weirdo." But she took the tissues, blew her nose, and then handed Olive back the tissues. Or tried to.

Olive put her hands behind her back.

"Oh, so you want to hug, but you don't want to hold my boogers?"

"I do not," Olive said. "And you just made it weird."

Katie sighed. "I know." She looked around, clearly for something to distract them, like she always did after she'd embarrassed herself. "Noah and Olive have been sneaking around."

"No," Noah said. "We're not."

Olive stilled, looking stricken.

Joe looked at his wife. "I honestly thought he had more game than this."

"We're not sneaking around," Noah said to the room while holding Olive's gaze. "It's out in the open. We're seeing each other and it's serious."

His mom, who'd just come down the stairs, gasped with delight, but before she could speak, Katie stepped forward. "Hold on!" she said. "I mean, yes, it's great these two pulled their heads out of their butts, but I have bigger news!"

"Bigger than your husband coming home from the hospital?" Noah asked. "Which, by the way, you could've told me. We'd have gotten here sooner."

"I called you like ten times! And never mind about that right now. Guess what?" She beamed wide. "Joe isn't going back to the job! He's going to take some time to fully recover, and then run the shop so Mom can retire and go travel with her friends."

Olive beamed at her. "That's amazing! I'm so happy for you, for all of you."

"Me too." Noah pointed at Joe. "But don't think I'm going to help you with the shop."

"You'll be too busy," Joe said. "I heard you'll be taking over Neil's job."

"You heard wrong." Noah looked at Olive. "I'm going to keep my job on this side of the country. For now anyway."

Joe looked at the way he was holding Olive close and smiled. "Nice."

His mom had been quiet. Smiling, but quiet. At the lull in conversation, she walked toward the woman Noah intended to spend the rest of his life with.

"I'm truly sorry," she said to Olive. "I never should have—"

Olive hugged her, then pulled back. "You did what you had to, and so did I. Let's look forward to what's ahead."

Noah's mom looked hopeful. "And what's ahead for you two? A wedding? Kids?"

Noah grimaced. "*Mom*."

Olive waved him off. "You know what? I'm going to amend my statement. Let's all spend a little more time in the moment before getting too far ahead of ourselves."

Noah grinned at her, never loving her more than he did in that moment. "Agreed," he said. "But just to be clear, I'm looking forward to this moment, and all the moments to come. With you, for as long as you'll have me."

"That might be a long time."

He nodded, his eyes reading her face, which was more fascinating than any book on the planet. "I'm counting on forever."

EPILOGUE

One year later

Olive headed down the third aisle of the thrift shop, which looked to be the 1960s collection. Noah was right behind her, Katie and Joe ahead of them both, walking backward, grinning.

"I'm scared," Noah whispered in her ear.

Olive laughed. "Big, bad federal agent is scared of Goodwill?"

"No, I love Goodwill. I'm scared of my evil sister—"

"Stop!" yelled Katie.

Olive stopped short so fast that Noah nearly ran her over.

"You know the rules of the night," Joe said, nearly chortling with glee. "You each have to pick something right in front of you from your side of the aisle to wear for the rest of the night, no matter where we end up."

Easy for him to say. On his turn, he'd ended up with a suit straight out of *The Godfather*. Katie had gotten a slinky gold-fringed cocktail dress that she couldn't stop twirling in, and the two of them looked amazing.

With a sigh, Olive started to turn to her side of the aisle, inadvertently knocking her purse off her shoulder to the floor, where the contents spilled out.

Including a rolled-up piece of tissue paper with a blue-and-pink ribbon tied in a bow around it. Heart pounding, she dropped to her knees and scooped it up as fast as she could, kicking herself for the ribbon, which might've been too obvious.

But her three dates all looked perplexed.

Noah crouched in front of her. "What's that?"

Her heart leaped anew and words failed her. So she handed the paper over and he very carefully unrolled it.

"It's from your medical group, the results of a blood test." He looked into her eyes. "Yours."

"Yes. I—"

"What's the matter?"

"Well . . ." She managed a shaky smile. "Okay, this is silly. I didn't realize it would be so hard to say out loud. I mean, we've talked about it, but neither of us were in a hurry, and—"

Katie's mouth fell open. "Ohmigod! *Yes!*"

Ignoring his sister, Noah scanned the report, swallowed hard, and looked at Olive. "You're . . ."

"Yes." Taking one of his big, warm hands in hers, she set it low on her belly. "Yes. I'm . . ."

"Pregnant!" Katie said loud enough for everyone in the store to turn and stare at them. "Sorry!" She waved them off. "Nothing to see here!"

Noah gave a single head shake, eyes still on Olive as he said, "You're . . . ?"

She grinned. "Do you think either of us will ever be able to say it?"

With a grin, he surged to his feet, pulled her to hers, and twirled her around in the narrow aisle, all in one smooth motion. Then he gently set her on her feet and put his forehead to hers. "We're going to be good at this."

She smiled. "Yes, I think we are."

"I can't wait to see you get all chubby," Katie said. "Oh! And your boobs will get bigger! That was fun. But don't think your big, cute news is getting you out of date night." She gestured to the clothing on either side of them. "On with it, guys."

"Not until I get a hug," Olive said.

"Okay, but just one," Katie said. "And you're not getting another until you push a baby out of your meow." She pulled Olive in, patted her on the back twice, and then pulled back quickly. "There."

"My *meow*?" Olive asked, brows up.

"You're stalling." Katie pointed to them both. "Grab your outfits."

Noah pulled a *Top Gun* flight suit—complete with a fake mustache—off the rack. "Hey, this isn't so bad."

Olive stared at what was right in front of her. "You've got to be kidding me," she griped, pulling out a legit pumpkin costume, which consisted of a leotard, tights, and a massive pumpkin to go over all of it, every inch a very bright orange.

Katie clapped her hands in delight. "The good news is that you can wear it for Halloween this year. And trust me, by then, you'll need the pumpkin part for your huge belly."

Olive nearly swallowed her tongue. It was real. She was going to have a baby.

Noah's arm snaked around her waist from behind. "Breathe," he said softly, chuckling when she gasped in some air.

"How are you not panicking?" she demanded.

"No need." He swung her around to face him and pulled her in for a big bear hug. "We've got this, Oli."

She fisted her hand in his shirt and stared up into his smiling eyes. "You sure?"

"Very. But I also have a surprise, one that I was saving for just the right moment." And he pulled a little velvet box from a pocket.

"And *this* is the right moment?" Katie asked. "In the Goodwill store?"

"Ignore her," Noah said, laughing when Olive gave him gimme hands for the box, finally taking it for herself, gasping at the beautiful diamond ring nestled inside.

"Yes!" she cried.

"Wait, he didn't ask you yet," Katie complained. "I wanted to see him grovel and beg you to marry him."

"Joe?" Noah said without taking his eyes off Olive.

"Got it." And Joe very gently wrapped an arm around Katie's neck and covered her mouth with his hand.

"I love you," Noah said to Olive. "I have since you showed up when we were fourteen years old. I'm going to love you and this baby—"

"Or babies" came Katie's voice, muffled from Joe's hand.

"For the rest of my days," Noah said to Olive.

She gave him a watery smile. "I love you too. And my knees are knocking."

"You should sit down."

She laughed. "I think I've got plenty of time for that in the coming months."

Noah grinned. "Are you saying our child is going to be a handful?"

"Oh, for sure," Katie muttered around Joe's hand.

"How long have you known?" Noah asked Olive.

"About a half an hour." And she hadn't known how she felt about it until she'd seen his reaction. "At my next appointment, we can hear the heartbeat."

"Or two," Katie said, still muzzled, not that it was stopping her. "What? Twins happen."

"Maybe I should sit down," Noah said.

And in the end, they both sat down, right there in the aisle, Noah first, Olive in his lap in his arms . . . right where she intended to be, forever.

And here's a sneak peek at the next book in Jill Shalvis's Sunrise Cove series, available Summer 2025.

CHAPTER 1

It was a terrible, no good, horrible day to die. For one thing, Lexi Clark hadn't yet eaten the rack of double-fudge cookies in her purse. And for another, her entire existence was still circling the drain after being fired and dumped all those months ago. Going toes up before she fixed her life would suck.

"Ladies and gentlemen, this is your captain speaking" came from the overhead speakers. "When we left Greensboro, the weather in Reno promised a fair day, but coming in for our approach, we've got high winds and a dropping temp. So buckle up, Buttercups, it's going to get a little bumpy." He clicked off, and then came back on, the speakers screeching, making everyone groan. "I nearly forgot the silver lining—those of you on the left have a gorgeous view of Lake Tahoe, which is deep enough to cover the Empire State Building. In fact, if the entire lake spilled out, it'd cover the state of California under fourteen inches of water. But no worries, since it's also two million years old, the odds of that happening are pretty slim." He gave a little laugh. "Okay, guys, hold on tight. We're coming in hot."

Awesome—and then a squeak of shock escaped her as the plane dropped, right along with her stomach. Her lungs suddenly refused to suck in air as her entire body broke out in a cold sweat.

"I need a snack," the woman on her left whispered, eyes squeezed shut, white-knuckling her grip on the armrest. "We flew all the way across the damn country without a courtesy snack and now I'm going to die hungry. Why didn't I just buy food?"

"Because a bag of chips costs seven bucks," Lexi gritted out, also white-knuckling the armrest, though she kept her eyes wide open because she had some twisted need to see death coming for her.

"Oh, right." The woman let out a breathless laugh that turned into a scream when the plane dipped again, yanking shouts, gasps, and Hail Marys from the other passengers as belongings went flying through the cabin.

Lexi reached out at the same time as the woman did, their hands blindly clasping tightly to each other. The cabin felt like a cyclone around them, the air filled with flying debris and more screams. When she'd boarded, she'd walked past first class with a twinge of envy, but now, seeing drinks and trays whip around while they fell out of the sky had her stomach reversing direction, getting stuck in her throat, making her glad she hadn't eaten.

They dipped again, so hard her body went airborne, giving her the unnerving sense of being a balloon on a string—until the seat belt yanked her back.

The woman at her side whispered, "The universe is going to keep us safe. The universe is going to keep us safe. The universe is going to keep us safe . . ." She squeezed Lexi's hand tight enough to crack bones. "Say it with me."

Lexi didn't want to blaspheme, but believed in the universe caring about her about as much as she believed in love. "Talking

the universe into doing anything for me is over my pay grade."
Like waaaay over.

"It's not," the woman said with sweet sincerity. "The universe
provides for anyone who puts their troubles out there."

The plane leveled out and everyone gave a gasp of relief as the
woman turned to look at Lexi. "See?" she said. "You just need
to ask."

Okay, worth a shot. Lexi closed her eyes. *Can I have a new
job? How do I lose the anger from being betrayed by someone I'd been
stupid enough to let into my life? Or soften the emotional blow of this
trip to visit my perfect stepsister, while I'm the opposite of perfect?*

The plane promptly banked right hard enough to rattle Lexi's
teeth and nearly roll them in a somersault.

"You might just be mouthing the words," the woman said,
squeezing Lexi's hand. "You have to truly believe nothing that
can stop you to be . . . well, unstoppable."

"Okay, then, I believe we're not going to crash and die in a
fiery death."

The woman's laugh was breathless. "I like you—" She ended
that sentence in a gaspy scream as the plane's nose dipped and
then—free fall.

More screams of terror pierced Lexi's ears. Her own. Everyone's from all around her. They were heading down, down,
down, right to rock bottom, where her life still sat.

"We're not going to die," her neighbor cried. "We're not. I'm
a professional manifester, so I've got this. We're not going to
die—"

Another terrifying drop and more wailing.

"Not going to die," the woman said, on repeat. "Not going to
die. We can't, because I haven't had a man-made orgasm in at
least a month."

A month was nothing. Lexi couldn't even remember the last time she'd had an org—

The plane dropped again, along with Lexi's organs . . . just as the plane hit the runway.

Hard.

They bounced a few times, the cabin utterly silent now, struggling against the g-forces as they screeched to a halt at the very end of the runway.

The woman still squeezing Lexi's hand let out a shaky breath, then turned her head and graced her with a big smile. "Whew. See? I manifested the no-death thing for all of us."

"Um . . . Thank you?"

She smiled. "I'm Summer, by the way." She dug through her pocket and came up with a business card.

Summer Roberts, CPO
Chief Professional Manifester

"Fifteen percent discount for friends and family," Summer said. "Contact me any time. What do you do?"

At the moment? A lot of whining, filling out applications that seemed to go nowhere, and more whining. But until six months ago, she'd been an overachieving, naive art appraiser, working for a company that handled closing down estates. She'd loved the found treasures, loved the histories of each and every piece, but to do the job, she went into homes after someone had died, where people were grieving, to put price tags on their belongings. To do that effectively, she'd had to learn to disengage herself emotionally.

Turned out, it wasn't a switch she could easily turn on and off.

Not that it mattered now since she'd lost the job.

The pilot was talking, apologizing for the rough landing as Lexi stared at Summer's card, wondering if she was desperate enough to believe she could actually manifest a better life for herself.

"Are you okay?" Summer asked.

Lexi nodded. "Yes."

Summer gestured beyond Lexi. The plane door had opened and people were scrambling to disembark. As the one in the aisle seat, she was blocking Summer from getting out. Letting out a breath, she grabbed her carry-on and joined the herd. She found herself standing in a crowded terminal, heart still pounding in tune with the headache behind her eyes. For a minute she'd forgotten why she was even here as she made her way through the throngs of people toward the escalator to exit the airport.

As she began the downward descent, she shook her head, still feeling shaken and lost. Her life. She could've lost it today, and while she was a hot mess, she didn't want to die. She wanted . . .

What? What did she want? Her sad little truth was that she no longer knew. Not with everything, every single corner of her world, turned upside down and inside out. Her own fault, of course. She'd disappointed herself, let herself down, which felt . . . unforgivable.

The escalator seemed to crawl down two full floors toward ground level, and she didn't even care, for once her impatience gone, beaten back by the lingering nerves from the flight. She had a case of vicious jitters, her limbs trembling like she'd consumed too much caffeine.

She shouldn't have come. But her stepsister Ashley, twenty-three to Lexi's twenty-eight, had called her out of the blue and asked her to. No, begged. She'd begged her to come.

And for reasons Lexi didn't want to think about too hard, she'd agreed.

She hadn't been back to her childhood home since she'd been ten. And would she even recognize Ashley? They talked on the phone every month without fail and texted in between, but they'd only seen each other a handful of times over the years, the last being at least five years ago. She pulled out her phone to access her Uber app, feeling anxiety tighten her chest.

Below, on the ground floor, she caught sight of a woman holding a huge bouquet of flowers and balloons that spelled out "HAPPY BIRTHDAY, STAN!" Lexi grimaced in secondhand embarrassment for poor Stan, grateful that no one would ever confuse Lexi for a flowers or balloons kind of girl. She hated being the center of attention—

"Lexi! Lexi, over here!" the woman behind the huge flowers and balloons bounced up and down. "Welcome home!"

Dear God. No. No, it couldn't be. Because not only was the petite redhead in the white tank top and flower power skirt her stepsister Ashley, but she also appeared to be videoing as well as narrating—

"Here she comes, guys, my big sister Lexi! Wait until you all meet her, she's awesome!" Ashley was saying, looking so happy it hurt to take her in.

Lexi stumbled off the escalator, not even looking at the guy who reached out and steadied her. "Ash? What are you doing here?"

"Picking you up, silly! As for this"—she tilted her head at her phone, still in Lexi's face—"I'm introducing you to all my friends."

Oh, for . . . Lexi reached out and hit the stop button.

"Hey, I was live."

Lexi eyed the balloons. It wasn't her birthday, nor was her name Stan. "Did you steal those?"

"Didn't have to. The grocery store gave them to me for free. The clerk told me the wife ordered them for her husband, but caught him cheating. Just another reason I don't date anyone with a penis." Ashley grinned and threw herself at Lexi, hugging her hard, smelling like cotton candy and forgotten dreams as she rocked them back and forth, making happy noises. "Hi! It's really you! You're here, you're finally back in Sunrise Cove after all these years!"

Lexi, who'd buried her heart six feet under years and years ago, told herself she felt nothing. A lie, apparently, since her arms came up and returned the hug. Catching herself, she tried to step back, but Ashley shook her head and tightened her grip. "Not yet."

Lexi let out a dramatic sigh, but the truth was, the unexpected human contact brought her something she hadn't felt in a while—comfort. Feeling eyes on her, she lifted her head and took in the guy standing at Ashley's side, the one who'd steadied her off the escalator, his gaze calm, quietly assessing, and looking . . . amused? He was tall. Clearly extremely fit in Levi's and an untucked dark blue button-down, a white T-shirt beneath that said *Fixologist.*

Whatever that meant. He had wavy dark brown hair, a few days of scruff on his face. Eyes a shocking blue gray—

No.

No way.

But she'd only ever seen eyes that searing on one person. Heath Bowman, her elementary school rival and archnemesis. Only, it couldn't be. How had the too-gangly, scrappy, trickster ten-year-old kid grown up looking like . . . *that?*

"She's turning purple, Ash," he said mildly. "You might want to let up on the grip."

Her sister's name shortened, matched with the affection in his tone, implied the two of them were close. Her sister was close with the kid who'd made Lexi's life a living hell.

At whatever he saw in her expression, his mouth quirked on one side, disarming enough that two women walking past tripped over each other. But his gaze never left Lexi. "Been a long time, Lex."

She wanted to growl at him for the nickname that no one else had ever called her. They'd been kids when he'd first used it, the boy who'd beaten her at everything she'd tried for: their second-grade ski race, the lead in their third-grade play, the fourth-grade spelling bee tournament, and the fifth-grade class presidency—for which he'd cheated by handing out candy for votes.

The rivalry between them hadn't been born from a crush. Nope, they'd been true childhood mortal enemies. Not that it'd mattered because that summer she'd gone to live with her dad on the other side of the country—and had ended up staying when Daisy, her mom, had let her gambling addiction blow up her life.

That had been when she'd first realized she'd had much bigger problems than one annoying Heath Bowman. "And you're here why?" she asked him.

Ashley's smile faded a bit. "He's my emotional support."

Lexi's heart stuttered as she turned to her sister. "Why? What's wrong?"

Ashley shored up her expression and shook her head. "Nothing."

Fine. Lexi would get it out of her later. In private. But if someone had set off Ashley's debilitating panic attacks again after she'd been free of them for years now, Lexi was prepared to go to war against them. "You didn't have to come," she said in her softest voice, one she didn't get much use out of these days. "I was going to Uber. Neither of you needed to take time away from your jobs."

"I didn't," Ashley said. "School just got out for summer. I would've loved to teach summer school, but kindergarten doesn't offer it."

Lexi turned to Heath, who lifted a lazy shoulder. "Being a nine to fiver isn't my thing."

Ashley gave him a look, and he smiled. A real one that met his eyes and everything—which she refused to acknowledge. Once upon a time, everything had come easy to him, making friends, melting teachers' hearts, schoolwork, everything, and clearly, he'd skated on charm and charisma right into adulthood.

"And I wanted to pick you up," Ashley said. "I wanted you to have a big welcome committee when you arrived, surrounded by people who love you."

Lexi bit back the urge to point out there were only two of them here, especially since she'd bet her last dollar that the taller of them had been dragged here against his will.

"I really appreciate you coming," Ashley went on. "I know you're far too busy for a visit, but . . ." She glanced at Heath. "Well, there're some things we need to fill you in on."

The "we" was deeply disturbing, but here wasn't the time or place. She'd dropped her heavy duffel bag while they talked, but reached down for it now, ending up in a tug-of-war with Heath.

Ashley laughed. "Mom once said you two could argue over what color the sky was. I didn't believe her."

There'd been a time when Lexi had been rotten enough to resent a five-years-younger Ashley, the daughter of Daisy's new husband, the one who called Daisy "Mom." But that had been a reflection of Lexi's complicated feelings when it came to Daisy, a woman who hadn't been the best mom—and absolutely nothing against Ashley, whose genuine sweetness and affection had easily torn down Lexi's walls. "That was all a long time ago."

Her sister smiled and nudged her closer to Heath. "If bygones are bygones, where's the nice-to-see-you-again hug?"

Lexi opened her mouth to say hell no, but caught Heath's gaze. His *amused* gaze. Dammit. Then Ashley nudged her again and she bumped right into the man. She really wanted it to be repugnant, but brushing up against his warm, solid frame, something equally warm unfurled in her gut. It felt like a live wire between them, and for the first time in months, she felt a tingle of something she didn't want to acknowledge.

Attraction.

Shock and annoyance as a betraying flutter went through her. And the only thing that made her feel better? Heath staring down at her, his amusement long gone, something pensive in his gaze now.

Ha! If she had to suffer, then she was glad he would too.

Ashley was watching them, surprise in her gaze. "Huh," she murmured. "Interesting."

Heath was still looking at Lexi. "It's . . . surprisingly good to see you."

She blinked at the words, at the surprisingly genuine tone, which threw her off guard. Had she misjudged him? Had he grown up into a more decent man than the boy had ever been? It certainly wouldn't have been the first time her instincts had failed her. Whether that came from her currently empty confidence tank or exhaustion, she needed to set it aside. Especially if he was going to be . . . nice.

When he leaned in close, she found herself more breathless than the rough plane landing had caused, getting goose bumps where she had no business getting goose bumps. She blinked up at him, head spinning. Wow, those eyes. They were warm and kind, and her smile came utterly unbidden as he whispered, "*Shotgun.*"

ABOUT THE AUTHOR

New York Times bestselling author JILL SHALVIS lives in a small town in the Sierras full of quirky characters. Any resemblance to the quirky characters in her books is, um, mostly coincidental. Look for Jill's bestselling, award-winning novels wherever books are sold, and visit her website, jillshalvis.com, for a complete book list and a daily blog detailing her city-girl-living-in-the-mountains adventures.

Read More by
JILL SHALVIS

— THE SUNRISE COVE SERIES —

THE WILDSTONE SERIES —

 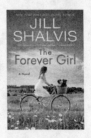